Samantha Tonge's passion, second to spending time with her husband and children, is writing. She has travelled widely. When not writing she passes her days cycling, baking and drinking coffee. Her bestselling debut novel, *Doubting Abbey*, was shortlisted for the Festival of Romantic Fiction best Ebook award. Her novel *Game of Scones* won the Love Stories Awards Best Romantic Ebook category. She lives in Manchester.

SAMANTHA TONGE

FORGIVE ME NOT

CANELO
US

San Diego, California

Canelo US
An imprint of Printers Row Publishing Group
9717 Pacific Heights Blvd, San Diego, CA 92121
www.canelobooksus.com

Printers Row Publishing Group is a division of Readerlink Distribution
Services, LLC. Canelo US is a registered trademark of Readerlink
Distribution Services, LLC.

First published in the United Kingdom in 2018 by Canelo. This edition
originally published in the United Kingdom in 2022 by Canelo.

Published in partnership with Canelo.

Correspondence regarding the content of this book should be sent to Canelo
US, Editorial Department, at the above address. Author inquiries should be
sent to Canelo, Unit 9, 5th Floor, Cargo Works, 1–2 Hatfields, London SE1
9PG, United Kingdom, www.canelo.co.

Publisher: Peter Norton • Associate Publisher: Ana Parker
Art Director: Charles McStravick
Senior Developmental Editor: April Graham
Production Team: Beno Chan, Julie Greene

Design: Brianna Lewis

Library of Congress Control Number: 2022947384

ISBN: 978-1-6672-0540-3

Printed in India

27 26 25 24 23 1 2 3 4 5

Martin, Immy, Jay.

*Out of the many thousands of words I write those will always
be the most awesome three.*

Chapter 1

The carriage slid to a halt, its doors opened and Emma stepped off the train. Like old enemies, scenes from the past ambushed her mind. They took her back to her last day in Healdbury – home as it had been then. She could almost smell the blood that had permeated her dress as she'd run away from her sister's voice. Yet today didn't feel like going back – more like going forwards. She gripped the pull handle of her suitcase, readjusted the rucksack on her back and with determined strides left the platform. Early June sunshine hit her face as she headed along the narrow path that led into the village.

Thank goodness she'd worn long cotton trousers, what with the straggle of nettles either side. Were the prickly leaves trying to safeguard the village from her arrival?

'Don't be ridiculous,' she told herself firmly.

Yet her chest tightened as certain questions persisted. Was this the right decision? Would Andrea and Mum take her back? What about her mother's health? The diagnosis had been long-term. Surely she couldn't have deteriorated that much?

And what about the suffering she herself had caused during that last Christmas at the farm?

She reached the first buildings in the village, trying to dispel negative thoughts. Compared to the Gothic architecture of Manchester, they looked Lilliput Lane quaint.

I

The occasional dandelion growing between paving stones punctuated the way instead of cigarette butts and discarded takeaway food. She squinted in the sunshine. On the pavement ahead was Mrs Beatty from the gift shop. The old woman stopped for a second and did a double-take from under her sunhat. A handkerchief fell from her hand.

Emma hurried forward and picked it up. 'You dropped this,' she said, and gave an unsure smile. The shop owner's lips pursed shut like the top of a drawstring bag and she turned away and crossed the road.

Emma's heart beat faster as she carried on past the post office and the Badger Inn. She glanced left into the butcher's window and a sense of relief flooded her limbs. Darts fan Bill was standing behind the counter preparing meat. He looked the same apart from his hairline, which had retreated even further. Perhaps her life, too, would just carry on as it had before. He caught her eye and wrinkled his nose, the sight of her more unpleasant than the smell of raw flesh. Still holding his knife, he went to the glass door and flipped the sign from *Open* to *Closed*. Well, it was almost five o'clock. Bill always used to shut the shop on time.

She pulled the case onwards, past the small Tudor church hall. To her surprise, a homeless woman had set up outside the supermarket across the road. She had asymmetrical dyed red hair, shaved short on the left. Locals steered clear as if they might catch the rough sleeper's bad luck.

As she headed up Broadgrass Hill, Emma drank in the sight of trees, flowers and insects. She pulled her luggage over to one side to let an elderly man she didn't know pass. He tipped his hat. Healdbury seemed impossibly lush after the greyness of the city, with its shades of green, colourful petals and tortoiseshell wings, and the scents that characterised journeys, be they of woody soil or fresh dewy grass. A dead blackbird lay in her path, wings broken, neck distorted. Emma released her case and crouched. Gloved with a dock leaf, she gently picked up the body and hid it in the verge's foliage. Then she wiped her brow on her arm. Combined with the afternoon heat, the weight of her luggage had become stifling.

She turned left into the dusty drive that led to her old home, and a bubble rose in her throat as she breathed in the sweet honeysuckle that grew all around a nearby birdbath. The last time she'd passed it, Andrea's angry shouts had accompanied the pounding of Emma's feet running away on frosty ground.

She coughed and walked towards the side of the farmhouse, passing a large patch of wild flowers. Further on stood a cluster of apple trees. A road veered off to the right that eventually doubled back on itself and led to the main entrance and parking space. It was lined with pink foxgloves, which were preceded each year by a carpet of forget-me-nots, Mum's favourite flower. With their yellow faces and tiny petals, a younger Emma had thought of them as the gentlest dance troupe as they swayed in the spring breeze.

She turned away and stared ahead at the kissing gate, more crooked than ever, with hinges that needed fixing. It stood in the middle of a mossy stone wall and provided a short cut to the front door if you were on foot. She and Bligh had kissed there for the very first time – only out of respect for tradition, they'd insisted. Emma could almost feel the splintered beams against her back as Bligh's lips pressed against hers.

Bligh. Tall, with the shortest beard. Tanned, with the whitest T-shirts. The firmest arms and the lightest touch. A man of contradictions.

Would he still be here? Had he gone to the police about what she'd done?

A shaggy blur of black and white charged at her from behind the farmhouse. She hurried forward, juggled her luggage around the kissing gate and dropped to her knees, pulling off her rucksack just in time as the Border collie lunged at her chest with a joyous bark. She fell backwards and her face crumpled as she righted herself.

'Dash! I've missed you so much, lad.' She buried her face in his white bib, grateful that he hadn't blanked her as well, and ran her hands through his tousled coat. Doggy breath hit her as Dash licked her face hard. Was he trying to remove the months – years – that had kept them apart?

'I should have taken you with me,' she croaked when he finally backed away and gazed at her, ears alert. 'A three-legged pet would have earned me lots of spare change. Talk about the ultimate underdog.' She gazed at the space where his front leg should have been. 'I wanted to,' she whispered, 'but at the time all I could think about was myself.'

The dog lay down and rolled on his back, begging for attention. His enthusiasm made Emma feel more optimistic. She crouched for a moment longer and tickled his stomach. It was her mum who'd saved him. She had heard that a local sheep farmer was putting him down: he couldn't afford the upkeep of an animal that couldn't keep up. Emma knew what it was like not to fit in, and like two halves of a lock slotted together, the doors to unconditional love had swung apart between them.

She gave his tummy one last pat and got to her feet, making her way around to the front of Foxglove Farm. Dash stuck to her side, lolloping with his familiar bounce. Before crossing in front of the windows that might betray her presence, she stepped back and surveyed the L-shaped building.

The wooden front door led straight into the lounge, with stairs going up to the bedrooms. Behind that was the dining room, and to the right of that the big kitchen and the farmhouse shop. Her eyes narrowed in the sunshine as she studied the building's uneven rubble-stone exterior, painted in the buttery limewash that had been applied during the final stages of renovation.

Emma could still remember the dullness and damp from when they'd first moved in. Mum had dreamt of creating a pretty chocolate-box cliché, with thatched roof, painted beams and colourful window boxes. All of that had been achieved, but now... What had happened? The paintwork was peeling and the limewash badly needed a refresh. The windows looked dirty. Mum had always prided herself on how they shone, despite the continual onslaught of dust. And the window boxes, the hit of the summer show, were missing their usual cast of petunias and geraniums.

She headed towards the front door, the loose ceramic name plate hanging lopsided. The doormat lay curled and weather-beaten. To the right-hand side stood the tallest sunflower, which hadn't yet bloomed. Emma wiped perspiration from her brow and reached for the cold metal knocker. This was it. She couldn't wait to see her family again so that they could all get things back on track. She'd missed the hugs. The laughs. The teamwork at harvest time. Recently she'd spent countless daydreams imagining a heartfelt reunion.

Dash nudged his nose against her thigh as if to say: *it'll be all right*. Emma scratched behind his ears and counted. Nothing. No footsteps. She rapped again. Sixteen, seventeen, eighteen… Finally she heard the thud of sensible heels on laminate and the door creaked open.

The house seemed so different but surely Andrea would have stayed the same? Surely life had just plodded on here – in fact run more easily, without the chaos that Emma had brought? However, the sight of the dark rings under Andrea's widening eyes blew this theory out of the water. Her long brown hair had been sliced shorter and was scraped back into a ponytail, with premature grey at the sides. She still had that scar above her top lip. Andrea and Mum had never been able to remember what caused it. Her feisty hazel eyes were now dull. She was still tall and tanned, but not as solid. She looked… fragile.

Emma's stomach twisted like the strongest bindweed. 'Hi, Andrea. It's me.'

Her older sister's lips rolled together before she slammed the door. The ceramic name plate fell to the ground and smashed into uneven pieces.

Chapter 2

Emma bent down and picked up the fragments of the broken sign before stacking them to the side. As she straightened up, she told herself sternly that Andrea's reaction shouldn't feel unexpected. Deep breaths. Dash had bolted at the noise but now returned to her side and nudged her leg again. Emma took hold of the knocker and rapped once more. This time footsteps quickly sounded and the door was yanked open.

'You'll wake Mum,' said Andrea between gritted teeth. 'She's having a nap. Just go away. You're not welcome here.'

'Andrea. It's so good to see you. Please. Just hear me out.'

Dash took matters into his own hands, gave a small bark and lolloped inside. Slowly Andrea exhaled. 'Fifteen minutes. That's all you've got. Then I've got to make Mum's tea.'

As Emma entered the house, a chill descended upon her, like a cloak designed to cool not heat. Why was Mum asleep at teatime, and couldn't she cook for herself? She gazed at the cream sofa and chairs. The white walls. The oak floor and coffee table. The vibrant watercolour of forget-me-nots Andrea had painted. Home. Her shoulders dropped with relief. At least indoors hadn't changed that much.

Or had it? At the end of the room, paperwork swamped the dining room table, next to a computer and printer, along with scattered jiffy bags and biros. Andrea sat down on the sofa and picked up a half-drunk mug of tea from the low table. Since her teenage years, she had always had a brew on the go.

'So?' she said abruptly, raising an eyebrow like a samurai lifting a sword.

Emma dropped her rucksack and sat down on an armchair opposite. Dash snuggled up to her feet. She ran a hand over the smooth upholstery. Mum had insisted on ordering the pale leather three-piece suite. 'Yes, it's completely impractical for a cluttered farmhouse and small children,' she'd said, 'but this is a slice of simplicity I need at the end of the day.' Her two daughters, aged four and nine, had made crowns out of cereal boxes, Andrea in charge of the scissors and glue, and used the luxurious chairs as thrones. Emma insisted on being Princess Diana. Budding gardener Andrea was happy to be Charles, as Aunt Thelma said he spoke to plants.

Now Emma met her sister's gaze. She'd practised this speech so often in her head, yet the crucial moment had deleted her thoughts.

Andrea consulted her watch.

'Firstly... I'm sorry,' said Emma.

'I've heard that before.'

Heat flooded her face. 'But I'm a different person now and—'

'What do you want me to say? Congratulations?'

Emma shifted uncomfortably.

Andrea looked up as the staircase creaked. 'Well done. You've woken her,' she said stiffly.

8

Emma stood up as Gail slowly descended the stairs. Her knees felt unsteady as she took in her mother's appearance. The short hair stuck up on top, grey strands now outnumbering the red. A crumpled blouse was half tucked into linen trousers, at the bottom of which, just visible, were odd socks. In her hand was a purple chocolate wrapper, her fingers folding it like a magician practising some trick.

Now and again during the last couple of years, Emma had dreamed of Gail holding her in that tight embrace that belonged solely to mothers and could salve the deepest upset. Like when Emma used to fall over and graze her knees, or worry about making friends, or when she lost her favourite teddy bear. Her mum would reassure her that her scrapes would heal, that friendships would grow and that Ted was just on holiday. Sure enough, he turned up a week later with a new jumper and longer legs. Mum said he must have had a growth spurt.

'Mum.' Emma stepped forward and held out her arms. At points during the last couple of years she'd found it hard to recall every detail of her mother's face. She'd forgotten the sparse eyelashes, and the age spot on the chin. Yet she'd never forgotten the bright eyes and the efficient manner that were now both missing.

Gail stood at the foot of the stairs and stared. She tilted her head to the side, then walked past Emma and sat down next to Andrea on the sofa. She picked up her daughter's drink, took a sip and put it back.

Emma looked at her sister, who gazed belligerently back. Mouth dry, she went over to Gail and crouched by her side.

'How are things?' she asked, and held her breath.

Gail's brow knotted. 'Who are you?'

Emma felt dizzy. No. This wasn't happening.

'It's me, Emma. Your younger daughter.'

'You can't be. You aren't shouting or swearing.'

Emma enveloped her mum's hands in hers. The frail fingers warned her off, squeezing too tight. 'I've… I've come back to help,' she said. She willed her mum to offer a flash of recognition, but there was nothing – the moment of semi-lucidity had passed.

Gail took back her hands and stared out of the front window, once again fiddling with the chocolate wrapper.

The leather armchair groaned as Emma fell back into it. 'What's happened?' she whispered. 'The diagnosis… This is much quicker than the doctors…'

'You can say the words. Early-onset Alzheimer's.'

That label had only been decided a matter of weeks before Emma left, and she'd never accepted it back then. Her vibrant, laughing, crusading mother going dotty? At only fifty-three? They'd made a mistake. Or if not, the inevitable wouldn't happen for years.

'But it wasn't supposed to get like this for—'

'How would you know?' Andrea asked, in a voice that sounded as if it were walking a tightrope. 'You never came to any of the appointments. It was me sitting with Mum when they told her the news.'

'I should have been there for her – for you. I know it must have been tough.'

'Tough? No, uncooked meat is tough. Over-kneaded dough. Chewing gum that's gone hard. But holding Mum's hand through the last few years as she's lost her bearings around the village… the farm… the house? As she's forgotten the names for places, objects and… loved ones? I've had to witness her distress as day by day she's felt less useful, and panicked by familiar surroundings that now seem brand new.' Andrea shook her head. '*Tough?* Try heartbreaking. That's a far more suitable word.'

'But what happened? Why has it progressed so quickly?' With fresh eyes, Emma glanced at the water-colour.

Forget. Me. Not. How could her mum not know who she was?

Her fists curled. It was so unfair. All the years... no, the *decades* of productive life Mum had been robbed of.

Andrea leant forward and rubbed her forehead. 'About a year ago she was rushed into hospital with appendicitis. They removed the appendix in time but she was never the same afterwards. It was as if the general anaesthetic had thrown her forward several years, into the illness. They had to move her to a private ward to recover, because she kept seeing things that weren't there during the night and waking the other patients.'

'Oh Andrea. That must have been hard on you.'

'Mum was my main concern,' she said in a voice with no tone, like a song that only existed as written notes.

'I wish I'd been here to support you both.'

'I'm glad you weren't.'

Emma flinched. 'How have you managed?'

'Just fine.'

'Please. Tell me the truth.'

Andrea's shoulders bobbed up and down. 'Bligh, of course.'

So he was still here.

'And Polly...'

The fifty-year-old landlady from the Badger Inn, married to Alan. Despite the age difference, Polly and Andrea were firm friends. They used to chat for hours in low voices, like Andrea and Emma used to before things got bad. The pair had a mutual love of Stilton and often shopped at the cheese shop in the village. Polly would invite Andrea over to the pub for a tasting evening in front of a DVD. When she visited the farm, Andrea allowed herself to relax, gossiping, joking and eating too much home-baked shortbread.

'Polly's gran had dementia and she used to look after her. She insists on sitting with Mum most Saturday afternoons, which is a godsend, what with that being the busiest day for the shop. She's also given me tips on how to keep Mum occupied. The hospital does its best, but…' Andrea sighed. 'Mum's still sleeping at night, which helps. But I caught her drinking undiluted squash last week, and I've had to stop her using the cooker and iron.'

Emma had tried to drink concentrated cordial once when she was little. Just in time, Andrea had spotted her mistake and patiently shown her how to dilute it.

'Polly's also great at doing an emergency shop if I just haven't had the time.'

What about Dean, Andrea's boyfriend? Didn't he help? Emma sat in a daze. She couldn't take it all in.

'You seem nice,' said Gail, and leant across to pat Emma's hand. Her eyes crinkled into a smile before she looked vacant again.

'Andrea? I'll be off now,' a deep voice boomed from the kitchen. Heavy footsteps sounded from behind Emma, then stopped abruptly.

Emma lifted her chin, jumped to her feet and turned around.

Chapter 3

Emma watched as Bligh ran a hand across his beard and blinked rapidly. White T-shirt. Blue jeans. His handyman uniform hadn't altered one bit. The air surrounding him still carried a hint of aftershave. With his Popeye arms and determined jawline, true to his namesake he looked like a mariner who could conquer the waves.

'This is a surprise, Emma,' he muttered.

He used to call her Emmie.

'What are you after?' he said in a firmer voice, and folded his arms. 'More money? Don't tell me – you're in some sort of trouble?'

'No, Bligh… I've come back to say sorry.'

'You didn't think about warning us of your arrival? I'd say that smacks of the old dramatic behaviours.' He glanced meaningfully at Andrea and Gail before once again meeting her gaze. 'Didn't you for one moment consider the impact of your visit?'

'I've come back to make amends. To help on the farm. I want to spend time with Mum and try to make things easier here. I want to make up for—'

'I want, I want, I want,' said Andrea. 'You just assume everyone will forgive and forget. We should ring the police.'

'And I... I wouldn't blame you,' said Emma, turning up the palms of her hands. 'You've got to believe how sorry I am. I hated my life back then.'

'Really?' Andrea snorted. 'To all appearances you were simply intent on having a good time.'

Perspiration ran between Emma's shoulder blades. This wasn't how her daydreams had panned out. 'You didn't really believe I was happy, did you?'

'Well I know I wasn't,' said Andrea, in a voice like a starched shirt – a voice Emma had become accustomed to during her last months at the farm. So unlike the gentle tones she remembered from their childhood days. Andrea had been the softest older sister, always letting Emma borrow her clothes or make-up as if the five-year age gap didn't matter. When Emma was little, Andrea would patiently play board games that must have bored her, and sing nursery rhymes even though her own taste in music had moved on to boy bands.

'This nice woman talks too much. Has she come to make my tea?' Gail tore her gaze away from the window. 'Fish on Friday. It is Friday, isn't it?'

'No,' said Emma. Guilt pinched her stomach. She'd been away far too long. 'It's actually Wed—'

'Yes, fish today,' said Andrea in bright tones. 'If that's what you fancy, Mum, I'll put the cod in straight away.'

Cod? But Mum was a strict vegetarian.

Andrea stood up, took a firm hold of Emma's elbow and steered her past Bligh, through the dining room and into the pine kitchen. Dash followed. The poppy-patterned crockery stood as proud as ever in the Welsh dresser, just like the soldiers that flower commemorated. The clock was different – bigger. The cupboards had child locks on them.

'Don't interfere with how I'm dealing with Mum.'

'But shouldn't she know it's not Friday? Isn't it best—'

'You have no idea what is best. How do you think she would feel if people continually corrected her mistakes?' said Andrea.

'I'd have thought it would stop the progression of the disease.'

'So, what if she asks you five times a day when she can visit Granny and Gramps? Do you keep breaking the news that her parents are dead? Force her to relive the grief? Or do you just say, don't worry, Mum, we'll see them later, and let her eventually forget the question?'

'But… we can't just let her give in.' Emma swallowed. 'She deserves—'

'Don't you dare tell me what she deserves, as if you have some say in this.' Andrea paced the chequered floor like a mutinous chess piece. 'Just go. It's for the best. I've got Mum to see to. The livestock. The shop. I can't look after you as well.'

'I don't need looking after any more,' said Emma quietly.

'What happened to your ambition of becoming a vet? What have you got to show for the last few years?' Andrea's ponytail swung angrily. 'You threw it all away and now you expect us to pick up the pieces?'

'It's not like that.' Emma concentrated on her breathing, determined to stay calm. All those hopes she'd had for a family reunion… she'd even given notice on her flat. How could she have been so naive – no, arrogant – imagining some kind of red-carpet welcome?

'Look. Great-Aunt Thelma…' Andrea rubbed the back of her neck.

'Is she okay?'

'She died a couple of months ago. Pneumonia.'

Andrea's voice was matter-of-fact. Emma gasped.

'She left us each an inheritance. Most of mine went on mending the farmhouse roof.' Andrea rummaged in a kitchen drawer. Finally she found a business card. 'Here's the solicitor's number. No doubt it's money you've come back for, so now you can go.'

Dear Thelma, with her wicked sense of humour and her affection for the soaps. When Emma had first met Joe, she'd told him how much her great-aunt would have liked him, talking for hours about *EastEnders*… but she couldn't think about Joe now. Not today. At Thelma's ninetieth birthday party they'd all joked that she'd outlive everyone. Emma wished she could have attended the funeral. She winced as Andrea took great care for their fingers not to touch on passing her the card. They'd held hands for years growing up, swinging arms as they walked to the shops. People used to comment on how lovely it was to see two siblings so close.

Andrea turned away. Bligh and Gail appeared. Gently he manoeuvred her around Dash. Gail went to the cutlery drawer and set the table for two people, putting out spoons instead of knives and forks. Then she sat down and busied herself folding and unfolding a napkin.

'Just go, Emma,' said Bligh.

Emma hovered for a moment. Swallowed. He was right. Her return was just making things worse. She wanted to kiss her mother but didn't want to add to her confusion. Instead, she gently squeezed the hand that had once mucked out the pigsty, picked and scrubbed fruit and sewn clothes. Gail looked up. Nothing registered. Emma glanced at Andrea's back, wanted to rub those stiff shoulders until they relaxed. Instead she walked back through the dining room into the lounge and picked up her rucksack. She coiled her fingers around the handle of her case and headed outside, accompanied by Dash.

She gazed across the farmland towards an ellipsis of clouds in the blue sky. In the distance, a weeping willow cried leaves into the small pond. In front of it was a bench, and the pasture for the few sheep and goats. To the left, the vegetable and fruit garden. To the right, the big chicken coop, where a hen clucked whilst taking a dust bath. Next to that was the pigsty, the sheds and the old barn.

Foxglove Farm produced jams and chutneys as well as fresh eggs and vegetables. They sold home-made fruit cake, and with a little persuasion, Andrea would hang her latest paintings in the shop. Or she used to. Emma didn't know if she did any more. She was self-taught, but she was good, and loved creating imagined exotic scenes from abroad.

Granny and Gramps had died in a car crash when Emma was little. The money they'd left had been used to give the three of them a fresh start up north. Gail had always fancied living near the Peaks, away from London. They never visited the capital again. She liked the wilder landscape. Undomesticated, she called it – unlike the animals she took in, which soon became pets.

Emma and Andrea had often giggled and said that Mum had to be the only vegetarian farmer in England. A centre for waifs and strays rather than a farm was probably a better description of the place. Two pigs had come with the smallholding. The previous owner was going to put them down but Mum persuaded him not to. They both died within five years, after a very happy life embellished with many biscuit treats.

The first sheep came from a big farm in the next town. Gail had heard the owner talking in the Badger Inn one day, saying how for a farm his size, emotions couldn't come into the shearing process. Targets had to be met and some sheep found the handling traumatic. He had one at the moment who was so jumpy he would sell her early for meat. Gail had interrupted. Said she'd pay him the going rate. Asked him to always send her the sensitive animals. She also rescued battery farm hens, and once a donkey destined for the foreign meat trade.

Emma's eyes narrowed. Currently there were two sheep, two goats, three pigs, hens and rabbits. Her mouth went dry as she walked over to look at them. The water bowls looked grubby. Fences and shelters needed repairing. The animals stood bored, with no items to encourage play or foraging. Her gaze moved to the vegetable patch. Wanton carrot tops dirty-danced with the breeze. A disapproving regiment of raspberry canes stood with plump, reliable lettuces at its feet.

She squinted in the evening sunlight and enjoyed the countryside soundtrack. If only she could record all the noises she used to find so pedestrian.

She spotted tomatoes growing in the greenhouse. From a trellis across the ceiling, cucumbers dangled like diving Zeppelins. A nose nudged her leg. She crouched and gave Dash a hug, then wandered across to the barn, which now had cracked windows and holes in the roof. Inside, it hadn't changed much. There were still the haystacks and bits of farm equipment, plus the sink they'd had plumbed in years ago so that they could prepare animal feed out here. Also a pen with dirty hay scattered across the ground, and in the corner, a scratched rocking chair Mum had bought years ago but never got round to renovating.

Emma looked at her watch. She could catch a train back to Manchester but she didn't have much money for a hotel. It was too late to get anywhere else. She collapsed onto one of the haystacks. Tomorrow was a new day. She'd work it out. Aunt Thelma's money would help, although she'd give it all away in a second to have just one lucid moment with Mum.

'She doesn't know who I am, Dash,' she said, and put her arms around his neck again. Her mum used to say that animals only judged you on the present. They didn't care about mistakes from your past and had no expectations about your future. Their behaviour around you – calm or on edge – reflected the person you truly were.

She closed her eyes and meditated for a few minutes. She opened her suitcase and took out her nightly readings. Then she filled her gratitude journal. Routine. Routine. Routine. Things she was grateful for today? Seeing her family. Acting like a grown-up and accepting the situation. Not shouting, swearing, making her mum cry – all the things she used to do.

She got a fleece out of her suitcase, wrapped it around her shoulders and lay down, finding comfort in the familiar hard ground. Dash snuggled up. Emma would get up early and leave without causing further upset. No one would know she'd slept here. In fact, she'd get up as soon as the sun rose and see what she could do to help improve the animals' situation before she left. She could at least clean out the water bowls and drag an old bench she'd noticed into the goats' enclosure. They'd love having something to jump onto.

She stroked Dash and with heavy eyes recalled once again the very last day she'd been able to call Healdbury home. How she'd woken up in that upmarket hotel. Seen the blood. Hurriedly driven to the farm and faced Bligh's fury when he discovered what she'd done. And then run.

17 months before going back

Emma stared at the dingy ceiling inhabited by her familiar eight-legged housemates. As a child, she'd imagined spiders to be the weavers of sparkly princess dresses that would entrap princes instead of snacks. She moved her focus to the walls and their nicotine stains the colour of overripe banana. Here, one day passed much the same as another.

A grunt sounded from her left. She rolled over, nose pinching in the winter morning air, and scanned the sparsely clothed male torso in the grubby blue sleeping bag on the stone floor. She shivered and studied the familiar dirty-blonde hair.

'Surprised we didn't freeze solid overnight,' she said, and shuffled over to him. She tucked her head under his chin and felt comforted by his warm breath. He hugged her back loosely and Emma clung on tight, tilting her face hopefully, but he pulled away. These days, Joe was always the first to break contact.

Unlike the weeks when they'd first met. The friendship had soon become affectionate. Joe would slip his arm around her waist and tuck his fingers in her back pocket. Emma would rest her head on his shoulder as they sat next to each other on the pavement at various locations in Manchester city centre. Being with Joe made this derelict building feel more like a home than just a place to sleep in.

Yet somehow they'd lost that natural ease and Emma was determined to get it back. She had plans. Their relationship was the way out of this mess. Since meeting Joe, an unfamiliar sensation had stirred deep within her chest. Was it hope? The desire to change? All she knew was that for the first time in months, a different kind of future seemed possible.

She turned back to the ceiling and reached out her right arm. Sight was not required to curl her fingers around the bottle she knew was there.

'Happy New Year,' she whispered.

She sat upright and as a treat allowed herself to think back to happier times at Foxglove Farm. Mum making strawberry jam. Andrea in the vegetable garden, as busy as a worker ant. Blue skies. Fragrant honeysuckle. Carefree pigs snuffling for imaginary truffles. And capable Bligh.

Sounded like the narrative of a children's story, didn't it? Of a book that no longer belonged to her.

'Joe,' she whispered, 'let's go out. Head down to the canal. There's some bread in my rucksack. I bet the ducks are as hungry as us.'

'Not possible,' he muttered. 'We've hardly eaten in two days.'

'I did say to go to the soup kitchen,' she said, half-heartedly. It wasn't her favourite place – cliquey at the best of times.

'What, with all that forced festive jollity?' He leant up on one elbow. 'No thanks. I'd rather keep it real.'

'You enjoyed those Christmas crackers. They've got to be the least useful thing anyone's ever given us.'

21

'The old dear meant well, and that plastic puzzle kept you quiet for, ooh…' his lips turned upwards, 'a good ten minutes.'

Her mouth broadened. 'Come on. I need a decent meal. So do you.' She reached out and took his hand. Joe pulled it away.

'Stop mithering me, Ems,' he snapped. 'You never know when to stop. We're not joined at the hip. You go if you want.'

He lay back down and wriggled into the sleeping bag. Stammering an apology, she tugged on her boots, grabbed her coat and headed out.

Half an hour later, she was standing in the queue for food, the merry jingling tunes depressing her mood. Stig stood behind her, having tied up his Staffie dog outside. As usual, he held a battered novel in his hand. They hugged briefly.

'Haven't bumped into you for a while,' he said, and pulled off his khaki bobble hat. As they neared the serving hatch, he stuffed the hat and the book into his rucksack. 'Thought I might see you at the Red Lion on Christmas Day for that free turkey lunch. They threw in a bag of chocolates and toiletries too.'

'Me and Joe just stayed in Market Street.'

The volunteers smiled as they dished out food. Emma and Stig carried their trays over to one of the long white tables. She inhaled the aroma of beef and gravy… creamy mash. A sense of nostalgia embraced her like an over-zealous aunt. The smell shouted school dinners. Christmas cooking. Sunday roasts in the Badger Inn. Oaktree Shelter's soup kitchen was a desperate measure, but at least her friend Beth was here today.

'It's made from scratch an' all,' said Beth with a slight slur, and gave a thumbs-up.

'Yeah, none of that tinned mince,' said Stig.

'Or that instant powdered potato crap,' said Tony, a tiny broccoli floret in his beard that looked like a tree growing out of uncultivable woodland.

'And as for this jam roly-poly with home-made custard…' said Emma. 'So much better than the shop-bought version.'

The four of them stopped shovelling food in for one second and smiled at each other.

'Listen to us,' said Emma, and wiped her mouth on her duffel coat sleeve. 'Quite the food critics, aren't we?'

'Me and the missus used to eat out once a week. Before she got ill.' Tony stared into the distance and started feeding himself on automatic.

'Seen Mad Hatter Holly lately, Beth?' Emma asked. She didn't like to call Holly that, but at least everyone knew who she meant.

Beth burped. 'Haven't you heard, chickie?'

'She got sectioned,' interjected Stig.

'About time. She needed to get back on her meds.' Emma stared at her plate and admired the cheerful yellow and red of the pudding.

'So where's that toy boy of yours?' said Beth, and smiled to reveal decaying teeth. 'I haven't seen him around so much.'

Emma couldn't remember the last time she herself had used toothpaste. When she was little, Andrea used to make her scrub her teeth religiously for two minutes every morning and night.

'Have you fallen out?'

She focused on the last mouthful of sponge. 'Joe is only two years younger than me.'

'He done a runner?'

'No.' Almost.

'He's thinking about it then?'

'London,' she replied in a flat voice. 'He's stopped coming back every night.' There. She'd said it without crying. Emma's friendship wasn't enough to keep him in Manchester, and that thought fuelled her thirst more than anything else.

A few days ago, Joe had announced his thoughts about a new start after… Emma swallowed… after more than just a kiss. It had been his twenty-second birthday. They'd both been out of it. Emma had lit a candle. Stuck it in an empty bottle. Said that in a fantasy world she'd bake him the most amazing chocolate peanut butter cake. He'd held her tight. Said she knew him so well. Then she'd done her best to sing him 'Happy Birthday'. She'd never reached the end. Their lips had collided. Their hands explored. She'd thought it felt so right, but just as things were progressing, he'd pulled back and now was more distant than ever. Why was it so wrong?

Joe was the first person in ages who'd made her feel normal, with their chats about telly and their visits to the canal. They both loved Jammie Dodgers and told each other when they had bad breath. They were movie fanatics and enjoyed casting friends into film. Tony was Harry Potter's Hagrid.

Beth rolled her eyes. 'You can't leave your head behind and that's the whole problem with leaving. It doesn't achieve anything.'

Emma shrugged.

Beth pushed her tray away and her hands hugged the steaming cup of coffee. 'So where you sleeping when he isn't around?'

'Not alone in that building. I go out, move around, keep to the street lights and CCTV cameras, walking, hoping no one will try to steal my stuff. I'll snatch a kip during the day if I can, somewhere busy.' Emma sighed. 'I don't need to tell you what it's like. I kept with Marta for a couple of nights last week – until her fella came back.'

'The one who beat her up?' Beth snorted. 'There's no helping some people.'

They looked at each other. Gave wry smiles.

'Well, if your boy does leave, stick with me if you like,' she said. 'I've found a decent place under a railway bridge. We haven't been moved on yet, and we pull together when strange faces turn up.'

Emma stopped eating for a second. 'Cheers, Beth. That'd be good.' Hopefully it wouldn't come to that. But it might. Joe was a special person. Everyone's friend. Sometimes she wondered why he'd stuck with her this long.

'Shower's vacant. Just ask for a towel,' hollered one of the kitchen workers.

'Guess I'd better have one,' said Beth. 'Get meself a bit of dignity. Yesterday a little lad told me I smelt like his dad's compost heap.' The brassy edge left her face for a second. 'He was right. And I could do with some new clothes – jeans, underwear...'

'My missus always wore nice undies. Loved Marks and Spencer, she did,' said Tony, and stared at his tea.

'Bet you liked them an' all,' said Beth with a grin.

'She looked right classy whatever she wore.' He looked up. 'My missus would make a bin liner look like the Duchess of Cambridge's latest clobber.'

'Show us your photo again,' said Emma gently.

Like a young lad sharing football cards, he eagerly zipped open the inner pocket of his rucksack. He held firmly onto the photo as he showed it to them.

'Took it myself,' he said, 'a couple of years ago on her sixtieth birthday.'

It was creased down the middle, with a stain on the right. Both flaws conveyed his post-mortem love. His life had fallen apart after she died. Emma gazed at the woman looking back at her. The slight tilt of the head that hinted she was shy. The smile that said: *I can't say cheese for much longer*. The eyes that promised: *but for you, I'll try*.

'She's beautiful,' said Emma.

'How did you manage to hook *her*?' said Stig, giving Tony's shoulder a playful push.

'Often asked myself the same question,' he said, and sat just a little bit taller.

'Wotcha got there, Tone?' asked a phlegm-filled Mancunian accent. A young man with tattooed fingers, in a torn anorak, snatched the photo away. 'Ooh, bet she was a right goer in her day.'

'Give that back,' shouted Tony, and lunged at the thief. They fell to the ground. The tattooed man laughed. They fought on the floor, Tony's arms flailing as if he were drowning, despite his large build. The scuffle continued until Stig managed to drag Tony away just before Emma got stuck in.

Staff threw out all three men, not sure who had started the fight. Desperately Tony knocked at the window and pointed to the ground.

Emma looked to Beth for help, but she'd disappeared into the shower. She dropped to her knees. Looked under the table. Scoured the floor.

Finally she found the photo, almost torn in half, just by the front door. Tony hovered by the entrance, gazing skywards as it started to snow – small flakes at first that rapidly morphed into featherweight sugar cubes. With a shaking hand, he took the snap from Emma. Stared at it for a few seconds. Put it back in his pocket. Emma leant forward. Smoothed down his wild hair.

She went back into the dining room and sat, elbows on the table, head in her hands. Bing Crosby's voice floated across the room, inspiring images of blazing fires, excited children, and gifts wrapped under a spruce. Would she and Joe ever share a Christmas like that? She *had* to stop him leaving. *Had* to make him see that they were perfect for each other.

'Shower's free again, chickie,' said Beth as she sat down beside her, rubbing her hair vigorously with a towel. It would have caught fire if it was kindling.

'Not today. See ya later.' Emma left and headed to the nearest newsagent. She needed something stronger than coffee to help her formulate a plan.

Chapter 4

Emma opened her eyes and stretched out on the barn floor. Dash nudged her nose. Of course, she was at Foxglove Farm. Her watch said half past five. The sun did its best to raise her mood. She'd spent a restless night listening to owls and feeling the familiar ache in her bones from sleeping on a hard floor.

'If there's one thing I've learnt from the past year, Dash, there's no point tying myself up in knots over something I can't change,' she said, sitting up and staring into his loyal eyes. Despite that, however, she still wished she could stay. She ran her hand across his forehead and behind his ears, and he tilted his head so that she could scratch the right spot. Then she meditated for several minutes, focusing on the morning countryside sounds that slid through the window crack. Once again, routine, routine, routine.

In front of the sink, she turned on the taps. The water ran cold. She pulled a small towel out of her rucksack and stood in her underwear. She washed her face and armpits, running a thumb across the smooth skin. When she was twelve, it had been Andrea, not busy Mum, who'd taught her to shave, declaring that hair removal cream was messy and smelt like Dash after he'd broken wind.

She examined her nails, glad to see that the pale polish wasn't chipped. She thought back to her group therapy and the transformation she and her new friends had undergone. Some had lost weight and got fit. Others had gained much-needed pounds. They'd got new hairstyles, too. Hers was bobbed now, and a light natural brown.

She pulled on shorts and a baggy T-shirt and packed her belongings before heading outside. With relish she breathed in the smell of manure and damp grass. Images came to mind of her and Bligh underneath the weeping willow. They'd been to an eighteenth birthday party in the village. It was shortly after he'd asked her out, and they were getting used to being more than friends. Sparks? As time passed Emma wondered just how many of those bubbly feelings for him had come out of a bottle. When she'd left, she had mostly missed his practical side – how he'd find her lost purse or put her to bed after a night out. Bligh was used to people needing looking after, like his dad. He was used to people hurting him, like his mum.

It made her question if she'd ever truly loved him, or whether she'd just taken him for granted because he tolerated what other people wouldn't.

Yet they had enjoyed many fun, carefree times before Emma lost control of her life, cycling along country lanes, Emma sitting on his handlebars. Never the academic, Bligh had worked for his handyman dad as soon as he could leave school. Sometimes she'd meet him after work and they'd take a picnic into the cornfields that Gail would pack. As a thank you, Emma always did the ironing when she got back. Her mum made the best cheese and home-made cucumber relish sandwiches, and would wrap up two slices of cake. Bligh's contribution was a bottle of cider. They'd lie on their fronts enjoying the feast and see who could spot a mouse first. As Bligh's parents argued more and more, he'd take refuge in Emma. She'd stroke his soft hair and hold him so tightly.

29

Now she made her way over to the animal enclosures and collected up the food and water bowls – though not before giving the rabbits a stroke and smiling as she pushed away goats keen to chew her T-shirt. She was determined to make the most of these precious hours back at the farm and do whatever she could to help, however small. She headed back to the barn and gave the bowls a thorough wash. The animal feed still sat in the large shed next to the pond. After checking that all the animals were enjoying breakfast, she examined the fences. Some needed reinforcing with concrete around the bottom of the posts. She relished working like this – every small achievement.

She caught the eye of a young postman about to walk back down the drive. He gave a cheery wave. It felt good to wave back. Bligh's car appeared, driving past him, and parked up.

'Emma?'

She looked at her watch. Seven o'clock. She headed over to Bligh. 'How come you're here so early?'

'Why are you here at all?' He gazed at the animals eating.

'I didn't have enough money for a hotel, so I slept on the barn floor. The first trains will be up and running now. Don't worry... I'll just get my bags.' She went into the barn to fetch her belongings, wishing these glorious hours back home didn't have to end. Bligh followed. So did Dash.

A haystack rustled as she dropped down onto it to tighten a shoelace. An ant marched across the ground by her feet. It carried a slice of leaf one hundred times its own size. Emma used to take it for granted that other people were strong like that; assumed that her behaviour never affected them as deeply as it hurt her inside.

Bligh stared at the top of her left leg.

She looked down at the pink scar. 'I got stabbed by a friend.'

'What kind of a friend does that?' he asked in an incredulous voice.

A friend like Mad Hatter Holly, who was just about to jump off a bridge. She was holding a knife in case anyone tried to ruin her plans. After Emma yanked her back from the edge, they'd fallen to the ground, and in frustration, Holly had stabbed her thigh.

'And how on earth could you sleep on the floor?'

'Best not to ask,' she replied, forcing a bright tone.

'So Andrea and I deserve no explanation? You turn up expecting to just slot back in?' He shook his head. 'This is no different to when you used to stay out all hours and refuse to tell me where you'd been.'

Her stomach clenched. 'Look… when I left, I found a place to stay. Almost got a job. But… things didn't work out. I ran out of money.'

'You had no problem spending it then.' He shook his head. 'Christ, how could you live with yourself after what you'd done?'

She avoided his eye. 'I looked over my shoulder for days and felt sick whenever I heard a police siren.' She wanted to say she'd felt bad during the days immediately afterwards, but at the time, she had just blotted out the whole sordid episode: the used condoms scattered across that hotel room's plush carpet along with empty bottles of champagne… the reckless car journey back to the farm, when she'd skidded badly outside the Christmas tree farm… 'Eventually I lost my bedsit.'

'What did you do?'

Emma swallowed. 'I was homeless for just over a year.'

31

'Forever the drama queen.' Andrea appeared in the doorway of the barn. 'Don't forget how my sister used to exaggerate at every opportunity, Bligh.'

Emma caught her eye.

'Just go,' said Andrea.

Emma stood up and lifted her rucksack, briefly squeezing her eyes as she bent over. Who could blame them? Getting better had sharpened her memory.

The three of them went out into the sunshine.

'By the way, a couple of the posts in the goats' fencing need to be reinforced,' said Emma. 'I've washed and refilled the food bowls, but the rabbits' are cracked and could do with replacing. And maybe consider dragging that old bench into the goats' enclosure. I'm sure they'd love to jump on top of it.'

Without looking back, Andrea disappeared into the farmhouse.

'Right. I'll be off. Look, Bligh... that last Christmas... I never meant to... The money... How did your dad manage?'

'He lasted just one month after you left.'

Nausea backed up her throat. 'He was a decent man – just like you.'

'Save it.' His voice had a dangerous edge.

'Bligh... please... it's Emmie, the girl you played chase with whilst your dad worked on the renovations; who made a sugar solution to save those exhausted bees down by Healdbury stream; who helped you bury that run-over fox.' She touched his fingers as if that might ignite better memories.

Andrea appeared at the back door with Gail. 'Thanks for coming in early, Bligh. I reckon we can pick most of the ripe strawberries today if we put our backs into it. I'm just going to give Mum breakfast.'

Emma and Andrea had loved picking strawberries as children. They had a secret rule – every third one went into their mouths. Emma loved the glossy red fruits with cream. Andrea preferred a simple sprinkling of sugar. When they were old enough, Gail taught them how to make jam. This prompted regular scone-making. Emma's scones never looked quite as tall as Andrea's, but Mum always insisted they were equally well-risen.

Emma longed for the old Gail. 'Why not let me stay for a few more hours and look after Mum? That way, you two can get on without worrying.'

'I'd like that,' said Gail. 'Breakfast with the woman who talks too much.'

Andrea folded her arms. 'You're joking, right? Why should I trust you?'

'Please. She's my mother too.'

Bligh clenched his teeth and looked from sister to sister. Gail's eyes had lit up and she walked towards Emma.

'Breakfast – that's all I'm asking,' said Emma.

'I'm hungry. I never get fed at this place,' whispered Gail. 'No one gave me dinner last night, but you look kind.'

Andrea paused. Then she sighed. 'Just for a couple of hours. But if Mum gets the slightest bit upset…'

'She won't. Thanks so much.' Emma's face lit up. 'I really appreciate this.'

Bligh shook his head and walked over to the kitchen door.

'I'm doing it for Mum,' said Andrea curtly. 'Just make sure your train ticket back to the city is one-way only.'

Chapter 5

Would Mum need to drink from a special beaker or wear a bib? Emma's eyes pricked when she saw two identical places set at the table with tumblers and napkins. Perhaps her condition hadn't become that bad. When they were little, she and Andrea used to think their mum was so sophisticated, with her strict table manners and weekend glass of sherry that she would sip during Saturday evening's tea.

'Just make sure she eats as much as possible. Her appetite's waned lately,' said Bligh. 'Sometimes she's more lucid and can hold a conversation. Others not. But we're lucky, most of the time she seems content.'

Emma looked at Gail. The big clock ticked. The room missed her mum's bustle and chat.

'Why the rush to start work? Can't the strawberries wait until your usual nine o'clock start?'

He shook his head. 'They're begging to be picked, plus I made a new batch of red onion chutney last week. I want to stick on the labels and put the jars out before I check the emails.'

'I saw the computer. What's with all the jiffy bags?'

'We've recently set up online – we need to stretch our reach. Profits have dwindled since a huge out-of-town supermarket was built around twelve months ago.

Its success has affected many other businesses in Heald-bury – the butcher's, the cheese shop and Phil's pet shop. It's early days, but our online sales are slowly expanding. There's definitely a market for delivering home-grown organic vegetables. We've already secured several regular customers in south Manchester, and it's not far to drive. As for the jiffy bags, they're for the smaller, long-life items such as pickles and jams.' Bligh turned to go outside. 'At least we've got a decent amount of stock now, stacked up in your old room.'

Emma winced.

'Right, I'll be in the shop if you need me.' He hesitated, as if reluctant to leave Emma in charge.

'You're the woman who talks too much,' said Gail, folding and unfolding a chocolate wrapper – a gold one today.

'Yes,' said Emma in a cheerful tone. She peered into the fridge. Blueberries. Her mum's favourite. 'How about pancakes?'

'Is Andrea eating with us?'

'No. She's picking strawberries.'

'Pity it's not tomatoes.'

Emma smiled. 'Why? They're the one thing you can't abide.'

'I like tomatoes. Can we have them on toast for break-fast?'

Emma stared.

'Is Andrea eating with us?' Gail asked again.

'No. She's busy outside.'

Gail lifted a glass of orange juice to her lips. The simple act made her seem so fragile. The way her hand shook as if she were in her ninth decade rather than her sixth. The detached look in her eyes. Would she miss her mouth?

35

And the parting in her hair wasn't quite straight. Emma glanced under the table. Yet again she was wearing odd socks.

'Do you still do needlework?' she asked.

'Sewing?' A vacant look came over Gail's face. 'How about those pancakes? I haven't eaten for days.'

As Emma made the batter, Andrea walked past the kitchen window and glanced in. She didn't catch her younger sister's eye but concentrated instead on Gail. The lack of trust penetrated the double glazing.

And who could blame her? thought Emma as she sat down with her mum to eat, ignoring the movement at the window as Andrea walked past again. After breakfast, while she did the washing–up, Bligh came in for a coffee. Was that to check up on her as well?

A couple of hours later, she and Gail were sitting on the sofa. Emma was surprised Bligh hadn't come back and told her it was time to leave. She'd glanced out of the kitchen window and spied her sister drinking out of a thermos flask. Clearly she'd taken every precaution to make sure their paths wouldn't cross again.

Emma fetched the photo albums from the side cabinet in the dining room. She and Gail flicked through them from way back. Gail hummed to herself just like she did in the old days. Now and then her face broke into a smile. Would she finally make the connection and recognise her younger daughter?

They came to a photo of Andrea aged about six months. She sat in a pram, holding a rattle. Emma looked away until the page turned. She looked back to see a print of herself just a couple of months after she'd left college, with the fake blonde hair, sprayed skin and dressy clothes she liked back then – all clues that the person she used to be had no confidence.

'That's your daughter,' she whispered, and held her breath.

Gail tutted. 'Caused trouble day and night, that one.'

'But... I'm sure she loved you.'

Gail turned the page without replying.

Emma collapsed back into the sofa and contemplated this uncomfortable return – the surveillance from Bligh and Andrea; the lack of recognition from Mum. Instantly her mind recalled the *whoosh* sensation she used to get from the first sip. How, with just one mouthful, the world became an easier place and seemed to have a space for her that was the perfect fit.

She stood up and paced the room, ending up by the front window. As she stared out at the pink foxgloves, Gail appeared by her side.

'I'm going for a walk,' she announced. 'In the village. It's Friday. That means fish for lunch at the Badger Inn.'

'No! I mean...' Emma softened her tone. 'I can make you a lovely lunch here. I don't think Andrea would want—'

'My coat... I'll just get my coat...'

Emma stood, unable to move for a moment. What should she do? Andrea wouldn't want her to take her mum out, of that she was sure. And there was no way she could face the pub's landlords, Polly and Alan. Not yet, not after she'd heard... She wasn't ready to think about it. Soon, but not today.

Gail gazed expectantly, like a child waiting to open Christmas presents.

How could she distract her? Keep her *doing* rather than just being? How had Andrea managed these last months?

37

Emma had been here only a matter of hours and could already see how challenging Mum could be.

She went to the patio doors at the back of the dining room and looked for Andrea. She dashed along to the shop, but Bligh had disappeared as well. When she got back, Gail had her winter coat half on. Emma tried to get it off, but Gail glared and pulled away. Emma considered shouting for help, but she didn't want to upset her mum.

'Okay,' she said reluctantly. Perhaps the fresh air would do them both good. She found a pad of paper in the kitchen and penned a note. She wrote down her mobile number, where they were going and at what time, and really hoped that would be enough.

She gazed at Gail for a moment, mourning the loss of her mum, her friend, the vegetarian, the needlework whizz, the animal carer. Gail had meant so many things to so many people. The dementia had reduced her to a singular being.

She managed to persuade Gail to wear her light summer jacket. There were some old Post-it notes screwed up in the pocket saying things like *Take tablets at ten*. When had she stopped writing them?

They walked along the dusty drive. Emma turned around, hoping to see Andrea or Bligh, but the farm looked deserted. They turned right and went down Broadgrass Hill. Emma pointed out colourful flowers. Gail stopped to pet a cat. When she stood up, her hand rested on Emma's. They ended up linking arms for the rest of their journey. Emma's chest felt lighter. Perhaps just a small part of Mum was in there somewhere.

They passed the butcher's. Emma didn't like to look in. Across the road, outside the supermarket, she spotted the homeless woman again, drinking out of a can. Familiar faces passed, smiling at Gail, not sure how to react to Emma. She looked at her mobile phone several times, to see if Andrea or Bligh had left a message. It was great that they'd let her spend time with Mum – she didn't want this walk to ruin it.

By the time they reached the Badger Inn, it had just turned midday.

'How about a lovely toasted sandwich in the teashop by the church?' said Emma brightly.

'Fish and chips,' said Gail.

A woman with a baby in a pram walked past. All Emma could hear for those seconds was the gurgle as the child woke up. When she focused again, Gail was already through the pub door. Emma closed her eyes for a second. This couldn't be happening. But it was. There was no going back now. This was the encounter she'd dreaded for months, meeting Polly and Alan. Pulse racing, she followed her mum in.

They were the first customers. Emma never used to like this pub much, with its old-school feel – the ping-pong table in the corner, not far from the darts board. She'd found the mahogany beams and magnolia walls unglamorous and wished for piped dance music instead of the jukebox. Yet now she gazed around and appreciated its charm. Like the small alcove in the corner, and the collection of badger ornaments on shelves along the tops of the walls.

Polly waved at Gail, and Emma took a sharp intake of breath. She noted the black shadows under the landlady's eyes, and how she had lost her curves. She still wore the boldest shades in make-up and clothes, as if she'd only ever discovered primary colours. She turned to Emma. 'So, the rumours were true. I meant to ring Andrea to find out if she was okay.' Polly crossed her arms, creasing the fifties-style swing dress. 'Alan!'

A distinguished-looking man with greying sideburns appeared around the side of the bar. His conservative clothes made him look like the black-and-white negative of Polly's bright lovebird outfit.

'Hello, Gail,' he said pleasantly. His gaze fell on Emma. 'You've got some nerve.'

Emma's knees felt unsteady as she thought back to rehab and what a friend there who'd visited Healdbury had revealed about Alan and Polly. It had caused her sleepless nights ever since.

'I… Gail insisted. We just want a quiet drink. Plus fish and chips for two. Please.'

Polly came around the bar, smiled at Gail and led her gently over to a table in the corner. She passed her a beer mat to play with. Then she whispered something in Alan's ear. He squeezed her shoulder before she headed out the back.

'You want a *drink*?' he said.

'Two… two Cokes, I mean,' she said, voice shaking a little. 'I don't—'

'Have you forgotten that you're barred?'

Emma walked up to him. 'No, I haven't, but look, Alan, I don't want a fuss. I'm really sorry… for everything.'

He snorted. 'I bet you can't remember half of the things you did – especially during the week before that last Christmas. How angry your actions made our customers. How it upset Bligh.'

'I can't undo the past, but—'

'Agreed,' said Alan. 'So bugger off.'

'But I can't leave Mum here on her own.'

Alan folded his arms. 'She'll be safer with us.' He proceeded to list Emma's many misadventures from the past – how she broke the toilet, threw up against the wall; how she hit on customers and once tried to do a striptease on a table. Like a pupil sent to the head teacher's office, she stood, ears burning, wishing some magical spaceship could beam her and Mum up and teleport them to somewhere more friendly.

The door creaked open behind her. Emma swung around to see Andrea and Bligh.

'What the hell are you up to?' said Andrea, face perspiring, sleeves rolled up.

'I just brought Mum out for lunch.'

'What was I supposed to think, coming into an empty house? I was frantic until Polly rang.' Andrea hurried over to Gail, scanning her as if she expected her to have come to harm.

'But I couldn't find you or Bligh.'

'One of the goats managed to get out again. We found him by the pond,' said Bligh.

'I left a note on the kitchen table.'

'Really?' He raised both eyebrows, then he, Andrea and Alan all exchanged looks.

'You think I'm lying?' said Emma.

'Would that be *so* out of character?' said Andrea.

Emma held onto the back of a nearby chair. What was the point in arguing? They'd all given her plenty of chances before. Chances she'd scorned. It wasn't enough to look clear-skinned and walk straight.

'Sorry. You must have been very worried.' She went over to Gail and knelt down. 'It's been lovely to see you,' she murmured. The beer mat fell to the floor. She picked it up and handed it back, then, using the table to

41

steady herself, pushed herself up. She caught Andrea's eye. 'Thank you for letting me have breakfast with Mum. I'll head up to Foxglove Farm and collect my things. By the time you get back I'll be gone. I'll forward you my address when I get a new place to live, just in case… Sorry for the disruption.'

She took one last glance at Mum and almost knocked a chair over as she left.

15 months before going back

Emma and Joe stood yawning in the March sun. He'd actually come back last night, and they'd scraped together enough money for burgers and doughnuts. It had almost been like old times as they'd huddled together to keep warm, telling jokes and singing songs. He'd even kissed her goodnight, albeit only on the cheek.

'Are you coming back tonight?' Emma asked, squinting against the bright rays that highlighted the blonde streaks in Joe's spiky hair. 'Tomorrow's Mother's Day, so people will probably reach into their pockets more than usual.' Like at Christmas, people's generosity was directly proportional to the number of bags they carried.

'Dunno. Don't depend on it.' A teenager skated past and almost hit Emma's legs. 'Oi!' shouted Joe and pulled her to one side. He squeezed her arm. 'Stay safe, Ems.'

'I could come with you?' she said, hating the neediness in her voice. She didn't understand. Why was he creating distance between them?

'Look… you know I think the world of you, but give this up.' He sighed. 'You and me… it'll never work out. You know why.'

'But I've been working on this plan – researching in the library...' Her stomach tingled. She'd held onto her idea as if she were planning a surprise party. Now it was time for the big reveal. 'Forget London. We could work abroad. Get away from all this.'

'Abroad? Are you crazy?'

'Yes. I mean no.' She gave a nervous giggle. 'Just think about it, Joe, we could easily do fruit-picking. With my experience in farming—'

'I haven't even got a passport. And where would we find the money for the flights?'

'I… I've still got to work out the details.'

'The basics, more like.'

'We could work it out together.'

He shook his head.

'But…'

He turned to go.

Cheeks flushed, she rummaged in her rucksack. 'Here. Take these. The soup run was handing them out last week.' She passed him a jar of vitamin tablets.

His face relaxed and he slipped the jar into his bag. 'Right. I'm off. See ya around.'

Vision blurry, Emma headed to the shops. She passed a travel agency and scrutinised the deals in the window. Spain. Provence. Tuscany. If only she and Joe could start life over again. Mothercare caught her attention next, and she peered through the glass at bibs and prams. One day she'd love to have kids. She'd try to be the best mum ever. Perhaps she'd have girls who got on as well as she and Andrea had. But not for a few years. She needed to sort herself out first. Until then, whatever Joe said, she just *knew* they were each other's answer.

43

Eventually she pitched up outside a gift shop, away from the centre. Children of all ages stopped off to buy cards, giving her their change on the way out. Emma sat cross-legged in front of an empty Starbucks cup, trying not to think about Joe. Just for a few seconds that donated coffee had made her feel almost normal – whatever normal was.

Was it a house with a white picket fence? A mortgage and business lunches out? During her more aware moments, she observed passers-by going about their daily business. Couples hand in hand. *X Factor* wannabe buskers. Browbeaten parents proudly watching toddlers toddle. Football fans giving their all to the latest chant. Young executives with their polished shoes and space-age phones.

She'd concluded that all being normal meant was being happy with yourself. Quite the street philosopher she'd become, like a Buddha who favoured company instead of reclusiveness.

She yawned and wished for another caffeine hit to take her mind off the physical niggles in her life, like continual acid reflux, toothache, cuts and bruises from falls, and that cough during the winter.

Joe was a coffee lover, latte being his absolute favourite. He came from London and didn't even know that goats produced milk. Painful as it was to talk about Foxglove Farm, she'd do so as Joe sat like one of the small children she'd enjoyed babysitting as a teenager, mesmerised by her anecdotes. Like the time Gail rescued two sheep from the same farm, one year apart. Clearly they remembered each other and skipped like lambs when they first met up. Andrea preferred plants, growing vegetables and harvesting fruit, but those animals' reunion brought

44

tears even to her eyes. Joe always said he could tell Emma would have made an excellent vet, even though she'd failed her A level biology twice.

For his part, Joe talked about London life. The clubs he'd grown up in with an older brother who had a lot of problems. His mum travelled the world as a lecturer whilst his surgeon Dad worked all hours repairing hearts. Neither realised anything was amiss until Joe's brother died from an accidental overdose. Initially they blamed Joe for not telling them. Then they'd been surprised when guilt sent him down the same avenue. A bigger contrast to Emma's rural life there couldn't have been. Yet she and Joe had clicked together like a seat belt and buckle.

The morning passed within hues of cider, everything beige and warm, as if the surroundings had been passed through the sunniest Instagram filter. So Joe wanted details for their new life abroad? Then Emma would work them out. The Starbucks cup filled halfway and she emptied it, stashing her takings in the pocket of her rucksack. A man in a sharp suit gave her a sandwich and told her about free cans of sports drink being handed out in Market Street. He had a good heart.

Mum had a good heart, Emma thought as a little girl walked past, her petite hand enveloped in a woman's. Would she still have backed Andrea's decision to throw Emma out if she'd been one hundred per cent well? The diagnosis had come as a shock. Yet secretly even Emma had known it made sense, like the end of an Agatha Christie novel that taunted you for not having seen the clues. Mum had always been a little forgetful – thanks to the menopause, they'd laughed. But then she'd started to forget basic words. *That thingamabob* became a favourite phrase. She would make up her own words – a belt became a waist tie. She was still their mother, though, and would laugh afterwards, brushing off mistakes. Eventually she started relying on Post-it notes and stuck them all over the house, reminding her of things to do and where stuff was. Yet when Emma had left, she was still tending to the livestock; still doing her needlework. Perhaps there was a chance she wouldn't get much worse for years and years.

How would she be spending Mother's Day tomorrow? With croissants and home-made jam for breakfast? One of Andrea's nut roasts for lunch?

Back in the day, Gail could have opened her own vegetarian restaurant with her spicy tofu curry and melt-in-the-mouth vegan beetroot chocolate cake. Every Sunday she insisted that the girls make dessert. When they were little, it might be a simple bowl of ice cream, with Andrea chopping fruit for the top and Emma squeezing on their favourite sauce. Emma would enjoy mothering her latest favourite toy, which meant feeding it her latest culinary creation. Soon, however, she was feeding school friends when the sisters gained skills and could produce the lightest sponge or chewiest meringue. Then they moved onto creating main courses. Gail respected their taste for the beef and chicken they'd grown to love due to Healdbury High School dinners.

'What the fuck are you doing?' Fingers dug sharply into Emma's scalp. 'This is my patch. EVERYONE knows that.'

Emma's face hit the pavement and her heart pounded. For a moment she wasn't sure what was going on. She heard jangling. Zips opening. Coins scattered across the ground. Grazed cheeks stinging, she opened her eyes. She dragged herself to her feet and rubbed the back of her head. Before she could focus properly, a fist hit the side of her face. She cried out and almost hit the ground again. The scenery swayed. A woman dressed in stained denim collected up Emma's money. Passers-by backed away. Some stared. Others pretended they hadn't seen.

'Leave my stuff alone,' Emma shouted, and lunged forward, but the woman swiped again, narrowly missing her target before she turned the rucksack upside down and shook out its contents.

Emma rubbed the side of her head. It felt sticky and wet. Like a caged animal, she paced from side to side. This wouldn't have happened with Joe. He was always meticulous about finding safe territory. She should have guessed this prime spot was already claimed. She'd got lazy and hadn't scouted the street the day before.

She should have stayed on familiar ground, amongst people who'd defend her. That was how she and Joe had first met – except then it was she who'd saved him. Two kids were trying to steal his money. He was out of it and couldn't protect his belongings. Emma had run at them screaming. Once they'd scarpered, she'd sat down with him. He'd insisted on sharing his takings.

Finally the woman threw down the rucksack and folded her arms. Emma shoved her few belongings back into her bag, grabbed her coat and, still feeling disorient-ated, slunk away. Eventually she found Beth, who took her to the nearest public toilets, tidied her up and gave her a chocolate bar – Beth's favourite Twix. Emma gave her half back. They went to the railway bridge and sat on the ground. Beth shared some wine she'd shoplifted earlier.

'Just a one-off, mind. I ain't going soft.'

'You're a good mate, Beth,' said Emma, and wiped her mouth.

Feeling fuzzy and calm, she hugged her knees. This was the last straw. It was time for her and Joe to leave England behind. She raised the bottle to her lips again, as grandiose plans formed of how to raise the money for those flights.

14 months before going back

It happened towards the middle of April, on a night when time seemed to get stuck. The evenings were much lighter now. This was good for takings. Joe and Emma had pooled their earnings and managed to raise the money necessary for a room in a bed and breakfast. That was a rare treat. Clean sheets. Hot water. Safety. A solid night's kip.

Cosy under the covers, they sat in bed, on the lumpy mattress, eating fried chicken. Joe had just smoked out of the window. Hotel staff became unfriendly if the wrong smell wafted out from under a door. With a satisfied sigh, Emma leant back against the soft pillows. She threw the empty takeaway box on the floor and downed the remains of a large brown plastic bottle.

Right at that moment, life was good. Leaving Foxglove Farm was the best thing she'd ever done. She was independent, answerable to no one – mistress of her own destiny. This was what life was about – having fun. She ignored the quieter voices in her head that asked how her mum was doing; that sometimes wondered, late into the night, if Andrea ever thought about her younger sister.

'Give me a cuddle,' she said, and burped. Life would be fantastic when they were living abroad.

'Fuck off, Ems,' Joe said in the same slurred tones.

Emma smiled and snuggled up to him. Her hand slid under his shirt and made contact with skin. She stroked his chest. He must have cared, because he held his fingers over

48

hers. His touch healed her recently familiar sense of rejection. Her hand spread out and soaked up the intimacy.

'Let's just pretend, for one minute, that we don't have to wake up tomorrow,' she murmured. 'That this night is our only existence and will last forever. Close your eyes. This could be our own proper house. We might both have jobs. Lots of friends. Money to spend on clothes. Let time stand still, Joe. Just for one night.'

She kissed him on the mouth that told bad jokes or offered comforting words. He didn't respond, so she pulled her hand from under his and moved it downwards.

'Emma... we shouldn't...' But eventually his breath became rasping. All she'd ever wanted to do was make him happy. Desperate kisses juggled with awkward limbs. Joe's eyes loomed above hers for a few seconds before his head turned away and he reached his height of pleasure.

Heat gushed through Emma's body and the room spun for a second. Yet why did she feel such a sense of emptiness when it was all over? Joe turned his back on her and lay separate. He must be tired. Yes. That was it.

Yet when morning arrived and both of them were in bed wearing no underwear, Joe still kept his distance. More than that, he lay as far away from Emma as possible and... her insides squeezed... why instead of the dawn chorus did she hear him quietly crying?

The sense of rejection returned.

He continued to spurn their closeness over the next few days. They hardly talked and instead communicated using a series of grunts and body language. It was like being in a bad marriage, just without the rings. Gold ones, that is, thought Emma one morning, as Joe lay in his sleeping bag blowing out rings made from smoke. She wished she could catch them. One could hang around her neck. Another on her wrist. Sometimes she missed wearing jewellery. She pictured yesterday's busy Mancunians in Market Street – the fashionable clothes, the pencilled eyebrows…

It made her feel a little less isolated to recall moments of kindness, like the young executive in a hurry who disappeared into a coffee shop and came back out to hand her a croissant and a cappuccino. Or the middle-aged postal worker who always stopped her bike to say hello and push fifty pence into her hand.

Emma tried not to dwell on those who'd do anything not to make eye contact. Legs would hurry past as if she were a concrete statue. She didn't blame them. Perhaps some felt uncomfortable. Maybe a few found it easier to believe that rough sleepers were scammers and no-good benefit cheats.

She stared across Joe and out of the dirty window. Reluctantly the sun climbed into the Manchester cloud. The early rush-hour traffic rumbled. A siren sounded in the background. Emma hadn't slept much.

Joe looked at her. Looked away. Stubbed out his cigarette. Sat up and packed his burgundy rucksack. Glanced back.

'It's for the best.' His voice broke. 'After the other night… you understand why I can't be around you now?'

No. Not really.

'Where will you go?'

'I'm going to try my luck down south again. My life north of Watford…' he gave a wry smile, 'obviously hasn't worked out. It's what I need. Starting afresh.'

'You serious? Are you thinking of getting treatment?'

He broke eye contact.

'Why not do that here? You had a permanent address for more than six months, didn't you?'

He nodded.

'So you're considered local. You qualify. If you feel ready to quit…'

'I do. You and me… what happened… it's given me that push. But I can stop on my own,' he said hurriedly.

Everyone thought that. It was known as denial.

'What about us leaving England? The fruit-picking?' she said. 'If we could just save a bit of money…'

'We've as much chance of flying to the moon.' Joe chewed the skin on the side of his forefinger. 'You'll be okay, right?'

'Sure,' she said in a bright voice. 'You know me. The street cat with nine lives.'

'Eight. Mad Hatter Holly almost took you with her when you pulled her back from jumping off that bridge.'

Neither of them spoke for a moment.

'I'll miss you,' Emma whispered. 'Please don't leave. And I liked the other night. I'm so sorry you didn't. I thought we were getting close. You and me, we go together, don't we?'

Joe didn't reply.

He couldn't leave. Not like her father had when she was little. With Joe, she'd finally begun to feel as somehow she fitted in.

They stood up. Joe rolled his sleeping bag and tucked it under his arm. Awkwardly he darted forward and gave her the quickest of hugs. 'I… I've got you a goodbye present.' His hand disappeared into the bottom of his rucksack.

Emma stared at the boyish face that so often tried to look tough. From the moment they'd met, she'd felt the urge to protect him, despite the street cockiness. Finally he pulled out a packet. Cheeks red, mouth curved upwards for the first time in days, he handed her a large box of…

'Tampons?' A smile spread tentatively across Emma's face.

'I had to get something that I wouldn't be tempted to keep for myself. And… well, they ain't cheap.'

'Too right,' said Emma. She took the box. A lump rose in her throat. 'It's quite the nicest present anyone's ever bought me.'

Joe's eyes glistened. 'It's been good, hasn't it? Us? You know – circumstances apart?'

'You've been a lifeline, Joe. Like… like…'

'Family?'

'Better than that,' she said roughly.

His face grew ugly for a second and he rubbed his stubble. 'Yeah, you're right.'

'We don't have to label what we have – family, friends, whatever… We've just been there for each other.'

He nodded. 'I'll miss our chats about movies and telly.'

'One day we should go into directing.'

'Nah. It'd be a crime to keep my good looks off the screen.'

'Well, I'll have to train to be your personal make-up artist then. You'll need all the help you can get to be camera ready.'

For one second it was just like old times. Then reality kicked in. Both their mouths flatlined.

'Look after yourself, Emma. Stay safe.'

'You won't change your mind? We can work this out, Joe.' Her voice sounded like a draught that had managed to escape. 'You told me about trying to make a go of it with that Kelly woman, before you ended up on the streets. Why not chance it again? I could make you so happy.'

His face hardened as he looked at the door. 'You *know* why. Don't make this more difficult than it needs to be.'

Emma swallowed. 'But how will we stay in touch? We could arrange to meet up in a couple of months. Decide on a meeting point either here or in London?'

'I can't think that far ahead,' Joe said, and made to go.

'Wait a minute...' She picked up a nearby newspaper and scrabbled around for a pen. She tore off a strip of paper and wrote furiously for a minute. 'Here's my address, back at Foxglove Farm. It... it's all I've got. I'm never going back there, but... I don't know... post can get forwarded. Perhaps one day...'

Joe sighed, snatched the paper and left.

Emma's day carried on carrying on, the sky becoming gloomier, her sitting in the dark, in the corner, doing what she did best. Eventually, in a haze, she packed up her belongings. Her supplies had run out. She needed to visit the supermarket.

How would she cope without Joe? How would he manage? She'd looked out for him. He'd looked out for her. Where would she go from here? Joe had stirred something inside that didn't just want to live from day to day any more.

She felt so alone.

She wiped her eyes and gazed around the room that had witnessed some of her happier moments over the last few months, like her and Joe curled up together, chatting through the night. He'd talk about his brother. How they'd shared a love of skateboarding and would plot against the latest nanny. And then there were the friendly arguments over who to cast in their all-time favourite films. The latest had been over *Jaws*. Beth, they'd finally decided, would be the mother on the beach who lost her son – she'd certainly slap honest police chief Martin Brody. *He'd* be played by Stig, one of the few friends both felt they could trust completely.

Buoyed by the thought of her imminent liquid escape, with ceremony Emma said goodbye to the spiders and her memories. There'd be no return. The door rattled on its hinges as she kicked it shut behind her. She left the building, and there on the ground, caught in a bush, a strip of newspaper fluttered in the breeze. The address she'd given to Joe. She delved into her rucksack for coins and walked straight past it.

Chapter 6

Emma left the Badger Inn and crossed the road without looking, heading away from Broadgrass Hill and the farm. Two cars hooted. A retired couple stared. Outside the supermarket, the homeless woman with the asymmetrical hair glanced up.

She continued ahead, down a road lined with shops. It used to be a favourite avenue, with several pubs and a takeaway for the appetite that always hit after closing time. She squinted as the pet shop came into view. She had once worked there part-time. She'd combined it with helping out at the farm, once the exam failures had quashed her dreams of becoming a vet.

Confused for a moment, she stopped. What was she doing here? She needed to get back to the farm and fetch her belongings. About to turn back, she narrowed her eyes as a figure caught her eye. Sitting outside on the pavement, wearing a khaki bobble hat and reading a book... She stared at the chocolate Staffie dog, then broke into a run.

'Stig!' There was only one man she knew who wore his woolly hat come rain or shine.

The man stood up. Under the gaze of curious passers-by she threw herself at him and they hugged.

'Whoa!' He stepped back and his face broke into a smile.

With red cheeks, Emma smoothed down her top. 'Sorry... it's just good to see a friendly face.'

'Nice to see you too. It must be over a year since I've bumped into you or Joe. I assumed you'd moved on. Looking good, Emma. You got into treatment?'

She nodded.

'And Joe?'

Emma mumbled something about him going down south and a difference of opinion.

Stig didn't ask questions. Just said he knew they'd been close.

'What are you doing in Healdbury?' she asked, still in a daze after the falling-out with Andrea.

'I could ask you the same thing.'

'This is where I grew up.'

'The farm?'

Emma tried to elaborate but just couldn't, and instead stood in silence. 'I'm sorry, Stig,' she said eventually. 'I've just come from... You see, me and my sister...' Her shoulders slumped. 'I'm not the best company right now; I need to clear my head. But it's great to see you again. I'll be back later.'

'Hey, no explanation needed,' he said, and studied her face. 'I'm not going anywhere.'

They hugged again and she headed through the village, taking a short cut to Healdbury stream. Sometimes she and Bligh had gone that way after school, popping into the bakery for an iced bun.

As the water came into view, her heartbeat no longer sounded in her ears. Instead she listened to the birds, wasps, the babbling current... Carefully she climbed down to the stream's edge, took off her trainers and sat with her toes in the water, squishing mud between them.

Bulrushes swayed side to side like pendulums. A frog plopped into the water.

Life was so simple back in the day, when all she and Bligh had to worry about was maths homework and how to convince their parents to let them stay out an extra hour. But now… She breathed in the algae smell and watched tiddlers circumnavigate her feet. Did they swim in families? If one lost its way, could it easily come back and fit into the shoal again?

Gail hadn't said much whilst eating breakfast. Emma hadn't known how to fill the silence. She wasn't sure there would be much more conversation with Andrea. More apologies would be pointless – the same with Bligh. So if words wouldn't work, that only left actions.

But what could she do to change their minds about her staying?

Her forehead relaxed as the sun warmed her face and the familiar surroundings took her back to her childhood. Dash used to love swimming for twigs that Emma and Andrea would throw into the stream. They'd laugh when he'd shake off the water and then go straight back in.

What was it her case worker Lou had said? *Manage your expectations. You've got yourself better, you've changed, but people won't know that. Give them time to get up to speed.* Blades of grass flattened as Emma ran her hand over the bank of the stream.

Lou was right. An instant reunion? That was never going to be possible. She could see that now.

She sat thinking about the past and all the people she'd hurt because she used to feel so isolated and not good enough, like some sort of misfit. Her mind switched to yesterday and the way she'd turned up so unexpectedly. She should have foreseen the shock that would cause. But it was too late now. She couldn't take back her thoughtless arrival.

She took her hand away from the turf and, like the blades of grass, stood upright. She brushed down her cotton trousers and put her trainers back on. Giving up was not the solution – but was it unfair on her family to persist?

As for Polly and Alan… one thing at a time.

She made her way back into the village and stopped at the baker's to buy Stig a sandwich. Then she headed to the pet shop, where he was sitting outside.

'I still can't believe you're here,' she said, and passed him the food before squatting down by his dog, the Duchess. She ruffled the Staffie's soft ears and ran a hand down her coat, feeling her ribs. Then she slumped against the wall whilst Stig put his book down and ate. She had forgotten how big the world looked from this angle. She studied the litter bin opposite and imagined all sorts of half-eaten hidden treasures. Friends on the streets used to kip in tall wheelie bins. Emma had never dared, terrified that she'd wake up being crushed in the back of a rubbish truck.

'What brings you out to the sticks?' she asked. 'I've noticed a few rough sleepers since I got back. There's a woman outside the supermarket…'

'Rita,' he said, and gave the Duchess some ham.

'And a couple outside the bank on Church Street. Plus a girl at the station.'

'She's called Tilly.' Stig stopped eating for a second. 'Have you heard of the Alternative European Arts Festival?'

'I saw it on the front of the *Manchester News* last week.' It had made her think of her mum. Gail would have loved to visit all the different exhibitions. There were collages made from rainforest leaves, and living works of art in the form of tattoos. It would have inspired her cross-stitching.

'It started three weeks ago and goes on until the end of October. Artists from across the Continent are visiting, along with local arts ministers and groups from schools. So there's been a huge clean-up in the city. Apparently it also happened during the Commonwealth Games in 2002 – rough sleepers were moved away to create a more pleasant impression.'

'Where have they all gone?'

'Stockport mainly. Some, like me, have come out further afield.'

'How are you supposed to manage without the shelters?'

'I won't lie, it's not been easy. I camp outside this pet shop in the hope that someone will give the Duchess a square meal, but there aren't many customers. I might have to move on – which would prove to be a popular decision with the locals.'

Emma raised an eyebrow.

'Oh, they haven't been abusive. And one mum brings me a takeaway coffee every single morning on the school run. But the majority...' He shrugged. 'They're just not used to it. You remember that sense of unspoken disapproval?'

'You still won't consider a hostel?'

'You know that's not an option for me,' he said gruffly, jerking his head towards the dog. 'I could never abandon her.'

He studied the pavement and gently turned over a ladybird that was stuck on its back. Stig wasn't an addict. He had talked about it once – the depression he'd suffered that made him walk out on his job as a geography teacher. He'd mumbled something about league tables and demanding parents.

'I've always wondered why you're called Stig,' Emma said. 'Is it after that bloke off *Top Gear*?'

'Nah. Everyone thinks that. It's from a book my grandad used to read me called *Stig of the Dump*. Stig lived in a den built from discarded rubbish. I can relate to that.'

'You still haven't contacted your mum and dad?'

'I can't. I was the first in my family to go to university. They'd be so disappointed. It's kinder to just carry on letting them think I'm missing.'

Emma knew that was an illness talking. Mad Hatter Holly firmly believed her family would be better off if she were dead.

'So, have you returned home for good?' he asked, polishing off the last mouthful of sandwich.

'Don't ask,' she said, unable to face giving details.

'Surely it's going to take a while to repair any damage?'

'Yes. Slowly, slowly, I guess. I've fantasised about some great reconciliation, but I realise now that I can't rewrite history; I can't erase all the hurt.'

'No, you can't. The past is done with. But the future is still a blank book. It might work out. Don't assume the worst. You haven't got a crystal ball.'

'One of my therapists told me that. I didn't appreciate it at first.'

Stig bent his knees up and wrapped his arms around them. 'There was this pupil I had once. Olly. Hard-working. Polite. I'd had a bad morning. Mock results were in. The head was disappointed with my class's results.' He nodded his head at a passer-by who had dropped a fifty-pence coin into his cup. 'I took it out on Olly. Humiliated him by making him stand in the corner for making some

60

wisecrack that was actually funny. I summoned him to my classroom at the end of the day. Apologised. But the damage had been done.'

'What happened?'

'It took several weeks, but eventually he made eye contact again and we moved forwards.' He put down the sandwich box. 'Exactly how long have you been back?'

'I arrived yesterday.'

'And how long was your drinking an issue before you ended up in the city?'

'I get it – you're saying that of course they aren't going to see me as any different after a couple of days when I ruined their lives for years.'

Give them time to get up to speed. Lou's words echoed in her ears.

'What have you got to lose by giving it another go? By giving it a few more days – or weeks?'

That was what Old Len from AA always said. Just give it time.

Promising to see him again whatever she decided, Emma headed up Broadgrass Hill, the air cooler as the sun disappeared for a moment. She could either collect her things and leave, or take the more difficult route. Actions and not words. Could that really be the way forward? She'd only been back one day, but already her mind kept returning to the farm and how she could help. She would love to do everything possible to return the place to its former glory. She could easily mend the tatty enclosures and shelters, and knew how to make the animals' lives more interesting using some discarded guttering and wood. She used to be a dab hand with a brush and could soon smarten up the farmhouse's peeling paintwork.

One of the best things about recovery was realising she had skills and could use them to do good; that she could be useful; that she counted; that she could make a positive difference, however small.

And then there was Mum… and giving Andrea a break; making up for the past – that was what really mattered. She inhaled and exhaled. Surely they could find common ground again?

By the time she approached her old home, she was walking with lengthy strides. She slipped through the kissing gate and walked around to the front. Barking loudly, Dash announced her arrival. It had just gone four. Andrea and Bligh appeared carrying full baskets of strawberries. Clouds had gathered above them. Creaking loudly, the barn door blew open and shut.

Andrea placed her basket clumsily on the ground and folded her arms. 'Where have you been?'

'I've decided not to leave Healdbury after all,' Emma said quietly.

'Are you for real?' Andrea shook her head. 'After everything you did to me and Mum?'

Bligh clenched his basket's handle tighter.

'No one wants you here. Not me, not Bligh, not Polly and Alan, not the villagers,' Andrea continued. 'You'll get Aunt Thelma's money. What's the point of sticking around?'

'I want to help with the farm – with Mum,' Emma said, in the same calm, steady voice.

'No chance,' said Andrea, and checked her watch. 'Just go, please. I've asked you more than once now. Don't make this harder on Mum or us.' She glanced up at the sky and disappeared inside.

Emma stood her ground. She couldn't quit after just twenty-four hours.

The back door flew open and her sister reappeared, chest heaving, cheeks the colour of goat's milk.

'What's the matter?' asked Bligh, striding over.

'It's Mum. The house is empty. I don't know where she is.'

Chapter 7

Bligh and Andrea talked in low, urgent voices. Where to start looking? The farm buildings? The village? The neighbours? It reminded Emma of the time Joe had disappeared, when they'd been spending every minute together. Off his head like never before. She'd been worried he'd get beaten up or run over.

After checking spots where he usually met his dealers, she had eventually found him in the Northern Quarter, outside a coffee shop. He'd got to know the owner, who always gave him a free hot chocolate or sometimes a cupcake. She said his quirky humour reminded her of her son, who'd disappeared three years previously.

'We need to think logically,' she said now. 'A good friend of mine called Joe went missing once. I tracked down his favourite places. Where are Mum's?'

'We don't need your help.' Andrea pursed her lips.

'How long was she in the house on her own?' continued Emma.

'I don't know… about an hour. She was tired and went for her usual afternoon nap.'

'Was she asleep when you left her?'

'No, but she was tucked up and quiet,' snapped Andrea. 'We got behind with the work, coming down to the Badger Inn after your little escapade – I didn't have time to wait for her to drop off.'

'I... I know how busy you are. Would you have seen her if she came out the back door, or must she have gone out the front?'

Bligh sighed. 'She could have walked straight past without us noticing, we were so focused on picking fruit.'

'What about the Badger Inn? It seems like her favourite place to eat. Do you think she could get that far?'

Andrea paused and then took a mobile phone out of her trouser pocket. 'I doubt it. She walks so slowly these days and probably couldn't find it on her own, but I'll check with Polly.'

'And I'll double-check around the house, just to be sure,' said Emma, and ran inside. She realised it was stupid to look under beds and behind curtains, but she was so worried, she couldn't help investigating every nook and cranny. She opened the big wardrobe in Gail's room and pulled out the clothes. Several Post-it notes fell to the floor. In passing, she noticed Mum's private wooden chest on the bottom, behind all the shoes. As children, she and Andrea believed it was full of treasure, as Gail always kept it locked.

'Mum! Gail! Are you there?'

Lastly she looked in the bathroom, even checking behind the shower curtain though she knew it was futile. Then she went back downstairs and out of the back door. Please let Bligh or Andrea have found her.

But they were both standing in the yard looking like geo-spotters without a map.

'She's developed a liking for tomatoes recently,' said Bligh. 'I'll check in the greenhouse.'

As he left, Andrea put away her phone. Her eyes glistened. 'Polly's gone outside to see if she's walking down Broadgrass Hill.'

Emma stepped forward to pat her arm, but Andrea pulled away.

'Look,' Emma said. 'We need to work together on this for Mum's sake, whatever you think of me coming back. Let's go to the end of the drive and check the land either side. If she was walking and tripped over and fell, she could be lying in the patch of wild flowers or behind the apple trees.'

Andrea paused, and then nodded.

Breaking into a run, they hurried around the side of the house and through the kissing gate, both calling out. It reminded Emma of when they used to play hide-and-seek. Once she'd stayed hidden for hours amongst the foxgloves. Andrea had given up looking. An anxious Mum had been furious. Was this how she'd felt, her mind imagining the worst outcome? What if she'd got onto the road and been knocked down? Or perhaps she *had* tripped over and was lying concussed.

'I'll check the wild flowers – you look amongst the apple trees.'

Andrea couldn't reply. Her arms shook.

'We'll find her, I promise. She's only been missing a little while.'

'Your promises don't mean anything,' said Andrea, and gulped before they parted.

Nothing. No clues either, like a dropped chocolate wrapper or one of her cotton handkerchiefs embroidered with a G in the corner.

'Where *is* she?' said Andrea as they stood at the end of the drive by the birdbath. She rubbed her forehead. 'I should have made sure she'd fallen asleep before leaving her.' She looked at her watch. 'And now we're getting behind with the strawberries.' Her fists curled. 'When is life going to give me a break?'

Emma could have said: *Now, because I'm back*, but she didn't. She just needed to listen. In the past she'd never done enough of that – she'd always been armed with a response she thought important or witty, or one that defended her old insecurities.

After more than two hours of searching, they were both running out of ideas. Mum wasn't in front of the pond or in any of the sheds; Polly couldn't see her along Broadgrass Hill and she wouldn't have had time to get further than that. Andrea went inside to call the police.

Eventually the two sisters and Bligh met up outside the barn. Andrea went into the kitchen to fetch glasses of water. Despite the drop in temperature, they needed to rehydrate. The three of them sat in the dust and drank. Andrea popped a mint in her mouth and offered the tube of sweets to Bligh. More clouds congregated in the sky.

'What if it rains?' she said. 'Mum feels the cold so easily these days. Or even worse, a storm? She'd be terrified.'

'I just want to give her a hug,' said Emma, '*when* we find her.' The sisters looked at each other.

'Are you thinking about Debenhams?' muttered Andrea.

Emma nodded.

One day they'd both got lost shopping in one of Manchester's biggest department stores. They'd only been six and eleven. Mum was on a rare shopping trip and lost sight of them in the women's clothes section. Emma had tried so hard not to cry because she knew Andrea was being brave, sliding her arm around her shoulder, telling her that *when* – not if – they found Mum, everything would be okay. Her grip had tightened as a strange man asked for their names. Turned out he was security, and within minutes he had reunited them with a distraught Gail.

'What did the police say?' Bligh took a large mouthful of water and wiped his mouth.

'They've sent a patrol car out to look for her and are coming right over.' Andrea slipped her mobile into her back trouser pocket. 'They were trying to sound reassuring. Insisted it wasn't uncommon for them to find and return residents to care homes. I explained that Mum had never wandered off before. They wanted to know what she was wearing. My mind went blank and I couldn't remember.' Her voice cracked as a spot of rain landed on her arm. 'I'll never forgive myself if something happens.'

'Oh, Andrea…' Emma reached out.

'Don't! If it wasn't for you, we wouldn't be in this mess.'

Emma stared into her glass. Where *could* Mum have gone? 'I know we've looked in front of it, but what about *behind* the pond? It's a long shot, but she used to love that view across the fields that border the motorway.'

'I don't let her down there any more in case she ends up on the road.'

The sisters looked at each other and put down their glasses. Gail never had liked being told what to do. Like the time the doctor ordered her to rest her twisted ankle – that advice hadn't stopped her digging up potatoes. And when five-year-old Emma's teacher had called her into the school one day and suggested she wasn't being supportive enough of homework, Gail had told her that the whole idea was ridiculous and that children of that age learnt far more by exploring nature.

'Bligh, can you stay here in case she turns up?' asked Andrea as the two sisters got to their feet. At a fast pace they left the yard, passed the animal enclosures and skirted the pond behind the weeping willow.

'Mum?' shouted Andrea.

Had they really heard someone mutter a response? They hurried past tall reeds and around to the back of the weeping willow. Andrea gasped as they saw Gail standing by a row of bushes bearing green berries, some of which had started to turn black. They hurried over.

'You had us worried,' said Andrea, voice trembling. 'Don't ever do that again.'

Their mum's expression didn't alter and Emma went to her other side, a wave of relief almost sweeping her off her feet.

Gail tried to spit something out. It was small. Black. Emma opened her mum's curled fingers and stared at five berries.

'What's the matter?' said Andrea.

'Blueberries,' muttered Gail.

Emma went over to the bush and studied the leaves as a rain shower fell. A shiver rippled across her back. 'Shit! Did you know these are deadly nightshade?'

'What? No. I mean... I haven't been down here for ages.' Andrea's hand flew to her throat. 'Are you sure?'

'They grew down by the railway bridge where I some-times slept. One guy ate them on purpose; heard they could make you hallucinate.' He'd almost died. Stig had dug up the plants so that no one else could give them a shot. That had been later in the summer, but this hot weather must have brought on some of the berries early.

'What do we do?' asked Andrea. 'Will she be all right? Should we give her milk to drink, or salty water to make her sick, or—'

'We need to keep calm,' said Emma quietly. 'Otherwise she might get upset.' Pulse racing, she stood in front of Gail. 'Her pupils aren't dilated. I don't think she's hallucinating.'

'That's a good sign, right?'

'I think so,' said Emma, but her voice wavered. As quickly as possible, she took out her phone and rang for an ambulance. It arrived within fifteen minutes, and by that time the sisters had led Gail around to the front of the barn and rung the police to say she'd been found.

Andrea insisted on going alone to the hospital with Gail. Wringing her hands, Emma stood in the yard watching the ambulance drive away. What if Mum took a turn for the worse? Emma wouldn't be there to comfort her or Andrea.

She turned and walked past Bligh, who raised his eyebrows. Before she did anything else, she had to dig up those deadly nightshade bushes.

13 months before going back

Emma yawned and rubbed her eyes as she sat outside the bank, along from Primark and Piccadilly Gardens. It was almost lunchtime, and specks of rain trickled down her cheeks as if saying sorry for ruining the late May bank holiday weekend. It was a good spot. She'd scoped it out for a couple of days and the regular rough sleeper seemed to have moved on. Just metres from the tram stop, she'd often pick up change from busy commuters, who darted into Costa Coffee before hammering on to the office.

People-watching, she listened to the diverse Manchester beat. Hurried high heels. The whistle of trams. The talented – and untalented – buskers further down Market Street. Students chatting as they headed to the Northern Quarter for a non-branded latte and cake. Mums pushing creaky buggies laden with brown paper Primark bags defenceless against the rain. Pub drinkers striding with a determination driven by the imminent opening time.

A young woman tossed a handful of coins into her cup as she walked past. Emma gazed at her glossy salon hair, the perfect foundation, those manicured nails. She couldn't remember the last time she'd thought about her own appearance.

A burp rose up her throat followed by a shot of acid. She took a glug of water. The nausea she usually felt had been particularly bad this last week. Last night's choice of drink had even been non-alcoholic.

Her throat buckled. She leant to her left and almost vomited the pizza slice she'd found boxed in a bin for breakfast. Her eyes watered and she hid her head under the sleeping bag and thought of her predicament. This was the worst thing about not drinking to oblivion – you had to confront your feelings. Because of that, she couldn't contemplate life without her crutch – yet recently she couldn't face the rest of her life with it.

How did you solve that particular conundrum?

Charity workers had tried to help, but Emma knew any offers of assistance would be useless until she hit her rock bottom; until the fear of changing felt smaller than the fear of staying the same.

Yet how much worse did it need to get?

Beth had reached rock bottom a fortnight ago. Her young son had been hit by a car and ended up in intensive care. She'd turned up at the hospital but they refused to let her visit as she wasn't officially the next of kin. Finally

71

broken, she'd registered with addiction services. Emma had shoplifted a Twix as a goodbye present.

Someone tripped over her leg and she pulled the sleeping bag away and jumped up to see a white-haired woman staggering.

'You okay?' she said, and took the pensioner's arm.

'Yes, thank you, dear. I'm as blind as a bat without my glasses these days.'

The posh tone reminded her of Great-Aunt Thelma, who loved visiting Foxglove Farm. Despite her advancing years, she'd muck in by weeding or collecting eggs, and she made the best apple crumble. Emma and Andrea would fight over the last portion. Emma screwed her eyes tight, determined not to think about Healdbury. Yet lately it was becoming increasingly difficult. She wasn't sure why.

She glanced over to the right and Piccadilly Gardens. The tops of the fountains danced. Their distant babbling reminded her of the village stream. How she and Bligh used to play there, catching tadpoles and feeding moorhens. They'd hit it off straight away as kids, sharing adventures good and bad. Like when they'd run a mile for charity, or got sick by bingeing on Easter chocolate. Bligh was a popular boy at school and Emma had eventually worked out why. He'd share his sweets as much as his time and never said no if someone needed help with their maths or learning how to shoot goals.

She yawned and struggled to keep her eyes open, despite rain spitting on her face. She'd been feeling much more tired lately. When she woke up, the afternoon was drawing to an end. Normally, at this time on a Monday, a tide of commuters would sweep in. But the bank holiday painted a different scene full of families and friends, and arms full of bags after a successful shopping day.

'You ought to get a job,' said a man who stopped in front of her and shook his head.

'And you ought to mind your own fucking business.' Mum would have told her off for saying the F word.

She looked up and watched heads bobbing along Market Street in the distance: Brazilian blow-dries, bald patches, peroxide blondes and throwback quiffs. She was just about to head over to the burger bar and badger the nice staff for a free coffee when her eyes narrowed. Her sleeping bag fell to the ground as she jumped to her feet, and she did a double-take at the sight of dirty-blonde hair.

No. It wasn't possible. But what if…? She stood on tiptoe, trying to find the familiar-looking figure again through the army of umbrellas.

Joe? Nah. He'd gone to London. She was being stupid. But the hair came into view again, on top of a slight frame carrying a burgundy-coloured rucksack. Emma threw her sleeping bag over her belongings and began to run, shouting at people to get out of her way and ramming into a woman's shoulder as she headed past a group of street entertainers. She skidded through puddles, and every now and again stopped to jump up and spot the distinctive hair. Soon she came to the Arndale entrance and the escalator leading up to the food hall. She could see Joe just ahead, about to cross the road that led to Marks & Spencer.

'Joe!' she called. 'Joe! It's Emma! Wait!'

A grin spread across her face. She and Joe were meant to be together. He'd realised that and come back. Her friendship was worth it after all. A burst of excitement drove her legs and finally she caught up.

'Joe!' She grabbed the familiar slender arm.

The arm was yanked away. Joe spun around. Emma's smile dropped.

'It's not you,' she said weakly.

The man's frown disappeared. 'Sorry, love. Tim's the name and I'm late for my shift.' He headed off.

Emma didn't move. She could hardly breathe; her lungs felt as if they'd been ripped out of her chest. A couple of teenage girls stared and pointed.

'What you looking at?' she snapped, wiping her eyes with the back of her hand.

Giggling, they hurried off, whilst Emma numbly turned around and began the long trek back to the bank. She'd often wondered how she'd react if the dad who'd abandoned her as a baby suddenly turned up. Would she run with open arms just like she had for Joe? Would her anger melt instantly at the prospect of finally feeling whole?

She stood for a moment, and stared vacantly in the window of Boots. When she finally focused, she found herself transfixed by baby merchandise. She leant up against the glass and studied the plastic potties and cute babygros. An image came to mind of herself pushing a pram. She'd have her life sorted then, with a home and a good job. On days off she'd meet fellow mums for coffee and always know just how to stop her baby crying. The other parents would ask her advice.

That vision of her future seemed further away than ever. She kicked a can on the ground and built pace as she went back to her patch. How could she have left her belongings? Primark came into view, and relief flushed through her system as she spotted her sleeping bag. Her rucksack was still underneath. She dropped to the wet pavement. The coffee cup containing a few coins had gone.

Emma sat hunched as darker clouds gathered and the breeze lifted. Joe wasn't coming back. She had to face that truth. Her head dropped onto her raised knees and she gazed into darkness. Yet even though Joe was out of her life, she still felt, just very slightly, that unfamiliar sensation that had appeared during recent months. It brought to mind phrases such as *turning point, enough is enough, this can't go on*.

A stray dog wandered over. Emma had seen it several times before. She stroked its head, reached into her rucksack and gave it the remnants of a sandwich. It peed up against a nearby bin and then wandered off.

Could she ever be brave enough to admit to people she'd messed up? She thought back to the chemist's window and the tiny babygros. She lifted her head as the word chemist gave her a jolt. She searched in her bag again and pulled out the goodbye present from Joe. Her throat constricted, making it difficult to swallow. She hadn't needed to use the tampons since he'd left. Perhaps her period was just late. But hairs stood to attention on the back of her neck. She had been feeling especially sick lately, and worn out.

No. It wasn't possible. Her body was in such a state of disrepair. She never ate properly, nor got enough sleep. Occasionally her periods were a bit erratic. It was no big deal.

There was no way she could be pregnant.

Emma pulled her anorak tighter as the skies opened. It tugged slightly across her stomach. She rubbed a hand over her abdomen. Was that distension imaginary, or due to her risky lifestyle? Funny how the prospect of creating a new life seemed more scary than losing her own.

Somehow she'd managed to put aside a tenner and buy a pregnancy test. It remained, unopened, in the bottom of her rucksack. Every time she walked down the street, prams seemed more prominent. Hungry bawls and jingling rattles drowned out the city sounds, as if there really was something in the proverbial water – or rain – that had made every woman in Manchester suddenly give birth.

A man walked past accompanied by a little girl wearing glittery trainers. She was skipping and tugging on her dad's hand to get his attention whilst he had a conversation into his phone. She caught Emma's eye and stuck out her tongue. Emma pulled a funny face. The girl waved as her dad finally slid his mobile into his pocket.

Emma had always assumed she'd have children one day, whereas Andrea was adamant that looking out for a little sister was more than enough. Emma didn't believe her. Nor did Mum. Oh, she never played with dolls and preferred plants to the animals… except, that was, when one of them gave birth. She hand-reared a lamb once, feeding it religiously through the night. Andrea was better than anyone else at getting the milk bottle angle just right.

Emma, though, had already worked out every detail of her motherhood by the time she was eleven.

'I'll have two girls. Like me and Andrea,' she'd declared to Bligh when they were paddling down at the stream one day. 'They'll be called Holly and Ivy after my favourite time of year. I'll be a vet. The girls will have their own ponies. We'll all play Animal Crossing.'

Emma liked the idea of mending people's pets. She'd be needed. Respected. She'd become a part of the owners' lives.

'What about you?' she'd said to Bligh.

He'd pulled a face. 'You know what my dream is. Mr Harris said it wasn't ambitious enough.'

The careers teacher had gone around the class asking each of the children to name their dream job. Bligh had said being a family man. The whole class had laughed.

'You can work for me, doing handyman stuff like your dad,' Emma said. 'And you can look after my children. You'd be ace.'

'What about your husband?'

She'd pulled a face. 'All that kissing stuff? No thanks. I'll be the only parent.'

So it wasn't as if she'd ever planned to be part of a couple when bringing up kids. Tentatively she pulled a magazine out of her bag. She'd found it in a bin. It was the Mothercare catalogue. She turned the first page and flicked through, admiring the stylish nappy bags and buggies that looked as if they belonged to a futuristic century. And weren't those dummies cute? Those socks so small? Emma would make sure her baby's toys were educational, like those sorting and stacking ones.

But I'm not pregnant, she told herself, and shoved the catalogue back into her bag. She opened a packet of biscuits that someone had given her and picked at the contents. But what if that bump across her stomach wasn't due to ill-health but was a child trying to make itself heard? The packet of biscuits fell to the pavement. Emma's chin sank onto her chest and she covered her face with her hands. Had her sense of denial crossed through the placenta? Could the foetus read her thoughts? Her last period had been a few days before she and Joe slept together, so… for possibly six weeks now, had it floated alone thinking nobody cared?

But Emma did care and would be damned if she ended up following her dad's example. He hadn't needed her. Or respected her. Or made her a part of his life.

She got to her feet. Grabbed her rucksack and not for the first time wished she had somewhere to store her belongings. Rough sleeping was hard enough without having to constantly lug your life around on your back like a snail. Carrying your emotional baggage didn't leave much energy to spare. She headed over to the burger bar, went into the toilets and disappeared inside a cubicle. Fifteen minutes later she was back on her patch holding a slim white plastic stick.

She inhaled deeply and then looked down at the test resting in her hands. She lifted it up, aware that it might be about to change the course of her life.

And there they were, as if the universe were sticking up two pink fingers to her face. Pulse racing, she leant back against the wall, feeling faint. She grabbed the small stick tightly and focused on the pink lines. Pink was an LGBT colour, the colour of fighters against breast cancer. It represented being proud of your identity, and survival. How could Emma live up to all that? And wasn't pink also supposed to signify romance? She'd messed things up big time with Joe.

And now she was going to be responsible for another life. That would never work.

Her hand reached for the bottle poking out the top of her threadbare rucksack. She pulled it out and paused mid air, staring through the plastic at the liquid's inviting caramelised sunshine colour. Then she let the bottle drop back inside the bag and instead fished out an orange flyer, staring at the information on it. She'd passed a mobile soup kitchen late one night. Got chatting to one of the volunteers. They'd handed her the flyer giving details of a treatment centre.

Her mind skipped back to the days before she'd started drinking all day. It used to be just on special occasions, with Mum and Andrea, and occasionally round at a friend's house – vodka and marshmallows in the bedroom with *Pretty Little Liars* playing in the background. How grown-up she'd felt. And then she'd failed her A level biology. She'd retaken it at a college in Manchester and made new, exciting friends. But when she'd failed a second time, she'd thrown herself into the party lifestyle, making her appearance more glamorous. Nightclubs Fifth and Factory were great for cheap shots. She was in with the in crowd and just the first mouthful made her feel accepted and loved. It gave her the sexiest moves on the dance floor. The funniest sense of humour.

Happy days.

It wasn't long before the weekend stretched from Thursday to Monday, and then every day of the week. If Emma wasn't out with the girls she'd take a bottle of wine to Bligh's. One bottle became two. Wine o'clock got earlier: midday, then the morning. Resentments grew – along with Andrea's disdain, Mum's disapproval and Bligh shifting to parental mode, calling her Emma rather than Emmie.

79

Her face screwed up and she tossed the pregnancy test away. It couldn't have been accurate. Her fingers curled around the top of the bottle and she lifted it to her mouth.

Darkness had fallen when she woke up with a thumping headache and a dry mouth. Late trams whistled. Amateur drinkers stumbled home, singing songs or having arguments. Someone had placed a sheet of cardboard over her. It was soggy now, like an over-dunked biscuit. She pushed it off. The early summer evening felt like a damp autumn night.

'Why did I have to wake up?' she said numbly, and gazed skywards. 'I'm done. What do I have to do to end things?'

'Get help, cock,' muttered a rusty Mancunian voice. 'And stop the pity party. It serves no purpose.'

Cheeks hot, she turned sideways to see a rough sleeper in his sixties. Stormin' Norman he was called. She didn't know why – something to do with him being ex-army. He knew Beth. Emma had chatted to him now and again under the railway bridge. He was sitting in a drenched sleeping bag and wore a military-style cap. He caught her eye. 'Just thought I'd keep you company until you woke up. There are some crazy bastards out there.' He offered her his cigarette. She shook her head. 'So, you want to end things? Why?'

'Because stopping drinking… it's impossible.'

'Thousands of alcoholics have done it.'

'I'm not an alcoholic,' she snapped. 'I've just… been down on my luck. I just want it over. I've had enough.'

'There are four ways of ending it.' He took a drag of nicotine. 'Prison. Psychiatric hospital. Recovery. Death. Not everyone has a choice. You're lucky. At the moment, you still get to pick.'

'But I'm stuck. I can't stop.' Her voice broke. 'And I can't carry on.'

'Perhaps that's because you're in a shit place at the moment. It'd be different with a clear head, with prospects, with help.' Stormin' Norman stubbed out his cigarette. 'I've decided to go and see my old case worker again. I tasted a different existence in rehab – remembered how things used to be. I'm going to stick to the programme this time. It isn't easy, but you know what they say – you don't get owt for nowt.'

He stood up and yawned. 'See ya around, cock.' He lumbered off muttering something about finding a doorway.

A small flash of orange caught her attention – the flyer leaning against a lamp post. She scrambled to her feet and stared at it for a moment as it shifted in the breeze.

She bent down and picked it up.

Chapter 8

It took over an hour to dig up the deadly nightshade bushes. Emma was glad of the distraction. Afterwards, she headed to the kitchen for a quick cup of tea. Bligh was labelling his red onion jars in the shop and rebuffed her offer of a drink. Next she dragged the old bench into the goats' enclosure and immediately one of them jumped on top. She scratched its head. She sawed an old piece of wide guttering in two and put one half in the rabbits' run to act as a tunnel, filling it with strawberry plant leaves. Dusk fell, and as an evening treat, she chopped up some apples for the sheep and hand-fed one with a black patch of wool on top of its head. He was an orphan they'd saved and named Spit because he never completely mastered drinking from a milk bottle. He'd taken it best from Andrea, who at one stage slept in the sheep enclosure overnight. Emma remembered doing that herself one summer when her favourite lamb fell ill.

Repeatedly she checked her watch. Why hadn't Andrea rung with news? When the sun started to set, Bligh drove to the hospital. Andrea wasn't replying to his calls or texts and he was worried. While he was gone, Emma swept the yard. Any evidence of the summer shower had quickly evaporated.

His car pulled up. Andrea opened the passenger door and got out. Emma laid down her broom and hurried over.

'How's Mum?'

Tears filled Andrea's eyes.

'Is she okay? Bligh?'

He nodded.

Andrea wiped her eyes and tugged out her ponytail bobble. 'They told me to go home. Mum hasn't been sick. She isn't hallucinating. They think she must have just eaten that one berry.'

Emma exhaled. Thank goodness.

'I'm just so worried,' said Andrea. 'What if they're wrong?' Bligh locked the car and came around to her side. 'Thanks for staying late, Bligh,' she continued in a flat tone. 'Go home. You've done more than enough; you must be as tired as I am.'

'Not until I've at least made you a hot chocolate,' he said. 'Have you eaten at all?'

She shook her head. 'I just wasn't hungry, and in any case I couldn't leave Mum's side. She looked so scared in the unfamiliar surroundings. What if she wakes up frightened tonight?'

'I'm sure she'll be all right,' said Emma.

'What would you know?'

'You told me yourself, Andrea, that the doctors weren't worried. They're just keeping her in overnight to be safe,' said Bligh. 'Try not to worry. She's in good hands.'

'Look, let me make us a drink,' said Emma, and without waiting for an answer, she went into the kitchen. She set out three mugs, spooned out hot chocolate powder and boiled milk in a pan. When she turned round, Bligh and Andrea were sitting at the table. Both looked utterly exhausted. Emma handed out their drinks and joined them. For a moment no one spoke.

'I've dug up the deadly nightshade bushes,' she said.

'Bligh told me what you've been up to.' Andrea put down her mug and gave Emma a cold stare. 'One afternoon of tidying up doesn't put straight the mess from the past.'

'I know. But please, let me stay a bit longer and help – try to put things right. I think you need me.'

Andrea picked up her mug again and sipped. 'You can forget staying here,' she said eventually, 'and I can't imagine anyone in the village wanting to put you up.'

'Then I'll sleep rough until I get something sorted and the inheritance money comes through.'

'Don't be so dramatic.' Andrea shook her head. 'That's not a solution.' She was still refusing to make eye contact.

'What about the barn for... for a couple of days, to start with?' asked Emma, bending down to stroke Dash, who'd snuck in the back door and was sleeping by her feet.

'But there's no furniture, no hot water...' countered Bligh.

She looked up. 'If Andrea doesn't mind, I'll use the bathroom in the house – but apart from that, it's more than adequate.'

'No.' Andrea shook her head. 'I said you can't stay here.'

'What about Mum?'

'I'm managing,' said Andrea, as if she were trying to convince herself. She screwed up her eyes and muttered something about one of her headaches.

'You look worn out. Today's taken its toll what with you having to go to the hospital on top of everything else, and... and I know I didn't help, taking Mum into the village.' Emma's voice softened. 'Please. Let me help, Andrea – for your sake as well as hers.'

'But she won't understand who you are if you call her Mum, and any confusion… that's when she's most scared.'

'Then I won't tell her who I am. I'll only call her Gail.'

'You'd really agree to that?' scoffed Andrea. 'Because this visit is simply about easing your conscience, isn't it? It's not as if you really care.'

I do, Emma thought, and pushed away her mug. More than you'll ever know. I hate the deep circles around your eyes. I'd do anything to stop Mum looking vacant and directionless.

'If that's what it takes, I'll not say a word. I'll take her out. Keep her busy. Help you two where I can if she's having a sleep or just contented to watch. I can help make jam. Man the shop. I can do the shopping and look after the animals. I'll more than pull my weight. And I've been thinking of some ideas to improve things on the farm. I can see money's tight. What about—'

'Whoa!' Bligh held up his hand. 'After everything – after today – you're asking for our trust?' He faced Andrea. 'You need to think very carefully about letting her stay longer. I don't want to see you and Gail hurt again.'

Bligh used to be someone who believed in giving people another chance. Like the friend at school who stole his Kings of Leon CD. Like the new grain supplier who muddled up the first order.

Emma held her sister's stare as if patiently waiting for an internet connection.

'I'm not lending you any money,' Andrea said eventually. 'And the *only* reason I'm agreeing to this – temporarily – is that I just don't have the time to give to Mum at the moment. She deserves some one-on-one attention – even if it's from you.'

'Thanks, I really—'

'Just keep out of my way. You can use the shower and the kitchen when I'm not around, but that's it. And if I find any money missing… if I smell anything stronger than tea on your breath, you're gone.'

Bligh pursed his lips, put his mug in the sink and abruptly left. The back door swung shut and the two sisters sat in silence as the rain fell harder.

'You should get an early night,' said Emma with a tentative smile. 'Remember what a night owl you were as a teenager? You were always reading or chatting on your phone, and there was that phase when you binge-watched *Friends*. Secretly you'd let me watch too, even though Mum said I was too young. I felt so grown up.'

Andrea actually met her gaze for a moment and then shook her head. 'You think I've ever had the opportunity for an early night since you left? You haven't got any idea, have you, what the last few years have been like?' She broke the brief eye contact. 'You've only been back a couple of days and already I'm sick of you saying sorry. It's as if you expect that word to magically shut down the past in the way that saying abracadabra opens doors.' She drained her mug. 'You know, I had ambitions too – away from Foxglove Farm.'

Emma's brow knotted as Andrea got up, brushed past and went to the sink. She ran some water and squirted in washing-up liquid. 'You always assumed that *you* were the one with big dreams. That reliable old Andrea was more than happy to keep Mum company on the farm.'

Emma's mind rewound to their schooldays. 'Is this about travel?' she said in a small voice. 'I remember now…

you were desperate to go to America. In fact you drew up a bucket list: you wanted to visit every continent by the age of forty.' And her paintings were usually set in foreign countries too. Was that it? Andrea was just over thirty now, and as far as Emma knew, she had never even holidayed outside of Britain.

'When you finally reached eighteen, I felt that perhaps my time had come. I'd helped Mum see you through to adulthood. I was twenty-three and ready to leave.'

As Emma listened, a tide of shame swept over her, pooling into all the nooks and crevices, so that when it pulled back, puddles still lingered.

'I had no idea.'

'Of course you didn't – your life revolved around having a good laugh, as you called it.' Andrea abandoned the washing-up and rummaged in a drawer, pulling out some paracetamol. She poured a glass of water and knocked back two tablets, then pushed the kitchen chair in and stared out of the window.

'You can stay for a few days, Emma, but then you must leave. Foxglove Farm, Mum, Bligh, me – this is no more your life than mine is to travel the world.' She headed to the dining room and switched off the computer. 'Don't forget to lock the door on your way out.'

Chapter 9

Somehow a few days stretched into two weeks. A fort-night at the farm passed as quickly as her life in the city had dragged. Each day Emma buttoned Gail's tops and brushed her hair, helped her clean her teeth and made sure she got into bed okay – all the busy things she would have been doing if…

She wrapped her arms around a cushion. Andrea still insisted on doing the bedtime routine. A small glass of sherry apparently helped Gail to sleep. Andrea would sit in her room until she nodded off. Emma walked past once, on her way from the bathroom, and heard Andrea quietly singing Gail a favourite eighties ballad.

Emma had seen lots of Stig and helped him whenever she could, along with the other homeless. More had trickled into the village. She'd started to talk to shop-keepers. A few answered her. Some, like old Mrs Beatty, didn't.

At the moment she was sitting in the lounge, watching the breakfast news – a new privilege of late. Soon Gail would wake up. Footsteps approached from the kitchen – her sister. Emma pretended to watch the telly.

Things had been awkward with Bligh since coming back, but at least they'd started to chat a bit.

'But weren't you scared the whole time you were on the streets of getting attacked?' he'd asked.

Yes. But there was no need to tell him that.

'Wasn't it difficult sharing personal stuff with a bunch of strangers in rehab?'

Emma found it hard to explain that no, her varied new friends all shared the same hopeless feelings.

And she had questioned him; discovered that he'd dated a couple of women.

'Neither relationship was serious, though,' he'd said. 'Not like…'

He didn't finish that sentence.

There hadn't been deep conversations with hugs, tears and jokes. But it was a start. Today she hoped to take their discussions further, as she could be asked to leave at any minute.

With Andrea, on the other hand, she realised it served no purpose to push deeper. Since that short chat about travel, her older sister had kept her distance. Emma didn't like to ask why she and her boyfriend, Dean, had split. Slowly she was realising that her old behaviours meant she'd relinquished any rights to intimacy.

Andrea came into the dining area holding a mug of tea. 'Bligh had to stay late last night to finish the repairs you started on the goats' shelter in case we got a storm or heavy rain overnight – you might have heard him. Although the forecasters got it wrong again. So I insisted he comes in a little later today. He asked if you could give him a hand with the jam-making.' She yawned. 'Mum can sit in the shop with me. Polly's coming over. She's baked Mum's favourite brownies.'

Emma nodded, forced a bright smile and headed upstairs as she heard her mum get out of bed. Eventually they both came down, Gail washed and dressed. She sat in the kitchen whilst Emma made blueberry pancakes. After eating, Emma took her outside to leave her with her sister. When she returned, Bligh was there wiping dirt off the fruit.

'Do you want a coffee?' she asked.

'Not at the moment.'

Emma watched him remove the soil and get rid of the green leaves with a knife by making a cone-shaped cut in the top. He'd always been practical, even as a child, identifying star constellations and tying complicated knots.

She opened the cupboard under the sink and glanced at a half-full sherry bottle. Bligh shot her an intense stare.

'I'm looking for a new washing-up sponge.'

'Andrea's had to start hiding the sherry from Gail in case she thinks it's squash and drinks a load.' His eyes narrowed. 'Does she need to hide it from you as well?'

Emma blushed. She'd seen the bottle yesterday, and all night the bad voice on her shoulder, from the old days, had reminded her about it, trying to tempt her to take a mouthful.

'It might be an idea.'

'You said you were over all that.'

'And I am – by keeping myself safe.' She closed the cupboard door and picked up a packet of sugar. She studied the label. 'It's already got pectin mixed in?'

'Time-wise we cut corners where we can.' Bligh rolled a few lemons over to her. 'Start squeezing the juice out. It's time to get the preserving pan on.'

She did as instructed, and then weighed out the sugar. Before long, the sweet mixture was bubbling. Emma took the clean jars and lids out of the dishwasher. Bligh had always enjoyed the domestic side of life when he was little. Emma would often find him cooking or folding washing with his mum when she called to play. When his parents split, he took over his mother's chores – his new word for the jobs he used to revel in.

'Thanks, Bligh,' she said, blurting it out as he removed scum from the top of the boiling liquid. 'Thanks for standing by Andrea. It's clear you've been her rock. I'm so grateful.'

'I would say my pleasure, but it's been hard – seeing her change.'

'I… I hadn't realised she'd missed out on so much.'

'She was in bits after your mum's appendix operation that worsened the Alzheimer's. Neither of them really recovered from that.' He skimmed off some more scum.

Emma tried to fight the cloying guilt by keeping busy. Carefully she tested the set of a spoonful of jam on a cold saucer, removed from the freezer. She gave the thumbs-up and Bligh started to ladle the mix into jars. Whilst roughing it on the street, she'd only ever thought of Andrea as having it easy. No one could be suffering as much as Emma was. Her sister had the farm, Mum, a life amongst the locals. But now she saw that meant Andrea had no time left for herself. Their situations couldn't have been more different, as Emma had spent the last couple of years focusing solely on her own problems. Yet like so many extremes, this meant there was common ground between them. Those feelings of isolation, and that no one truly understood their predicament.

Without thinking, she stuck her finger in the leftover jam mixture, with the intention of having a lick. She needed a sugar boost. Chocolate bars and sweets had helped with the initial cravings, and now the habit was proving hard to give up.

'Ow!' She jerked back and banged into the table. The jar nearest the edge toppled onto the floor and smashed.

Broken glass and red liquid splatted across the tiles. Hurriedly Bligh and Emma bent down to pick up the pieces of glass. A large dollop of scalding jam found its way into Bligh's palm, and Emma suffered a small cut.

Shaking his burnt hand, Bligh sighed as they stood up. 'Wait there. I'll get you a plaster.'

'I don't think so.' Gently she manoeuvred him over to the sink. 'A small cut will heal quicker than a burn. Your wound is the priority.' She switched on the cold tap and held his palm underneath. She had forgotten how big his hands were. She recalled them carrying her up to bed after yet another night of carnage, and the same strong hands gently caressing her curves. Sometimes she'd giggled. Found it funny. Sober sex? Had she ever really had that?

Eventually she let go of his hand and cleaned up her own wound. Wincing, she covered it with a square of kitchen roll. Bligh tried to help.

'It's okay,' she said, and pulled away. 'Thanks, but I can manage on my own.'

He stared at her. 'Where's the jumping up and down? The squealing? That's how you always used to react to the slightest pain.' He sat down at the kitchen table. 'The Emma I know never managed alone. All the scrapes... I became a dab hand with antiseptic cream and a bandage.'

For a few minutes the sound of running water cut between them like a time portal – him in the past, her in the present.

'Remember what you used to call me?' he said.

Emma sat down.

'The fixer,' he said. 'Mediating between you and an angry Andrea – paying back your debts.'

He went to stand up, but gently Emma held his arm. 'Please. Don't go. Let's talk about it.'

Bligh hesitated for a moment, then with a stony expression sat down again.

'Yes, I did call you that, even before my behaviour started to get out of control. At school you were always there, lending me your homework to copy if I'd not gone mine done.'

'I thought you really loved me, you know.' His voice quietened. 'But over the last year or so, you just saw me as someone to sort out your problems, didn't you?'

'I thought the world of you, Bligh.' The wooden chair creaked as she shifted from side to side.

'And was this Joe person, the good friend you mentioned when Gail went missing… was he another fixer?'

'No. We helped each other.'

'I couldn't believe my luck when you agreed to go out with me, after years of us just being friends. Even as kids I knew you only liked me because I got you out of trouble. Like when I took the blame for Dad's broken china teapot.'

'I admit that caring side of you always appealed, because…'

'What?'

'My dad…' she said.

'You never had one.'

'Exactly. Then you came along. Looked out for me. You were always so strong.'

'You're saying that you saw some school kid as a father figure – that's pretty messed up.' He got to his feet and made for the door.

'Bligh. Please. Stay. We need to talk. It's just… you gave me hope that not all men were losers like him. Every time you stood up for me, it made me feel good. I couldn't believe my luck, either – couldn't believe you thought of me romantically.' All the girls in the class had admired his dark looks and easy manner, not that Bligh ever seemed to notice, laughing off love notes in his locker as his male friends' idea of a joke.

'Don't lie,' he said roughly, and folded his arms.

'I'm not. Honest.'

'Honest? That word used to be your tell. *Honest, Bligh, I'll be back for dinner. Honest, Bligh, I'll never do it again. Honest, Bligh, this is the last time. I'll give up tomorrow.* I eventually worked out that *honest* meant the complete opposite.'

Emma hadn't counted on other people's memories being quite so detailed, as if they were reading from the memoir of someone she used to know. The new Emma was an empty book. It was up to her to fill it with positive words.

'Remember all the dates we went on at the beginning, just before I started college?' she said. 'We lay in the fields amongst the wild flowers, holding hands, watching clouds. And we'd paddle in Healdbury stream, arms around each other's waists. Before I got ill, those simple moments meant everything.'

Bligh's arms dropped to his sides. 'Even if they did, that phase didn't last long. Once you started at that college in the city, you only wanted to go out with your friends. And that wouldn't have mattered if you'd included me.'

'I remember offering to shape your eyebrows once.' She looked at his forehead and wondered why.

'Yeah – it was obvious you didn't think I fitted in with your new crowd.'

Emma stared at his palm – the burnt skin. Scars never healed. Oh, they faded. You could cover them with make-up. Invent an entertaining story to explain them away. But they'd always be there, reminding you of the truth.

'And then you stopped calling me the fixer. You chose another word instead.'

Emma scrolled back through her memories. She drew a blank.

'What?' she said.

'Maybe I should leave you to figure it out,' he said, and the stony expression returned. 'Why did you have to come back, Emma – just when I was managing to put all of this to rest?'

He left to check on Andrea and Gail in the shop. After finishing tidying up, Emma too went outside. Dust flew into the air as she slid down the wall by the back door and landed on the ground. Dash ran over, panting, candyfloss-pink tongue hanging out. He nuzzled her neck and lay down, his head on her knees. Briefly, old, familiar negative thoughts jumped into her head: *I hate myself. I'm a bad person. I wish I was dead.*

'Why are you so forgiving?' she whispered, and stroked his ears.

He licked her hand.

Bligh's mum had met someone else during his last years at high school. The signs had been there. She'd started staying out at night. Bligh talked of his parents' arguments and did everything he could to keep his mum happy, regularly baking her favourite coconut cake and doing the housework. But it wasn't enough to stop her moving away. She was keen for him to visit often, but his dad became fragile and faced problems that forced Bligh to stay. He hardly talked about his mum, but when he did, his face flushed and his voice wavered as if sadness blew on sound waves like a breeze.

Was that why he'd stood by Emma for so long? Because belonging to something, however screwed, was better than the prospect of being alone?

Until she'd finally gone too far, even for Bligh, and had thrown his misguided loyalty back in his face.

Emma could hardly find the strength to get back on her feet. It reminded her of days spent on the pavement in Manchester. How numbness crept into her legs, which buckled when she finally stood up. But sitting here moping wouldn't get the rabbit hutches clean. And it wouldn't help Andrea or Bligh, who'd hardly had time to sit down since that Christmas she left.

She straightened up, brushed herself down and mulled over a proposition she'd been meaning to put to Stig.

12 months before going back

Emma sat in a chair opposite someone called Ben. She was beginning to regret dialling the number on the orange flyer. The small office at Stanley House wasn't as friendly as the waiting room, with its comfy soft chairs and piped pop music. The only sound here was a clock ticking. The chairs were wooden. Emma squinted in the artificial light.

For the first time ever, her problems were *official*. That word made her throat constrict. She was in the system. Ben was the assessment officer. She'd thought he'd be wearing a suit; that more than ever in her life she'd feel that she didn't fit. What a relief to be met by a T-shirt, jeans and tattoos.

After breathalysing her, Ben filled out the top of a form and consulted a stand-up calendar on his desk. It was June the fifteenth. Emma rarely knew the date. He pushed the paperwork and pen across. 'First things first. Fill this in.'

Her eyes scanned the questions, and pages rustled as she gave details about her drinking habits, medical history, financial and family situation, criminal record and drug use – at least she could skip those last two sections. Her insides felt numb. Her writing hand shook. The complex horror of recent years had been reduced to a list of scribbled answers on a page.

'And now for the most important question,' said Ben in a voice loaded like a gun. A gun that made her afraid, because when it went off, the race would start – the race to facing her problems head on. 'Why are you here, Emma?'

Was that a trick question? 'I want to stop drinking. For good.'

'Nice one. I agree that's the right option for you.'

Her brow furrowed.

'Some people come in with ideas about simply cutting down.'

'I just want you to make all the craziness go away.'

Ben leant back in his chair. 'For the treatment to work, you are going to have to stop first.'

His words didn't compute for a moment, and when they did, instinctively her hands covered her face. 'Are you messing with me?' she asked eventually, looking up. 'That's your job, isn't it? That's why I'm here. What's the point if you expect that to happen before I even start?'

'We'll sort out a detox – at the end of that, you'll be dry. But this isn't about stopping; it's about staying stopped, and to do that, you have to change the way you think.' He handed over a box of tissues. 'Only you can do this, Emma. We're here to offer support, but you've got to take responsibility for yourself. That's what recovery is about.'

Emma stood up and paced the room. 'But I've tried so many times. I… I can't do it on my own.'

'You're braver and stronger than you think.'

Under any other circumstances she would have laughed. An addiction worker quoting Winnie the Pooh?

'Proved by the fact,' he continued, 'that you've brought yourself here. Admitted you've got a problem. That takes a lot of guts. And in my experience, the people who succeed are those like you who self-refer – not the people forced here by relatives, social services or the courts. Honestly, there are lots of positives.'

The chair rocked as she slumped back into it, but after a moment, she sat up a little straighter than before.

'And you won't be on your own. We'll offer you as much education and mental rewiring as we can.'

She blew her nose and followed him back out into the waiting room while he fetched her allotted case worker. The baby. She was doing this for the baby. She mustn't run out of the door.

But *case worker*. How had it come to this? They were for people who'd grown up on deprived council estates. For underage single mums who needed support. For people with mental health issues. Not Emma. She'd got a couple of A levels and grown up in a village where the worst crime was sabotaging a neighbour's efforts for the summer fete bake-off.

A door left of reception opened and a woman with tousled greying blonde hair appeared. Black-framed glasses. Flowing floral shirt. Baggy slacks. Flip Flops.

Emma liked the Flip Flops. Someone prepared to show their curled toenails and cracked skin was familiar with imperfection.

The woman consulted her clipboard and peered over the top of her glasses. 'You must be Emma. Emma Bonneville.'

Sounded posh, didn't it? She never mentioned her surname on the streets. It was French. So was her father, apparently. That was all he'd given her – a name no one could pronounce.

She stood up, heaved her rucksack over one shoulder and followed the woman through the door and along a corridor. They stopped outside a small room and went in. It was sparse, like the other one.

'My name's Lou. Lou Burns,' the woman said, and they sat down. Lou opened her laptop on a nearby table and rested Emma's paperwork on her knees. 'I've looked through your details.' She put down her pen. 'Tell me about when it all started to go wrong, Emma. How long have you been drinking heavily?'

'I wrote all that on the form.'

Lou took off her glasses and placed them next to her laptop. 'This is your first serious attempt to get sober?'

'I tried lots of times on my own,' Emma said, 'but it never worked.'

'And your family – are you in contact? You haven't written down a next of kin.'

'They've disowned me. Everyone has.' Tears trickled down her face. Was this what getting better was going to be like? Her body expelling liquid instead of taking it in?

Lou studied her for a moment. 'You must feel very lonely. Well, you aren't alone any more. We're here to help.'

A tiny light ignited inside Emma's chest. She'd felt lonely for such a long time, even when she'd lived at the farm surrounded by family and animals.

Lou put her glasses back on. 'Okay... let's get things moving.' She handed over a timetable of therapy sessions. 'We offer a lot at Stanley House. And after your detox I'll be pitching a case for you to go to rehab. If you attend regularly here, that will strengthen your case.'

'Strengthen my case?'

Lou stopped tapping at her laptop for a moment. 'Our funding is stretched. You've got to show willing, Emma. I'll refer you to our Listening EAR programme – EAR for Education and Reduction. It's two hours of group therapy, here, three times a week.'

'*Group* therapy?' She failed to keep her voice steady.

Lou reached out and squeezed her arm. 'I know it's tough. But rehab is group therapy too.'

'But all our stories will be different.'

'On the surface, yes, though I think you'll be surprised. The feelings of fear and despair, the reasons for using... they're usually pretty much the same. It's a level playing field. Even the facilitators have had problems in the past.' She sat back and stared hard at Emma. 'So are you up to the challenge? Do we go ahead?'

Emma clenched her fists tight. She could do this. She couldn't go on waking up every morning wishing she were dead. And more importantly, the baby deserved the best chance.

'Yes. Please. I haven't meant to sound ungrateful. It's just I'm so confused at the moment...'

'I understand. This is a massive step.'

'There's something else.' She took a deep breath. 'I'm about eight weeks pregnant.'

Lou's face remained expressionless.

'I only found out recently. I'm worried. What if I've done some damage?'

Lou tapped furiously at the screen for a moment. 'Right, well this changes everything. We'll have to get you a detox immediately. It's too dangerous to do during the second trimester, and that's not far off.'

'Can't I have some time to think about it?' Emma's scalp felt tight. 'I've heard terrible stories from friends about seizures and hallucinations.'

'That's why it should be done in a residential detoxification service.'

'In hospital? With doctors and nurses?' Her face fell. 'They'll think me the worst person ever.'

'People aren't there to judge – they're there to look after you and baby,' said Lou calmly. 'I'll have to inform social care as well.'

'No! Please! They'll—'

'They will help you make the best decisions. Everyone is here to support you. Of course you have options, Emma, regarding the pregnancy. I can fetch you a leaflet, and if you decide—'

'I'm keeping it,' Emma blurted out.

Where had that come from? It didn't make sense, but then sometimes, in life, the most important things never did. In school they'd once touched on chaos theory – to expect the unexpected. Perhaps that was what this was. Your stereotypical order of life was: get a job, fall in love, move into a house, get pregnant. Perhaps this chaotic decision was right but simply a case of working things backwards.

Then there was Joe. What would he have wanted? Would he approve of her decision?

'The social care duty officer will sort you out with emergency accommodation – a hostel,' said Lou. 'We should be able to book the detox for later this week. It's

101

really important that you keep on drinking until you go in. It can be dangerous to stop suddenly after months or years of abuse. Then, once you're out, your hostel worker will work on finding more permanent accommodation whilst I concentrate on getting you a place in rehab.'

'I haven't got much choice, have I?' Emma mumbled, and attempted a small smile.

'There is always a choice. You could run away, back to the obscurity of the streets. But you know this situation is just going to get bigger and bigger – literally. And you rang our number. I get the feeling that maybe you're ready to stop running. Running from yourself. Running from responsibility.'

Emma's next words came out in a whisper. 'It's scary.'

'It is,' said Lou in a quiet voice. 'This process means you've got to deal with your feelings for possibly the first time in years. But we're all on your side, Emma. And after treatment – if you want – recovery services will give you the tools to build a different life.

She could picture it now. Her and the baby in their own little flat. A pram. A cot. They'd make friends at play-group. Emma would purée vegetables and get up at night whenever the baby cried. And when it got older, they'd be best friends. Watch movies together. Go shopping. Eat pizza. Although Emma would always be a mum first, and set rules about staying out late and getting homework done. There would be pleases and thank yous. And tidy bedrooms.

She thanked Lou and took a large mouthful of tea. It scalded the back of her throat, but she hardly noticed and rested a hand across her stomach. Everything would be all right now.

Chapter 10

How much had changed in a year, thought Emma, as she strolled into Healdbury. Today, the twentieth of June, was her sobriety birthday. For three hundred and sixty-five days she'd not picked up. How was that even possible? Last night she'd caught the bus to her favourite AA meeting. She'd chaired for the first time. Old Len had sliced up a chocolate cake. Another member handed her a card signed by everyone.

Now she crossed the road with Dash and walked down towards the village. Sparrows chirped, leaves rustled and a distant ice cream van played a perfect earworm melody. As she approached the supermarket, the mundane chat of shoppers took over, accompanied by Smooth Radio escaping a car. As usual, Rita with the asymmetrical hair sat there. Emma stopped for a quick chat and handed over a packed lunch that she'd prepared for her at the farm before leaving. Then she headed on down the road and turned left. Stig sat reading outside the pet shop.

Emma stopped for a moment and rummaged in her purse. A big gold disc smiled up at her. It was AA's first-year sobriety coin. She took it out. Her friend from treatment, Rachel, had given it to her a few weeks ago. She'd kept it safe until today, and now she kissed it with ceremony. She'd taken it as a sign that, one year on, it was time for her to take the next step and earnestly start helping others while she had the chance – before she had to confess and face head on the worst thing she'd done in the past. She stared at the coin for a moment and then slid it back into her purse.

Dash pulled at the lead. He and his new friend, the Duchess, greeted each other with sniffs and metronome tails. Emma handed Stig a packed lunch as well.

'I've just got to speak to Phil in the pet shop before I change my mind about a plan I've got, and then I'll come back out. I've a proposition for you.'

Stig sat upright and smiled. 'It's a long time since I've had one of them. Leave Dash with us if you like.'

Nerves strumming the inside of her stomach, Emma passed him the lead. Then she took a deep breath and pushed on the door. The bell rang as she went in. The shop was empty of customers. She glanced around at the plastic bags of food and the two fish tanks that smelt of algae. They needed a good clean, as did the hamsters' cage. She'd enjoyed her days working here until things got out of hand. She'd turn up with a hangover more often than not, and resent how the job dirtied her polished nails.

Phil was doing a crossword. He looked up and adjusted his cap. Straggly greying curls poked from underneath. A scowl crossed his unshaven face.

She approached the till. 'Hi, Phil.'

'Emma,' he said, looking back at his crossword. 'Why are you here?'

'Firstly, I… I'd like to apologise for… for everything. Looking back, I'm surprised you didn't sack me sooner and I'm grateful for all the chances you gave me here – and elsewhere. Like that time I threw whisky at you in the pub. I was totally out of order.'

He tossed down his pencil. 'That was nothing. Not compared to what came after.'

Her shoulders tensed.

His newspaper rustled as he folded it up and stuck it under his arm. 'Always mithering me, you were, to buy you a drink. Same for the other men in the pub. Polly and Alan only put up with you for as long as they did because of Andrea and Gail.' He shook his head. 'What you in here for now? Because if you're looking for your job back, you can forget it. I could never trust someone who stole my car.'

Of course. Andrea had told her about it afterwards. Emma's eyebrows knitted together. It had been late at night. The off-licence was shut. She had reckoned the motorway services would be open – they sold what she needed. So she'd stolen his keys from... off the pub table, that was it, and told herself he'd never notice. She'd be there and back in half an hour, which she might have been if she hadn't fallen asleep at the wheel and smashed the front bumper.

'Can you remember how much the repairs cost?' she said in a quiet voice. 'I'll bring a cheque in this afternoon.'

'You don't even know, do you?' he said, and jabbed his finger in the air. 'Bligh and Andrea bailed you out. It wasn't cheap, either. The windscreen had to be replaced. If it wasn't for Bligh, I'd have reported you to the Old Bill. Just get out.'

'But... it's just... Phil...' She hadn't told anyone else about her idea yet. 'I want to set up a soup run to help the homeless people coming into Healdbury. The charity shops here are overflowing with spare clothes I could also hand out, and the farm always has surplus produce. I'm going to go door-to-door asking businesses for donations.'

'Good luck with that.'

Emma swallowed. 'Some of the rough sleepers like Stig outside have dogs. I wondered if you'd consider donating a few tins of dog food and—'

'You're serious? Like I'm really going to encourage more piss-heads like you to visit our village, let alone to look after animals that deserve far better owners.' He jerked his head towards the window. 'That Staffie looks like it could do with a right good feed. It's shameful that bloke just using it to get the public's sympathy.'

'Stig's not like that. He loves the Duchess to bits. You know, when I was on the streets a vet used to visit the homeless dog owners in Manchester to check over their pets. He'd walk around at night with his rucksack full of tablets and jabs. He said many of the dogs were happier than some of his registered patients because they were so loved and in the company of their owners twenty-four seven.'

'Likely story. Go away. I'm not in the mood for this crap.'

'I don't drink any more, Phil,' she said in the same steady manner, despite her knees feeling as if they might give way. 'I'm really sorry for what I did, and—'

'Have you forgotten how you threw up on top of my stock of best cat toys? How you *borrowed* twenty quid out of the till?'

'But—'

'Healdbury's a decent place – a place for families, pensioners, hard-working folk. I'm not doing anything to swell the influx of time-wasters and scroungers.' His newspaper fanned open as he threw it down. 'Some of us work damn hard to earn a living and end up paying towards benefits for people like you.'

Head down, Emma hurried out of the shop.

'Emma?' Stig looked up.

She sat down next to him.

'What's up?'

She rolled her lips together and didn't speak for a few moments.

'I want to start a soup run, Stig. With your help. I thought about setting one up in the barn for just a few hours each week, but I looked into it online and there are just too many rules and regulations. Whereas if I provide a mobile service, just turning up on the street with my food in a backpack and perhaps carrying a foldaway picnic table… well, that's okay. I could make soup, sandwiches and… Not everyone in the village will approve, but…' She gave a wry smile. 'Like you've said before, sometimes you need to give things more than one shot. So next I'm going to ask at the bakery if they ever have any waste stock. I thought we could do it two evenings a week up at the station, say from seven until nine. What do you say?'

'I think it's a great idea. I wouldn't ask the cheese-monger, though.'

'Ted? Large build? London accent?' She shrugged. 'Suitably named, I always thought. I used to think of him as a big friendly bear of a man. He always gave me a small slice of my favourite smoked Cheddar when Andrea and I passed his shop. He actually said hello to me the other day. I was almost too surprised to reply.'

'Is that his name? Yes, he's the one.' Stig pulled a face. 'He walked past a couple of days ago talking loudly about setting up a petition to get the rough sleepers moved on.'

'I'm surprised. He's a charitable sort, playing Santa at primary school and helping out at boy scouts.'

'Well I wouldn't knock on his door for donations. He told his grandson off for giving me ten pence. Told me to clear off. That Healdbury had enough problems. I guess his business is struggling as well. Hard times change people.'

They exchanged looks.

'So what happened with Phil?'

'I had hoped he'd donate tins of dog food. I guess it might be harder work than I thought to get donations from the villagers. Still...' Her voice brightened. 'Foxglove Farm has more than enough spare strawberries and early potatoes. Plus spring onions, tomatoes, peas and cucumbers. Mum's got a recipe book somewhere, specifically using the fruit and vegetables grown at the farm – she hand-wrote it herself. All that's left to do is ask Andrea.'

Stig burst out laughing.

Emma plucked a daisy growing between cracks in the pavement. 'I know. Talk about leaving the most important thing until last. I've no idea if she'll agree. Or if any of the villagers will help. No one can forget what I used to be like, and why should they?'

Although she'd rather Mum had recalled every sordid detail than forgotten to the extent she had.

'*I* know I'm different now, but they can't see that yet. I thought coming back would mean a happy end to a challenging year.' She shook her head. 'What an idiot.'

'Then perhaps you need to adjust your idea of happiness,' Stig said, and raised an eyebrow. 'To most people my life looks pitiful, but I'm no longer under stress. I have the Duchess. I'm answerable to no one but myself.'

'So you're happy?'

'My life's bloody hard most of the time – you know that – but if you offered me my old job back tomorrow, I wouldn't take it. And what exactly is happiness? Having a bit of peace, perhaps that's a better goal.' Stig put down his book. 'My dad has his own painting and decorating business – said he always wanted something better for me. But you know what? He and Mum have a good life. They aren't in debt. Go on holiday once a year. They live in a terraced house, but the neighbours are like family.' He shrugged. 'You're sober now. Maybe anything else is a bonus. Don't give up on Healdbury, Emma. I've only been here a short while, but can see it's got heart.'

'Despite Ted and the others who don't want you here?'

'All the businesses have adverts in their windows for each other's goods. I got chatting to the baker yesterday. He stopped to give me some change. Apparently everyone's pulling together to try to survive in the face of the big supermarket that's taken so much business. He said not to take locals' hostility personally. Most of it was probably because profits are so low and they're worried about anything that might make the village look less attractive to people with money in their pockets. Apparently Ted's whole family is finding it hard to cope. The grandkids are living with him and his wife whilst their widowed computer-consultant dad travels the country doing better-paid contract work. At the moment, his income is the only thing keeping the cheese shop afloat.'

'By the looks of it, Phil's shop is definitely in trouble too. No wonder he was in a sharp mood.'

'The baker told me Phil is on the brink of bankruptcy – of losing everything. And his wife left him for another man.'

'*What?* Poor Phil. I can't believe it. He and Sheila seemed made for each other when I was working for them. I never thought those two would break up.'

'Apparently he's desperate to find a lodger; he's been trying for weeks.' Stig squeezed her arm. 'It must be tough coming back, but remember, it's not just about people giving you a second chance – it's about you giving them one back. Everyone is fighting their own battles. You know that.'

Emma mulled his words over as she made her way up Broadgrass Hill and back to Foxglove Farm. He was right. She needed to think more about the other person's situation. She rubbed her elbow as it brushed against a nettle. Seeking forgiveness was harder than she'd ever imagined, and the lack of it stung. But perhaps the real sting came from her realising she'd had a sense of entitlement.

Her ears felt hot as she looked back over the last few weeks and how she'd arm-wrestled her way back into her family's life, with little thought for them. How she'd forced her way back into the village without considering the problems her old neighbours might be facing.

She was still fiddling with the daisy, and gazed now at its bowed head. It could never get its old roots back, but placing it in water might give it a second life. She and her family had cut ties two and a half years ago, but perhaps there was a way of taking the relationships in a new, different direction.

She gathered pace as an idea took shape. It would involve bracing herself to talk to Phil again – and then to Bligh and Andrea.

Chapter 11

Emma sat on the bench in front of the weeping willow tree, Gail next to her. They both wore large sunhats. Gail was flicking through a small fabric sample book. Emma had tried to buy it from the local curtain shop, thinking it might please her seamstress mum, but when they'd heard it was for Gail, they wouldn't take payment. Andrea had grudgingly said it was a good idea. It made a change from fiddling with chocolate wrappers. Gail loved sweet treats yet clothes hung off her as if she'd gone shopping alone and bought the wrong sizes.

'Emma would like this,' she said, having stopped at a square of material for children's curtains patterned with pigs.

'Your daughter? You remember her?' Emma's pulse danced.

'She used to beg her sister to paint the pigs. A little devil she was for giving them biscuits.' A cloud passed across her face.

'And now...?'

She continued flicking through.

The not knowing whether Gail knew who she was was hurting less. Seedlings of something – acceptance, perhaps – had sprouted inside her. An understanding that this was how it was. She had to deal with life on its own terms – as it was now, disconnected from the past.

She glanced at her watch. She'd asked Andrea and Bligh to meet her here during their lunch break. Ahead of her grazed two sheep, with their new lamb, and some goats. She stood up and walked to the fence. One of the goats ran over. She tickled its head. Straightening up, she squinted in the sunshine. Yesterday she'd positioned several upturned crates and big logs in the field. The goats were agile, and it was as if their hooves were made of Velcro as they mounted and clung to any surface or angle.

She looked up and saw her sister and Bligh approaching from the distance. When they neared, she gestured for them to sit down next to Gail.

Andrea glugged water from a plastic bottle and wiped her mouth. 'What's so important that I have to give up my break?'

When they were little, the girls often shared a bottle of water when helping Mum plant or harvest. Some children might have baulked at drinking out of the same container, but the two sisters didn't worry.

Emma took off her sunhat, dropped it to the ground and rubbed her sweaty palms down her cotton shorts. 'I've been thinking.' She looked at Bligh. 'You were right. I shouldn't have just turned up without warning. I've imposed on you both.' She looked at Andrea. 'I know it's been difficult for you having me around – and in the house during the evening.'

The bottle squeaked as Andrea squeezed it tight. 'Just spit it out, Emma. Coming back hasn't been such an easy ride as you expected. You've got bored and now you and your inheritance are heading back to the city.' She shook her head. 'How very predictable.'

Emma sat down in the grass, legs crossed, in front of her sister.

'You're right,' she said, and looked up. 'It hasn't worked out quite as I expected. That's because, as usual, I've only been thinking about things from my point of view. So I've got a suggestion to make.'

Gail got up and started walking around.

'I meant what I said when I came back – I want to help and make amends. But I realise now that expecting to simply slot into your lives like a missing part of a jigsaw... that was unrealistic, because the overall picture has changed. So...' she cleared her throat, 'I'll move out. Give you breathing space. I'll get here early each day – without needing to come into the farmhouse for breakfast or a shower – and I'll stay for as long as you need me, looking after Mum, working in the shop, whatever. Aunt Thelma's money will tide me over for a while.'

Andrea screwed the lid back onto her water bottle.

'What do you think?' said Emma.

'Where exactly will you stay?' A pinch of relief flavoured Andrea's voice.

'With Phil Brown.'

'At the pet shop?' asked Bligh incredulously.

'You're joking?' said Andrea. 'He tore a shred off me a couple of weeks ago – blamed me for you coming back, thought I'd tracked you down, said I hadn't learnt my lesson. He kept going on about his car.'

'We've talked. Come to an understanding. He needs money badly and has been looking for a lodger. I need a place to stay. The room is basic, which is why he hasn't been able to fill it, but compared to a barn... He insisted I pay two months' rent up front, which is fair enough, and he can ask me to leave at a moment's notice.'

'Wish I'd been there when you asked him. Well, it's up to you,' Andrea said stiffly, and got up. 'We managed perfectly fine without you, and we can do again.' She walked straight past Emma and rubbed Gail's arm. 'Egg on toast, Mum? And I could do with a cup of tea.'

'There's just one more thing... How's it going with the tomatoes?' asked Emma.

Andrea look puzzled. 'Even better than usual. The extra warm weather has meant it's a bumper harvest this year.'

'Great, because I've got a favour to ask.'

'I wondered how long it would take,' Andrea said, in a tired voice.

'I've decided to set up a soup run for the homeless who have been forced into Healdbury. Could I have our spare produce that doesn't get eaten, frozen or made into jam? I've found Mum's old recipe book full of ideas for using the farm's fruit and vegetables.' It had been stuffed at the back of Gail's wardrobe next to the wooden chest. 'Remember that cucumber relish she used to make? And the onion soup? She used to swear by putting a tablespoon of peanut butter into it.'

'I'd forgotten that,' said Andrea, her voice lacking the usual formality for a second. 'It kind of worked.'

Emma nodded. 'And you said there were a load of clothes Mum can't wear any more because the fasteners are too fiddly. Perhaps I could hand those out as well.'

Andrea stared.

'What's the matter?'

'What's the catch?'

'There isn't one.' Emma threw her hands in the air. 'What do I have to do to prove that I've changed? Just name it, Andrea. Anything, because I'm running out of ideas here.'

'Don't you get it? It's too late. It's just not in me to trust you again. Give it up, Emma, like we had to give up on you all those months ago.'

'No. No, I can't do that. I won't. Not yet,' said Emma quietly. 'We can work this out. I'm sure of it. We just need time.'

Time was one thing she had never valued in the old days. Whatever she'd wanted, she'd wanted *now*. She had left the farm for the city full of unrealistic dreams, believing they'd be easily achieved.

Andrea opened her mouth and then sighed. She looked at her watch. 'I'm not going to argue. My energy is better spent elsewhere. Use the overripe or damaged produce if you must. Just don't get under my feet.'

She linked arms with Gail and the two of them headed off to the farmhouse.

Emma got up and sat next to Bligh. They watched the staggering lamb try to walk straight.

'Phil Brown. Really?' He shot her a probing stare.

'I feel sorry for him, actually. He's on the brink of losing everything. In fact I noticed some tubs of paint stacked in the barn. Could I have them for him? His shop's exterior could do with a makeover.'

'I guess so. I'll drop them off tonight on my way home after work.'

'Great. I'm packing up my stuff now, so I'll see you later.'

'Why don't you wait until this evening? It's on my way. I can give you a lift.'

For a second she sensed the old familiarity.

'Thanks, but I've got to go into the village to talk to Stig about recipes for the soup run – I may as well take my stuff then.' She stared at him. 'You know… I remembered that other word I used to call you. It wasn't very nice, and I'm sorry.'

'No, it wasn't. But you had a point. I *was* a doormat. I let you trample over me. I smoothed things over with the locals and paid your credit card bills. I didn't even end things when I heard how you threw yourself at Dean.'

Bligh was right. He was always clearing up her mess, and the more he did, the angrier she became. In her twisted mind she'd decided his compassion was enabling her behaviour and therefore he was to blame. A proper boyfriend, she'd tell herself, would have dumped her – made her face up to her decline.

As for Dean, it was as Emma had feared – she'd made a drunken pass at the man her older sister was hoping to marry.

'You were so strong,' she said.

'Or was I weak? I should have been able to keep you safe, but I failed miserably.' He sat down again. 'I hated myself after you left. Hated that I'd let you treat me like that. And I'd re-enact scenarios in my head. I should have refused to buy your drink. Made you face people and apologise yourself. Then maybe you wouldn't have had to leave; perhaps you'd have finally agreed to go to the doctor. Andrea wouldn't have been left to cope.' He bit his lip. 'At the time I thought I was doing the right thing, but later it felt as if everything was my fault.'

'Bligh. Please. Don't *ever* think that. There is only one person to blame and that's me. Don't ever change. That's who you are – helping people, seeing the best in them. I didn't deserve your loyalty, but other people aren't me.'

He stood up and rubbed the back of his neck. 'Did you ever truly love me, Emma? Because from where I'm sitting, you just used me. You said I made you feel good.

Was that all it ever was? Fixer. Doormat. What about just *Bligh*? Why did I always have to serve a purpose?'

His phone went, and he hid the flash of anger and answered it. Emma left to start packing.

Chapter 12

Emma was still thinking about Bligh's question when she headed to Phil's later that afternoon. Had she really been such a selfish girlfriend? Since coming off the streets, she'd asked herself that over and over again. At times it had consumed her, along with thoughts that she was the worst sister and daughter to boot. However, after treatment, she was able to tame the shame; guilt was more constructive, a sense that she'd done bad things but that didn't make her a bad person. This was one firm message from therapy that had given her the strength to come back to Foxglove Farm.

What a relief to start letting go of the self-absorption, as if she'd been wearing blinkers that had been removed to let in a wider view, although she still felt the fear in the pit of the stomach about her last day in Healdbury and her reckless actions. She still couldn't face dealing with that. But it wouldn't be long now before she confessed to Polly and Alan and faced the consequences. And then all her plans to help her family would have to come to an end. But until then…

Feeling hot and sticky from the walk down Broadgrass Hill, with the rucksack on her back, Emma pulled her case up to Phil's door.

'I'll be back out in a second,' she said to Stig, who was staring at a tatty copy of one of the Harry Potter books.

It was upside down. 'I've found Mum's old recipe book. There are some brilliant ideas in it.'

He gave her a thumbs-up but didn't make eye contact. His woolly hat was pulled down further than usual, despite the smothering heat.

'Everything okay?'

'I'm not sure how long I can stay around.'

Emma crouched down. 'Stig? What's happened?'

He lifted his head. 'That Ted, the cheesemonger, he's just gone in to see Phil. He told me to leave by the end of the week or he'd report me to the RSPCA; said they'd say they saw me kicking the Duchess – make sure she was taken away.' His voice wobbled. 'I can take a lot. But lose her? Never.'

Emma stood up and took a deep breath, then entered the shop. Ted was standing at the counter talking to Phil. She put down her rucksack.

Ted ran a hand over his bald head. He'd had a little hair left the last time she'd been in the village. 'Emma. Glad to see you looking well. Well done for turning things around.'

'Oh. Um… thanks. Thanks, Ted. That means a lot.'

'How's it going at the farm?'

She shrugged. 'As good as can be expected after everything that happened.'

'I hope it works out for you. I'm sorry about how things have turned out for Gail.'

This was more like the Ted she used to know – yet he'd been so harsh towards Stig.

His fingers tightened around a bundle of papers. 'This is the petition to get the council to move the rough sleepers on. So far I've got over sixty signatures. Phil said you're friends with that chap outside. Can't you have a word? That way we can avoid any nastiness.'

'A petition? I'm glad you're going to do it properly then, Ted, instead of threatening people that you'll lie about their dog.'

He flushed.

'These people have nowhere to go,' she continued quietly. 'They've been chased out of the city for appearances' sake. When that international art festival is over, they'll go back. Their presence here won't last forever.'

'And I'm not unsympathetic, but them being here is a risk to everything we value. Healdbury's crime rate is low. It's safe to walk the streets at any time of night. All that will change if more of them appear, and I can't hold on for them to leave of their own accord. My livelihood will suffer.'

'What – because of a handful of homeless people? They aren't even near your shop.'

'But it looks bad. I've got a potential investor coming over next week and I don't want him thinking this is a rough area where businesses might be broken into.'

'Have any of them caused trouble so far?' she said calmly.

'No, but who knows how many more will turn up? Increasing numbers will bring down house prices, and what about drugs? There will be an increase in petty crime and—'

'Drug addicts won't move here, it's too rural,' said Emma. 'They'll stay near their dealers.'

'Ted's done his research,' said Phil. 'One council takes this matter very seriously and has brought in fines to stop the homeless sleeping in doorways. The last thing customers want is to have to step over a tramp. With rising prices it's challenging enough to make ends meet as it is.'

'Have a word, Emma – and give up your idea of a soup run,' said Ted. 'We're a fair-minded community, you know that, and I don't want to get the authorities here unless we have to.'

She pursed her lips.

'What?' said Phil. 'It's easy for you to take the moral high ground, but you haven't got a mortgage or a family to support.'

'That's the whole point,' she said.

Ted raised his eyebrows.

'It's ironic. A good number of the people I got to know on the streets were just like you two once.' She gazed from one man to the other. 'I used to eat in a soup kitchen with a man called Tony. He'd often set up by the black bin outside Debenhams, in Market Street. He had a good job and used to do charity work with the Round Table. But then his wife died of cancer and he subsequently lost everything, because he couldn't cope. Tony represents a lot of professional people who due to debt or redundancy or mental health issues have ended up on the streets. There isn't as big a gap as you might think between you and them.'

Neither of them replied.

'We all used to be friends. You saw how easily someone's life can spiral out of control when they aren't happy,' said Emma. 'Haven't you ever had a double shot to ease the stress of a long day? And Stig outside isn't addicted to anything apart from books.'

The men looked at each other.

'I'm grateful for your welcoming words, Ted. Really I am. But how can you appreciate that I've changed yet not give the homeless out there a chance? Don't they deserve our help? Even the government has finally recognised their plight and set targets to deal with—'

Ted's lips formed a firm line. 'I am glad to see you back, Emma, but you caused a lot of damage before you left. Should we tolerate such reckless behaviour from these people? No, because the village is suffering a difficult enough time as it is. The kind of help they need is available in Manchester and Stockport. We pay our taxes to provide that. There's nothing for them here and they don't need you setting up some sort of lifeline that will mean they never return to where they came from. I have to think of my family – the local community. It's a big enough job looking after the people who've grown up here at the moment, let alone anyone else.' He looked at Phil. 'I'll let you know when the meeting is.' He nodded to Emma and left.

'Meeting?' said Emma.

'To discuss our plan of action. Some villagers, like you, are giving these people handouts. They need to know this will only exacerbate the problem.'

Emma sighed.

Phil delved into his pocket and pushed a key across the counter. 'From now on you can use the private entrance out the back.'

Emma picked up the key. 'I've just got one condition.' Clearly this was a day for asking favours. Andrea had agreed to Emma using spare produce. Perhaps this request would be granted too. 'No drink in the house.' For her own good, and also because she was worried about Phil himself.

'You're having a laugh, right?'

'I can't live anywhere that's got alcohol. Or you'll have to hide it.'

'So you expect me to give it up?'

'Only at home. If that's so much of a problem, perhaps you need to ask yourself why.'

'How dare *you* try to give me advice?'

'Say what you like, Phil. I've been rejected by those closest to me, so you can't hurt me any more.'

He broke eye contact. 'I'll drink at home if I damn well want to.'

'If I see it, I'll be moving out.'

'Don't forget I've got your money up front.'

'So for the sake of not drinking you'd throw out a lodger? Doesn't that ring alarm bells?'

'You're a fine one to talk.'

'I am. Because I've been there. I threw everything away and ended up in the gutter. Don't follow my example. Because believe me, it's no picnic trying to get back those things of value.'

'I've already lost Sheila.'

'And now you have two choices. You can wallow in self-pity. Stop fighting for your business. Go under. Or, like Sheila, you can build a new life. Why not prove you're stronger than me, Phil, and start to make changes before it's too late?'

Months of treatment had made her used to saying it how it was. Social niceties had often been bypassed.

'We used to get on, didn't we? Me working here with you and Sheila? We had laughs. You even invited me and Bligh to dinner once.' She gave a small smile. 'I felt really grown up.'

'Yeah, so grown up you vomited in our front garden on your way home.'

A tide of heat rose up her neck as she picked up her bag. 'Bligh will be dropping off some paint later. How about we freshen up this place? And a while back I met someone on the streets who used to co-own a pet shop. I've got some ideas – if you want them – that might bring in business.'

'What... and then we'll become friends again and everyone will clap you on the back and say how much you've changed?' He folded his arms. 'Are you crazy? People don't forgive and forget. Life's not like that. That's why I'm on my own now.'

He disappeared out to the back. Emma closed her eyes for a moment and then followed him, dumping her belongings in the hallway and going into the kitchen. It was small. Pine. There were no curtains at the window, and empty hooks stood out from the walls. Clearly he'd not replaced a thing since Sheila left. The room lacked her singing. The notes of her flowery perfume. The homely smell of the bread she loved baking. The sink was filled with dirty mugs. Empty takeaway boxes stood stacked on the table. Phil sat on one of the chairs, his head in his hands. Next to him was a half-empty bottle of whisky.

'You're no bloody martyr, you know,' he muttered.

She sat down opposite him. 'Never said I was. Just trying to become a better person.'

He looked up and his hand reached for the bottle. 'You've clearly come back to try to make up for the past and all that crap. Well take it from me – it's never going to work. I cheated on Sheila a decade ago. One stupid mistake. She's been harbouring a grudge all this time and finally got her own back. Except she fell in love and actually left. Ten years and I still didn't get forgiveness, so if I was you, I wouldn't bother seeking it from other people.'

'How is drinking going to help, Phil?'

'Makes me feel better.'

'Until you wake up tomorrow hating yourself and promising it'll never happen again.'

Phil concentrated on the bottle.

'I *know*, Phil,' she said quietly. 'That's where I've been.'

He moved the whisky nearer.

11 months before going back

It was a humid Friday morning. The fourteenth of July. Emma had been out of detox for two weeks. Perhaps she'd have her own flat soon. That had been the plan, with her and Joe's baby due in January.

For such a long time there'd been no sense of a yesterday or a tomorrow. It was so long since she'd spent even one minute planning for the future. Since considering taking steps to get better, however, ideas had popped into her brain that focused on cots and prams. These ideas had become something else then; she'd created a story around first days at school and built up images of herself waving her daughter off to university.

Something had told her that her baby was a girl. Josephine, she'd be called. Joe might have liked that.

She swallowed and looked around the minimalist whitewashed room at Stanley House, with the flipchart easel in front of a half-moon of chairs. She'd started the Listening EAR programme last week, straight out of detox, despite what had happened. This was her sixth session. One of the facilitators, Dave, came in. In defiance of his receding hairline, he still managed to scrape back some sort of wispy grey ponytail. He wore his standard attire – T-shirt and voluminous explorer shorts.

He switched on a fan and she gave a weak smile as he passed around a clipboard for them all to sign in. Then he started with the usual catch-up – going around the room getting everyone to say how they'd managed since the last session two days ago.

Emma tried to focus, but instead, in her mind, the unexpected scenes of her last day of detox just played over and over. She had gone to the bathroom, marvelling at how clear-headed she felt. She'd washed her hands trying to pretend that she hadn't just seen pink spots – that the cramps in her stomach were simply due to too many vegetables at lunch. She'd got herself a coffee. Tried not to double up. But the pain was too bad and those spots had returned, like traffic lights designed to halt pregnancies rather than cars. They had turned into a stream that couldn't be stopped.

She had lost her.

She'd lost Josephine.

Potential decades of life wiped out in a few hours.

A kind doctor had checked her over. Said she wasn't to blame. Early miscarriages weren't uncommon. The foetus just wasn't viable. Nature's way, perhaps.

The voice on her shoulder tried to persuade Emma that her former habits would fill the void, and the old her would have taken oblivion over reality any day of the week. This was all new, facing feelings head on. Her case workers supported her with sympathy and cups of tea, but what was the point of recovery now?

Night after night she'd lain curled up in her bed at the hostel, listening to shouts from the room next door as sirens approached, unable to sleep after years of simply passing out. Heart thumping, she would think about her lost baby and how the future now seemed like a blank screen. The emptiness, the loneliness made her want to join in with her neighbours' hollers. She'd go on to recall the hurt and trouble she'd brought to her family. Instead of releasing her to darkness, closing her eyes just made her see more. The huge upset she'd caused Mum, Andrea and Bligh. The smaller things she'd forgotten, like the villagers' disgusted expressions… it was all coming back now.

The emotional up and down made her realise just how much she missed Mum. She did. And Andrea too. But most of all she missed her Josephine and the littlest pair of arms that might one day have hugged her tight as she hugged back too.

Everything seemed so hopeless.

'Boring you, are we, Emma?' said Dave.

With a jolt she came back to the present. *A right bastard, Dave is, but his heart's in the right place,* one of the others had said to Emma on her first day. She'd been scared of him to start with.

'So how about you?' He raised a wiry eyebrow. 'What's been going on since Wednesday?'

She shrugged.

He held her gaze.

'Okay… you want the truth? It's like it's the end of the world. Like I'm the worst person ever. Like everyone must think I deserve to have lost my child. At moments I don't see the point in staying sober.'

'That's some pity party. You like wallowing, don't you?'

Her face flushed. She shifted in her seat. An accusation like that somehow held unquestioned truth when it came from a fellow recovering addict.

'But mostly I'm disappointed that you've already forgotten everything we did in the last session.'

Her brow knotted.

'Negative thinking. Go on. Just analyse your last few sentences. How about *it's the end of the world*? What are you doing there?'

Okay, so the universe as she knew it hadn't come to a halt. She still got up and washed. Still set her alarm when she went to bed. 'I'm catastrophising,' she said, and bit her lip.

'And *everyone must think I deserve to have lost my child*. I see you've still got that crystal ball. Wish I was that special, being able to mind-read.'

Her cheeks felt hotter. Dave was right. She shouldn't assume what people thought. In fact, everyone in the group had been really kind.

'And *I'm the worst person ever*,' she interjected. 'I've given myself a label, haven't I?'

'Bingo. Do that long enough and mentally, labels stick. *I'm a bad person* is a common one.'

The rest of the group nodded.

'Perhaps you have all done bad things, but you've also been ill,' he continued. 'Your habits, your behaviours and choices might have been bad – that doesn't make *you*, intrinsically, a bad person. Not if you're prepared to do what it takes to change yourself and make amends.'

He looked around the room. 'That session on negative thinking is one of the most important ones you'll do, folks. You've got to rewire your brains. So now I'll ask you again, Emma – how are things going?'

'I've had a lot of cravings since… since it happened. But I've followed suggestions – went out for a walk or drank a glass of water or read a book.'

He nodded.

'And my case worker is getting rehab sorted. One we're considering is based on a tough boot-camp style, whereas another gentler one calls itself a therapeutic community. Yesterday we visited one in Sheffield that is between the two. Lou thinks that one is best.'

'What about our discussion on moving forward from former friends in order to safeguard yourself from old behaviours?'

'I went to the library to use the computer to get my mates' contact details. But when I scrolled down my accounts, I realised they were really just drinking partners.' Her scalp had prickled as she'd studied the online photos. Facebook, Instagram, her posts had been all about showing off and duck pouts. She could hardly bear to look at the selfies and those bloodshot eyes, or listen to the videos narrated by her slurred words. 'So I've deleted all my accounts. I'm making new friends in AA now.'

She realised she *was* making progress. Perhaps things weren't quite so hopeless after all. Bit by bit she was taking charge of her life, and something warmed the inside of her chest – a small sense of self-respect that had kept away for so long.

Dave gave her a thumbs-up. 'It's so important not to isolate. Meeting new, like-minded people is the way to go. So lastly, let's go back to what you said at first, about not seeing the point in staying sober...' He paused. 'We care, you know. Me. Your case workers. Your new friends in here. We want you to reach the end of this journey,' he added in gentler tones. 'We want to help.'

'But it was my pregnancy that brought me here.' She swallowed. 'Now that's gone... I can't help wondering why I'm bothering.' Joe had left. Now Josephine. Struggling to fight the self-pity, Emma wiped her eyes. She had to stay strong.

'It doesn't need to have been for nothing,' he said. 'Not if you carry on. Stay well. Build a future for yourself. Wouldn't staying on this road make everything that's happened worth something?'

He moved on to the next person, his usual brusque tone restored. Emma zoned out of the class. Turning her life around... changing things for good... of course, Dave was absolutely right. Making something of her life, contributing – that would make Josephine's brief existence significant.

Especially if... A shiver shot down her spine. Her throat ached as she contemplated going home. She hadn't called Foxglove Farm home for a long time. But recovery had made it hard to block out thoughts about Mum and Andrea and how they were coping now. It asked uncomfortable questions, like had they really abandoned her, or had her behaviour forced them to let go?

What if everything wasn't their fault after all? All those second chances they gave her after her false promises – how had she repaid their patience? By continuing to hurt and humiliate them; by treating Bligh and his dad so badly.

She stared blankly at the flipchart and felt so confused. Who was this new open-minded, rational Emma? She felt like a stranger.

But in that instant, she knew what she had to do. To make Josephine count, she would put all her energy into completing the rehabilitation process, and then as soon as possible go back to Healdbury.

Chapter 13

Phil sat at the kitchen table and kicked his feet against its pine legs like a teenager.

'I don't want pancakes for breakfast. I'll sort myself out. You're my lodger, not my mother.'

Emma winced.

'I've made too many,' she said, and set down a pile in front of him. She sat opposite him and reached for the pot of honey.

'Three weeks here and you think this is your gaff.'

'Nope. If it was, I'd have curtains back up in here by now.'

Phil glanced at the window. 'Hadn't really noticed. Guess I could get some,' he said grudgingly.

'Or blinds…' Emma shrugged. 'Might be more practical.'

They ate in silence.

'On the plus side, the bare window means we've got an amazing view of today's sunrise. What a fabulous pink sky.' Emma studied his face as he turned to look. Having stuck to soft drinks for a while, he looked like a different person. The dark shadows around his eyes were less pronounced. He'd shaved and got on top of his washing and ironing. Routine had become part of his life again. He'd even embraced her suggestion of using Bligh's paint to smarten up the shop.

'Have you thought any more about my idea?' she said, and sipped her tea.

'Even if I thought it was worth it, I haven't got the means to advertise.' He turned back and cautiously prodded a pancake as if it were alive.

'Yes you have. I can help with posters and ask local businesses to pin them up. We're heading past the middle of July now – it's not long before school breaks up. You could take in hamsters, gerbils, guinea pigs and birds while people are away on their holidays. I'd help you look after them.'

He put down his fork. 'It won't work, you know. People – including me – aren't ever going to be taken in. Why don't you just drop this bright and breezy front?'

She raised her eyebrows. 'You don't think people can change?'

'All those years, since I had that one-night stand, Sheila made me think she'd forgiven me and never said a harsh word. But just before she left, the resentment, all the old bitterness I thought had disappeared, poured out. So no. I don't believe people can change – and memories certainly can't.'

'But you were the one who had the affair, and you changed.'

Phil didn't answer.

Her mum had forgotten lots. Her memories had altered. Or rather, they'd disappeared and left a confused mind to fill in the gaps. Yesterday she'd asked Bligh if he was her boyfriend and held his hand. Emma was still known simply as the woman who talked too much.

Emma rolled up a pancake and picked up her tea in the other hand. Her chair scraped as she stood and headed into the garden. She sat on a worn plastic chair, mug by her side. Morning dampness lent the air notes of grass and soil. A speckled thrush landed on the lawn nearby. She tossed small crumbs of batter. Minutes later a blue tit and a sparrow shared the spoils.

Even Andrea couldn't help smiling at the idea of Gail and Bligh dating. The sisters had always teased their mum that she had a secret crush. Laughing, she wouldn't deny it and regularly made him his favourite steamed treacle pudding. That was back in the day, when Bligh's world revolved around Emma, like a planet that had finally found its sun. And just lately, just occasionally, she'd felt that old pull between them again.

When she returned inside, Phil had done the washing-up. Ignoring his glance, she put her mug by the sink. He'd got a tape measure out and was holding it up to the window.

'I won't be back until late,' she said. 'I'm at the farm all day. Andrea has agreed to let me prepare the food there for tonight's soup run.'

'Good. I'm sick of this place smelling of onions.' He said something else, but she didn't wait to hear – didn't want to hear any more of his negative comments.

–

'Honestly, I wouldn't mind if he was perfect, but you should see the state of the bathroom after he's had a wash,' she complained to Stig with attempted cheerfulness as they walked through Healdbury that evening. He'd met her at the top of Broadgrass Hill at a quarter to seven and was helping her carry the rucksacks and an old picnic table she'd found in the barn. Emma had filled flasks with rich tomato soup and made cheese sandwiches with the cucumber relish recipe out of Mum's recipe book. 'Phil's default setting is just plain rude.'

'But he did let you move in,' said Stig as they passed the Badger Inn. Laughter and chat wafted over from the beer garden out the back.

She sighed. 'And I am grateful. Since moving out, things have improved at the farm. Bligh and I actually sat down and drank coffee together this afternoon.'

Stig steered the Duchess away from a broken bottle smashed on the ground. At that moment, Ted from the cheese shop approached them, pointing to the glass.

'We didn't have any of that before you rough sleepers moved here.' He took out his phone and took a photo. 'Evidence for my next meeting with the local council.'

'Ted... please,' said Emma. 'It's a Coke bottle. Anyone could have dropped it.'

He jerked his head up towards the station. 'Quite a crowd there now, waiting for your handouts. The bins are overflowing and the bushes stink of urine. I've just been up there to take notes.' He rubbed his forehead. 'No wonder my migraines have been coming back.'

'Get some lavender oil in. Always used to do the trick for me when I was teaching,' said Stig.

'Teaching?'

'Stig's a geography graduate,' said Emma.

Ted's cheeks reddened and he loosened his shirt collar before answering his phone and walking away.

Stig and Emma called in to the bakery and then approached the station. Rita and young Tilly were waiting. Tilly wore scruffy pink and white jogging bottoms and a stained T-shirt that said *Unicorns Suck*. The young couple who begged outside the bank were also there, plus an older woman who'd been in Heald-bury a week, camping out next to a bin opposite Ted's shop. Then there were several rough sleepers who hadn't appeared before, including one with a Labrador.

They all sat smoking and chatting. It was a warm summer's evening and Emma was beginning to wonder if she should have made cold fruit smoothies instead of soup.

This was the fifth soup run they'd done now. Wednes-days and Fridays, they'd decided upon. Seven until nine. Rita smiled as they arrived and helped them off with the rucksacks. Stig set up the table.

'I'm dead grateful,' she said and tossed her asymmetrical hair, 'but please tell me it's not that peanut soup again. Even I'm not quite that desperate.'

Tilly grinned.

'You're in luck. We've had a glut of tomatoes up at the farm this year,' said Emma, 'so it looks like global warming might have saved you.'

'That's one thing I miss,' said Stig, passing Tilly a sand-wich before helping himself. He opened it, took out the filling and gave the bread to the Duchess. 'The geography field trips I used to go on. The last one was to Iceland to see the impact of climate change. The kids were really switched on.'

'That must have felt so rewarding.'

Stig ate the cheese. 'Our planet's always fascinated me. It was a toss-up between doing geography or physics at university. One plus of living on the streets – I get to study the night sky for free.' He set out the cups and poured soup. Emma handed them out.

'It's clearer around here, away from the city lights,' said Tilly. 'Just look at that full moon – and I saw a shooting star last night.'

'Me too,' said Rita in between mouthfuls. 'Makes a change from seeing nowt but the city's amber street glow.'

'Nature – keeps you going, doesn't it?' said Stig.

Emma bent down and ruffled the Duchess's neck. 'Me and Joe used to go down to the canal to feed the ducks. It would make me feel human, just for a moment.'

'I used to live in the country – down south,' said Tilly, and cautiously sipped her soup. 'The neighbours had sheep and pigs. Me, Dad and Mum were in our element. Mum couldn't wait to take on chickens rescued from battery farms. Never thought I'd miss the smell of pig shit.'

'How did you end up here?' said Emma.

'Mum died when I was twelve… she'd only been ill a few months,' Tilly said in a flat tone. 'Dad got married again. She persuaded him to sell up and we moved to London. I had to catch the tube to school – hated every minute. Dad and me started arguing all the time.'

'Must have been hard,' said Emma gently.

Tilly drained her cup. 'I ran away in the end. Dad was treating me like a baby – setting curfews, not letting me drink. I bought myself a train ticket to get as far away as possible.' She pulled a face.

'How old are you?' asked Stig.

'Isn't it rude to ask a woman's age?' she said, and drained her cup.

Emma, Rita and Stig exchanged looks. On close examination, behind the grime, this woman looked more like a child – a child with swollen red eyes, bitten nails, and collarbones that protruded like bike handles.

'How long ago was this? Have you contacted your dad?' asked Rita.

Tilly didn't reply.

'Didn't you hear me this morning, Emma?' said a deep voice. Footsteps approached, and Emma turned around to see Phil carrying a bowl and a plastic zip bag. He looked at the Duchess and put down the bowl. She went over to it eagerly. The Labrador joined her. Phil opened the bag and dog biscuits tumbled out. The two pets wolfed down the food.

'I told you to pop back tonight to collect these biscuits. They've gone out of date.' He stood up.

'Cheers,' said Stig. 'She's been living off scraps for the last few days.'

'No problem. My stock isn't exactly flying off the shelves. I used to have a Staffie. She's a beautiful dog.' He handed Stig the bag.

'Thanks, Phil,' said Emma, unable to keep the surprise out of her voice. 'Would you like a cream bun? She picked up the box of spare cakes from the baker's and lifted the lid.

He wiped his perspiring forehead with his arm and then took a bun. After demolishing it in three swift bites, he nodded, gave the dogs one last stroke and headed off.

They sat chatting, and as time passed, moonlight and cigarette ends lit up the dark. Rita shared how she'd escaped an abusive husband. He'd liked everything to be perfect – food tins lined up, shelves dust-free, books sitting in alphabetical order. He'd lost it when she'd finally rebelled by getting her lopsided haircut.

The young couple from outside the bank had been brought up in care. One of the rough sleepers Emma didn't know suffered from bipolar. Everyone had their own story that had led to the same outcome. As the summer evening chill descended, Emma emptied the last of the flasks into cups. All the sandwiches and cream cakes had gone.

She glanced at her watch.

'Half past ten! How's that happened?' she exclaimed. A few of the rough sleepers had used the station toilets and were now lying in their sleeping bags under the safety of the CCTV cameras.

Tilly picked up Gail's old recipe book that Emma had brought so that Stig could help her choose future meals. On the front, Andrea had written *Foxglove Farm Delights* in big fancy letters, and drawn a border decorated with images of carrots, eggs and various fruits. Tilly flicked through. It was A4-sized, and stains brought the recipes to life: jam, melted chocolate and cheese sauce.

'This is awesome,' she said as she carefully turned the pages, which were curling slightly at the corners. 'It's like something from medieval times.'

Emma burst out laughing. 'Well it's not quite that old, but I guess most people bookmark favourite recipes on the internet these days. It started off as a scrapbook. Mum would tear recipes out of magazines and stick them in. But then she became more experimental and made up her own. She got me to write them up for her in my best handwriting. Andrea designed the front and got the cover laminated at school.'

'Did your sister do the illustrations inside as well?' said Stig, peering over Emma's shoulder.

Emma nodded. She hadn't seen Andrea draw or paint since she got back. No surprise, really. Her sister barely had time to eat and drink.

Tilly pointed to a recipe. 'Strawberry and white chocolate cupcakes? Yes please!'

'How about you and Rita visit the farm tomorrow with Stig, and if I get time, I'll make some.' Emma studied the bags under Tilly's eyes. Her slight frame. She could be as young as fourteen. 'It's at the top of Broadgrass Hill, the other side of the village. Come over at seven. You can see the animals. Have a wash if you like. Grab a bite to eat. Once the shops are closed, and commuting is over, Healdbury gets pretty deserted, so you won't miss many passers-by.'

She hadn't asked Andrea's permission, but all she could think of was Tilly.

There were many ways of losing children, she decided. Miscarriage. Alzheimer's. A falling-out.

'Not sure,' said Tilly, eyeing her warily. 'You're not going to report me to services, are you? Or the police? I'm not going back, and no one can make me.'

'Just think of all that pig shit to smell,' said Stig.

Tilly paused, and then her face split into a cheeky grin.

They cleared up every bit of their own litter and then some more, just so that Ted had no reason to complain. Then Emma, Stig, Rita and some of the others headed back into the village. When they reached the crossroads where you turned right, down to the pet shop, Stig sniffed.

'Do you smell that?' he said. 'It reminds me of Bonfire Night.'

The others nodded and crossed the empty road. They hurried past Phil's. Thanks to the street light directly outside, they could see thick black smoke swirling inside the cheese shop.

Chapter 14

'Ted and his wife and the grandkids sleep upstairs,' said Emma. She dropped her rucksack and delved into her pocket. 'Crap. I've forgotten my phone.' No point in asking if anyone else had one. 'I'll call 999 from the pet shop.'

'Bring a large blanket if you can find one,' shouted Rita as she and the others ran towards the cheesemonger's. Stig stopped to tie the Duchess to a lamp post, leaving his belongings by her side. She whined as he rushed off. They reached the entrance door and banged and hollered as loudly as they could.

When Emma came back out with Phil, one of the upstairs windows was open.

'The hallway's full of smoke,' Ted shouted down. 'Me and Shirley have managed to get into the kids' bedroom, but now we're all stuck in here and the smoke's coming in under the door.' The pitch of his voice veered from high to low like car tyres skidding out of control. 'I don't know what to do. Help us! Please, someone!' His head disappeared.

Nearby residents appeared in their nightwear. Children's screams cut through the summer night. Phil and Emma ran to help. 'What's this for?' said Emma as she handed a blanket to Rita.

'The kids, at least,' said Rita. 'We can catch them if we spread this out and hold it in the air.'

'Isn't that dangerous?' said Emma. 'What if they jump in the wrong direction or the material tears?'

'Perhaps we can get in and reach them.' Stig sounded hopeful and pulled hard on the door handle.

'Don't be stupid, man,' said Phil. 'You'll get yourself killed.'

But Stig looked at the other rough sleepers and they nodded. One scouted around for something to throw. He found a brick and went up to the shop's entrance.

'You can't just—' Phil's voice was drowned out by the sound of breaking glass as the brick fell through the front pane. The Duchess barked frantically.

Stig put his arm through the hole, fiddled for a moment and opened the door. Smoke billowed out. He coughed for a few moments as he stood and listened to the crackle of flames, then pulled his coat collar over his mouth and nose and stepped inside. Phil grabbed his arm, but Stig shook himself free. A couple of the other homeless lowered their heads and followed him in.

'Ted! How are you all doing?' shouted Emma skywards as the Duchess barked even louder. Phil hurried over to calm the dog down.

'The little ones are having trouble breathing. Is the fire brigade coming yet? I can't stop the smoke getting in.' Ted's voice sounded hoarse. 'Please, please hurry!'

Emma looked at Rita. She shook the blanket and a group of them formed a circle and pulled it tight.

'You sure this will work?' asked Emma, palms sweaty. What if she lost her grip when the kids' weight hit the material? They might break their backs, get concussion or… She inhaled and breathed out, pushing away pessim-istic thoughts.

'There was a fire in a women's refuge I stayed in once. The fire brigade got stuck in traffic due to an accident. We had no choice. We didn't think it would work but it turned out fine.' Rita nodded her head vigorously. 'We can do this.'

Emma looked up at Ted again. Wondered if they could wait and see if Stig and the others got through, or the emergency services arrived. But the kids were only small and could easily choke on the smoke.

'Yes. Yes we can. Come on. Ted!' she shouted. 'Get the kids to jump. One at a time. It's okay, trust us. We'll catch them. It'll be all right.'

At that moment, Stig and the other men staggered out of the building, faces blackened, eyes streaming, coughing and retching.

'It's no good,' Stig spluttered, a glistening red burn on his forehead. 'Visibility is practically nil and you just can't breathe. Everything is too hot to touch.'

'Hurry up, Ted,' Emma yelled. 'Get them to jump. *Now!*'

'Children, don't be afraid,' shouted Rita. 'This is a magic blanket. It'll feel like the softest trampoline.'

Sobs travelled through the air. Small, scared faces peered down. Footsteps came running. It was Polly and Alan. They grabbed the blanket too. First a little girl jumped, screaming as she fell. Polly hauled her off and took her away to comfort her. Then her brother landed. Alan took care of him. Sirens finally sounded, and in a flash, a fire engine and an ambulance appeared in the street. Emma wrung her hands as a ladder was raised. Everyone stared up at the window.

Eventually Ted and his wife climbed to safety. He was wheezing badly. His wife saw him to the ambulance and then hunted out her grandchildren.

The next couple of hours passed in a blur. Another ambulance turned up and everyone who'd gone into the shop was checked over. The crowds cleared. Eventually the flames were put out. Emma congratulated Rita on her initiative. She hugged the children and promised them they could visit the farm to feed the pigs in a couple of days. Villagers appeared carrying trays of steaming coffee and sandwiches and handed them out to everyone. The teashop's owner offered Stig a free lunch the next day, and the hairdresser told Rita to call in for a wash and blow dry.

Ted came over, shaking his head. 'You could have been killed,' he said in between coughs. 'You don't know us. Why would you help?'

Stig wiped his eyes. Black streaks still covered his face. He looked years younger without his bobble hat, which hid a thick mop of chestnut hair. 'Strangers have helped me often enough on the streets. Saved me from a beating. Given me food.'

'You're a hero – and your friends,' said Ted's wife in an unsteady voice, eyes red, hair dishevelled. 'I'm not sure I'd have been that brave for people I didn't know, let alone people who'd been trying to drive me out of town.'

'Maybe I am. Maybe not,' said Stig. He shrugged. 'I've got my physical life to lose, yes, but no wife, no kids, no career...'

Ted's eyes glistened. He held out his hand. Tentatively Stig shook it. The cheesemonger then went round to every single person who'd helped and did the same before clambering back into one of the ambulances. To be on the safe side, the paramedics wanted the children checked over at the hospital.

Phil came across, talking to the Duchess. He handed the lead to Stig and dropped his bags at his feet. Stig got to his knees and spoke gently to his dog, stroking her head and ruffling her ears.

'You'd better come back to the pet shop for a shower,' said Emma, and looked at Phil. He nodded.

Stig stood up and wiped his nose on his arm. 'Nah, I'm okay. The wash basin at the train station will do. I'll head up there now. Fill Tilly in on all the gossip. Are we still invited over to the farm tomorrow night?'

'Of course.' She gave him a hug.

A paramedic from the second ambulance came over. 'Look, mate – Stig, is it? – can't I change your mind? We're getting off now. You really need that burn dressed properly at the hospital. Otherwise it won't heal properly.'

'Thanks, but no. I'll just give it a wash. It'll be fine.'

'Why on earth not?' Emma raised an eyebrow. 'It could get infected.'

His mouth set in a firm line and he looked down at the Duchess.

'Leave her with me until you get back,' said Phil gruffly. 'And your belongings if you like. You can pick them up first thing. The Duchess will be fine – I'll make sure of that.'

'Hop into the ambulance then, mate,' said the paramedic.

Stig hesitated. Then he knelt down again and promised the dog he'd be back. 'Cheers, Phil,' he said. 'But watch out. She turns nasty during a full moon.'

Phil noticed Stig's expression and mirrored his smile.

As Stig accompanied the paramedic back to his luminous vehicle and clambered in, Phil caught Emma's eye. She was staring at him. 'What?' he said.

On the spur of the moment, she hugged him too.

9–7 months before going back

'Hands up all of you who blame someone or something else for your addiction,' said Tess.

Emma's hand shot up along with everyone else's. It was late September. The first day of rehab in Sheffield. No sooner had she been shown to her room than she was called down to join an initial getting-to-know-you session. She sat in a bare white room, not dissimilar to the one where she'd done the Listening EAR sessions back at Stanley House.

No prodding was required for people to reveal exactly who they accused – their boss, their lover, a neighbour, work, society's expectations, friends, that teacher in Year 10... Since stopping drinking, Emma had been having doubts about whether Mum, Andrea and Bligh were to blame, but her father was still in the frame. Andrea's dad had died when her sister was three, but Emma's had run off. She'd never felt good enough because he chose to leave; never felt as if she fitted. So surely her problems were his fault?

Tentatively she smiled at the woman next to her, Rachel, who was also from Manchester, dressed in leggings and a baggy denim shirt. Rachel winked back, and discreetly offered a boiled sweet before slipping one into her own mouth. She was chatty, and before the session started had already found out where Emma grew up and introduced her to everyone else.

Tess said, 'The truth is, there's only one answer and it applies to you all.'

Emma sat upright on the hard chair.

'There is only one person or thing to blame – yourself.'

Rachel swore. Everyone else sat wide-eyed in silence.

'Thousands of people around the world have your challenges but they don't use because of them.' Tess explained how other people dealt with their feelings. Perhaps they talked them out. Meditated. Went swimming. Read a good book. Whereas everyone in that room used substances to change the way they felt and to escape.

An uncomfortable sensation washed over Emma as rain pitter-pattered against the windows. She thought about Mum. What she'd been through, widowed then abandoned. She hardly ever complained. And then there was Bligh, whose mother had run off and who'd then had to suffer the worry over his dad… the way he'd coped was to carry on being hard-working and reliable.

Whereas Emma…

Rachel took a while longer to grasp what Tess had said. It came out that she used to drink to try and fit in, and unreservedly blamed her mum for what made her stand out – the ginger hair the other children would laugh at, the unhealthy food that made her pile on weight. The next evening, over dinner, she and Emma swapped stories from their school days. Emma realised how lucky she'd been, with the farm, the support of Andrea and Bligh, and her mum's home-cooked meals.

'I grew up in a tower block,' said Rachel, putting down her knife and fork. 'We lived off takeaways and frozen food. Mum often left me on my own overnight to work her second job in a care home.'

'That must have been frightening,' said Emma.

146

'I never felt alone thanks to the noise from our neighbours. Their arguments and slammed doors were kind of comforting. Most nights I watched box sets. I could win *Mastermind* if my specialist subject was *The Vampire Diaries*.' Rachel shrugged. 'The ironic thing is, my dad would have stayed around and helped. But Mum knew he didn't love her. She got pregnant after a one-night stand. Apparently he offered to do the decent thing – even bought a cheap engagement ring from the market. They were just kids. But Mum's a proud woman. She told him to do one and never let her parents find out who the dad was.'

'My dad couldn't get away quick enough. Have you ever thought about tracking yours down?'

'Yeah, but Mum… she's never even told me his surname. She's as tough as anything, you know – how she sticks up for herself with the housing people and at work – but if I mention my dad, this look comes over her face like… like a kid who's been blocked on social media by their mates. My gran talked to me about it once, a couple of weeks before she died – said Mum got called a slag at school when she showed and had to leave. Gran said mentioning the pregnancy just brought back too many painful memories and I should leave the subject alone.' Rachel shrugged. 'But what about me? It's painful knowing nothing about my dad.' She looked at her watch and groaned. 'I can't be doing with this bed at ten o'clock malarkey. They're having a laugh. It's like freshers' week in reverse.'

'You went to university? I didn't get the grades.'

'Yeah. Mum was ever so proud, bragged to all her friends, yet told me I was an embarrassment when I just scraped a third in the final year, due to my partying. She

147

seemed more bothered about what her mates thought than my health.'

'Does she know you're here?'

Rachel drank some water and wiped her mouth with the back of her hand. 'I haven't rung her for over a year. I could be dead for all she cares.'

'Scary, isn't it? Doing the Twelve Steps. Just number one seems hard.'

'I already love Tess – but don't tell her that,' said Rachel, and dimples popped into her full cheeks. 'She's bossy. Calls us out for our behaviours. Tells it like it is. I need that. She's the first person whose opinion I've taken notice of for a long time.'

Rachel had made the mistake of saying she just wanted a normal life.

'You can scrub that word for starters,' Tess had said. 'It doesn't exist. Whereas *ordinary* – there's nothing wrong with that, and it's the opposite of what addiction makes you desire.'

She was right. A few drinks inside Emma and she thought she was the big I am. She wanted status, and if she couldn't be the village vet, she'd been determined to find it another way. But perhaps the simple things really were more important. These days she relished a pretty autumn leaf, a refreshing cup of tea – or making new friends like Rachel.

There was nothing wrong with being ordinary. Emma was just beginning to realise that.

'There's so much truth in everything she says. I mean, Step One is all about accepting you have no control over drink. It's funny how I never saw this in the past.' She shook her head.

'Did you ever try to stop?' asked Rachel, and patted her generous stomach. 'For me, it's the same with food. No willpower. I've tried replacement meals, starving…'

'Yeah, I tried alternating soft drinks with shots, having spritzers or mocktails. I tried buying mini bottles of wine instead of normal-sized ones, and only drinking after seven p.m. or at weekends.'

'Me too. I was so desperate towards the end. I remember one night I woke up frantic. There was nothing in the house and the shop near me was shut, so I drank mouthwash.' Rachel shook her head. 'Honestly, all the detours I'd make before and after work, trying to find a different supermarket or wine merchant. I was so embarrassed going into my usual stores, convinced the cashiers knew I had a problem. In fact I'd often buy a birthday card at the same time so they thought the wine was for someone else. Wasn't it creepy what Tess said? So obvious.'

Emma raised an eyebrow.

'You know…' Rachel cleared her throat. '*If you have to try so hard to control something, really it is controlling you.*'

Emma nodded. She liked Rachel, with her caring ways once you cut through the banter. She'd been the first to grab the tissue box today in the group, to hand to a man who'd started crying. Rachel admitted that she talked so much to cover her nervousness. In spite of the illness that had drawn them together, she managed to laugh at life – and laugh at herself.

With just one hour to go before bed, Emma suggested they look through their work booklets once more before the next day. This had become something of an evening routine. They'd take it in turns to meet in each other's bedroom. Rachel always had a stash of biscuits and Emma soft drinks.

On one such evening several weeks later, in November, Emma heard the expected knock at her door. A smiling Rachel came in. Her clothes hung more loosely and her mottled complexion had cleared. Today they'd been working Step Four.

'Which is utter hell!' Rachel had declared.

It dealt with character defects in depth.

'Resentments is the big one, folks,' Tess had said that morning. 'Addicts replay and replay them in their minds, obsessing, until they take over. To get well, you need to admit your own role in the situation and wipe the slate clean. Let's think of some small examples to start with. We've just had Bonfire Night – does that remind you of anything relevant?'

Emma's memory involved Joe. They'd shoplifted some sparklers and written each other's names in the night air. She'd drawn a love heart. He'd got sulky. Consequently Emma felt a huge resentment.

'It was because of my... my low self-esteem,' she admitted to everyone now. 'And maybe a little pride. And fear – the fear of being alone. I couldn't accept that he didn't feel the same way about me.'

Low self-esteem. Pride. Fear. Thoughtlessness. Selfishness. The list went on. Emma was seeing herself with fresh eyes. It made for uncomfortable viewing.

'Hellooo. Anyone in?' said Rachel, and playfully tapped Emma's head.

Emma grinned. 'Sorry.'

Rachel headed to the bed and sat on it cross-legged. Emma joined her. They both opened their booklets.

'These inventories we have to draw up – of everyone we've ever resented in our whole life. It's not easy.'

Rachel nodded. 'I know. For me, it's everything from friends and family who told me to stop drinking to complete strangers who've made nasty comments about my weight.'

'I can't believe the rubbish I've held onto for so many years. Villagers in Healdbury who—'

'Healdbury? So that's where Foxglove Farm is? Nice place.' Rachel shuffled into a more comfortable position and offered Emma one of the granola cookies from her bag. She was choosing healthier options these days and had stopped buying fizzy drinks.

'You've been there?'

'About a year ago. The village worked as the halfway point for meeting a new client. Most customers were happy to discuss web design over the phone, but some liked to meet up to show me material that would help me understand the whole concept. This client was a self-employed potter and brought in a range of his kitchenware. I thought a pub would be nicer than motorway services.' Rachel smiled. 'I always remember places by their food. This pub did amazing fish and chips.'

'So it had nothing to do with being able to drink?'

Gently Rachel pushed Emma's shoulder.

'Do you miss your job?'

'No. It paid well – that's why I did it, and the only reason I took computer studies at university – but now...' Her cheeks flushed. 'I'm thinking about doing that training course Tess mentioned, at the end of treatment. I want a job that does more for me than just line my pockets, and helping people through the Twelve-Step Programme should do it.'

'Rachel, that's brilliant! This time next year you could be working alongside her.'

'Maybe – and without the temptation of boozy lunches. Sitting down most of the day didn't help my eating either. It'll be a complete change of lifestyle but I finally feel as if I'm discovering the real me. I always thought it was that chunky little girl who sat in watching telly every night, stuffing her face, but looking back, that person was just a result of circumstance.'

'Which pub did you visit in Healdbury?'

'Now what was it called...? The Badger Inn.'

'You've got a good memory.'

'Not usually, but it's a difficult place to forget – great food aside.'

'Why? All those badger ornaments?' Emma wiped crumbs from her lips.

'No. Because of the landlords... what were they called? Polly and...'

'Alan.' Emma stopped chewing for a moment. 'I lost count of the times they barred me. That's one couple I know for sure won't be pleased to see me return to Healdbury.' Heat flooded her face as she recalled the week before that last Christmas. Out of all the embarrassing things she'd done in the pub, this was the worst. She'd stolen the charity box from the bar. It was for a local cause – Emma didn't know what, and at the time she didn't care. She must have taken it in blackout, because she didn't realise until she found it hidden, days later. It was extremely heavy, so most of the regulars must have chipped in. Polly and Alan always said that a sense of community was everything, and would never forgive her for stealing from the village.

'It's so sad about their son,' Rachel said.

'What, Ned? He must be nearly eighteen now. What's happened? Is he okay?'

152

'No… no, he isn't, Emma. I'm sorry… He died in an accident.'

'What, Ned? Surely not.' Emma shook her head. 'That's so terrible. He was a kind lad. He saw me crying in the street once and offered me a stick of chewing gum. I can't believe it. Are you sure? He was so young.'

Rachel rubbed Emma's arm. 'I'm afraid he got knocked off his bike doing his paper round. It was a hit-and-run.'

Emma put her half-eaten biscuit on the bedside table. 'Poor Ned. Poor Polly and Alan. They had fertility treatment to have him, you know. He was their only child.' She shook her head again. 'It just doesn't seem possible. They were always so proud of him.'

'I know, it's just so tragic, and to make matters worse, it happened early one Christmas Eve.'

Emma's body gave an involuntary shudder, and coldness crept across her back like a winter chill, settling into her chest.

No. That was a stupid thought. She'd been drunk, the roads were icy and she'd been using her phone at the wheel that last day she drove back to Healdbury after leaving the hotel in Manchester, so she hadn't actually seen the animal she'd hit, but if it had been a boy on a bike, she'd have definitely known. No question. People didn't kill other people without having some idea.

'Which Christmas Eve was that?' she asked weakly.

'It must be two years ago now… that's when you left home, right?'

Emma ran to her bedroom sink. Her body went into spasm and red pasta sauce from dinner splattered across the white basin like blood on ice.

Ned? No, please, universe, she thought, please let this be a mistake and he's still alive; please don't let it have been me. I hit a fox. Or a sheep. Not a sweet, much-loved son.

Memories flashed into her mind. Leaving the hotel. Blood on her dress. Somehow managing to drive out of the city centre. The winding road as she approached Healdbury. She'd been looking at friends' photos on Instagram – her phone on the passenger seat – and singing at the top of her voice to an old One Direction hit on the radio. Suddenly her body was thrown forward. The car had hit something and skidded. She'd struggled to keep control of the wheel and screamed. Screams turned to manic laughter as eventually the car slowed...

Rachel hurried over and rubbed her back. 'You're shaking,' she said, and ran the cold tap. Emma scooped up mouthfuls. Rachel passed her a tissue. She wiped her eyes and blew her nose.

'It must be such a shock,' said Rachel, and gave her a hug.

Emma pulled away. She didn't deserve kindness.

'I... I wonder where exactly it happened,' she said, without meeting Rachel's eye. Another wave of nausea rose at the back of her throat, and fear gripped her, like the terror of waking up after blackout and wondering what she'd done. She collapsed onto the bed.

Just as she'd thought she was leaving the nightmare of living on the streets, of losing Joe, of miscarrying Josephine, another black hole of despair had appeared and she was falling in head first.

'Just past the Christmas tree farm, on the outskirts. I remember driving past it on the way back. Apparently Ned loved his paper round because most of it served isolated customers, away from the village, and he didn't have to carry as many newspapers as his friends. The police think he left his bike outside the farm because the driveway was so icy. He delivered the paper on foot, and when he walked back to his bike...'

'Was anyone caught for it?'

Rachel shrugged. 'Dunno. Didn't like to ask. I don't think so, though, not when I was told about it.'

Emma nodded slowly, but inside, her mind raced. Within minutes she'd pleaded a headache and seen an understanding Rachel out of her room, declining her friend's offer to hunt out an ice pack. All she could hear was the words *the Christmas tree farm*. That was where she'd hit something that morning.

She drew on the tools she'd learned about to control her negative thinking and took a deep breath. Mustn't catastrophise. Mustn't tell myself I'm a bad person. She'd seen hit-and-runs in the movies. If she'd knocked a person over, they'd have been tossed into the air. There was no way she wouldn't have known about that.

Not even if you were drunk and tired and more bothered about your friends' social media than how you were driving? asked a small voice in her head.

Chapter 15

'Have you heard this, Bligh?' said Andrea as he came over from the greenhouse carrying a basket of cucumbers. He was preparing some vegetable boxes for delivery. The internet orders were providing a modest but steady income. 'Emma has invited some rough sleepers to visit Foxglove Farm and they're arriving in a couple of hours.'

Andrea stood in the sunshine just in front of the barn, hands dusted with soil. Emma and Gail were sitting outside – Gail on the old rocking chair, and Emma on one of two deckchairs; she always put an extra one out in the hope that Andrea or Bligh might join them. Nearby, an upturned crate served as a table for their mugs. Dash lay next to them on the ground next to a small children's trampoline. Emma had found it discarded by the roadside and had spent the afternoon mending the leg. It would be perfect for the goats to jump on. She'd also created interesting feeders for the rabbits using toilet paper tubes and hay. Gail had been able to help.

'I did mean to ask.' Emma had struggled to find the right moment. Andrea had been snappy all day. The boiler had broken. The plumber had done a temporary fix but said they'd need a new one soon. That meant finding a large sum of money they didn't have. Plus she had found a load of empty beer cans behind the weeping willow.

She'd half-heartedly accused Emma before conceding it was probably local teenagers.

Gail had been quiet all afternoon – she wasn't sleeping well at the moment. This had allowed Emma to spend most of the day fixated on the memory of Polly and Alan from last night. The way they'd comforted Ted's grand-children and calmed them down, then offered the whole family free lodgings until they got themselves sorted out.

She couldn't put off the inevitable for much longer. She'd hardly slept herself last night and woken up in a sweat having relived that crazy car journey. Mentally she'd listed all the things she might have robbed that boy of – university, marriage, maybe kids, a great career. Tales of prison life that she'd heard at AA kept her tossing and turning as well.

But if there was one thing she'd learnt from the months of treatment, it was to listen to the voice of conscience in her head. If she didn't keep that happy, sooner or later she'd start drinking again, and that hell was worse than any prison sentence.

'I'm sorry, Andrea,' she said. 'I know it's short notice, but I'm really worried about this girl, Tilly… she's a runaway. Someone should do something, but I'm not sure what. I bet she'll really love feeding the animals.'

'What about Mum? She'll only get confused.' Andrea folded her arms. 'I won't see her hurt.'

'Nor would I,' said Emma.

'I've only got your word for that, and frankly that's not worth much.'

Emma couldn't suppress a sigh.

'What?' snapped Andrea. 'You think I'm being harsh? Well I was the one who had to listen to her sobbing night after night after you left, blaming herself for your departure, telling herself she'd failed as a mother.'

A lump formed in Emma's throat. Andrea would rarely commit to a proper conversation, so her frustrations would burst out suddenly as if they'd come from a piñata that only her younger sister's presence could rupture.

'And the farm can't afford to have anything stolen,' said Bligh. 'Although I guess they did help save Ted. The Badger Inn was full of talk about how brave they were when I dropped in at lunchtime.'

'They'll stay outside the farmhouse,' said Emma. 'Stig and Rita are all right.'

'Stig?' Andrea rolled her eyes and sighed. A weary expression crossed her face. 'I want them gone by nine o'clock.'

'Thanks, I really appreciate it. Could I use the kitchen to make sandwiches? And I promised Tilly those strawberry and white chocolate cupcakes – you remember, the ones we loved?' Emma lifted the recipe book off the upturned crate and stood up. 'Your illustrations were brilliant.'

'You can have the kitchen, but tidy up afterwards and keep an eye on Mum. Use the cheese, not the ham – the price has just gone up, and with a new boiler to think about...' She rubbed her forehead. 'This is the last time you can use our bread and other ingredients that aren't surplus though, Emma. Money's tighter than ever.' She about-turned and headed towards the shed behind the barn.

Emma swallowed any reply and Bligh gave her a curious look. She told Gail about the cupcakes, and arms linked, they went indoors. Bligh picked up his basket and followed them. He set the cucumbers down on the table and put the kettle on.

'I could murder a cup of tea. Gail? Emma?'

Emma nodded. 'Thanks for your support,' she said, getting flour out of the cupboard.

'I'm beginning to see signs of change. Like just now – you took Andrea's comment on the chin.'

A warm feeling radiated through her chest. 'Thank you.'

'I'm not a forgiving man, but Dad was, and in honour of his memory I'm trying to see things for how they are now. Although I'll never forget that Christmas and what you did to him,' he said, voice thick.

'I know, and I'm so sorry.' It sounded like such an empty word. 'And I'm grateful you didn't report me to the police.'

'You always took my loyalty for granted,' he said in a tight voice. 'Don't make the same mistake again.'

A chill replaced the warm glow as they fell into silence. Gail helped Emma beat the cake batter. They spooned it into paper cases, splashing it down the sides.

'You're a clever girl,' said Gail when the cakes went into the oven.

Emma's spirits lifted as they looked at each other and smiled. She began to chop the strawberries, then filled the washing-up bowl with soapy water and asked Gail to clean the utensils, knowing that she'd have to do them herself again later. Bligh had gone into the dining room to work at the computer.

When the cakes had cooled, she melted white chocolate and let Gail pour it over the tops. Their roles had reversed. She remembered Gail teaching her how to ice. Was this nature's plan? To have parents teach things to their children because one day they'd need someone to show them the way again? Daily Emma had to remind Gail how to clean her teeth. Brush her hair. Wipe her nose. It took patience to pass on skills that would never improve. There was still so much her mum had to lose.

They pressed cut strawberries into the white topping. Emma hesitated before putting one of the cakes on a plate. She carried it through and tentatively handed it to Bligh.

'Verdict?' she asked.

'Passable,' he replied, and wiped his lips.

Briefly both their mouths quirked up. For a few seconds it had seemed just like the good times. Andrea came in, took off her boots and headed up to the bathroom. The loo flushed, and when she came back down, Emma offered her a muffin.

'No thanks,' she said without looking, and took a tube of mints out of her pocket. She picked up her boots and returned outside.

'Perhaps she'll have one later,' said Bligh, who had come through to the kitchen.

'Maybe.' Emma kept her tone bright.

He stared. 'What pushed you to finally get yourself sorted? You must have known it would be tough coming back.'

Emma put down the tea cloth. 'I got pregnant.'

There. She'd said it.

'*What?*'

'It was as much of a surprise to me.'

'But... I don't understand. I mean... where's...?' He leant against the wall.

'I lost the baby. But the pregnancy had to mean something, right? So I used it to help me focus on becoming a better person.'

'And you faced that alone?' His teeth clenched together.

Gail pottered, taking mugs out of the cupboard and putting them back.

'I managed.'

'What about the father?'

Emma looked down.

'You should have got in touch. Despite everything, I'd have helped you.' He stepped forward and hugged her tight.

How Emma had craved such an embrace during those months in the city – but now she could see that was only because a hug from Bligh usually meant he was about to solve yet another of her problems. She no longer needed that escape from facing up to managing her own life.

She didn't doubt that Bligh would have been the perfect person to help in such a situation – he'd wanted a family for so long now, and would have stepped in and raised the child as his own. He had so many good qualities, all underpinned by a sense of decency. It was strange. He got that from his mum, who'd been an active member of the community. She'd often taken part in charity events, and had helped out on the farm more than once if Gail, Andrea or Emma fell sick. But then she'd left Bligh's dad for a younger man and no one in the village understood why – except, years later, Bligh. He'd cleared up Emma's mess yet again, paying for a shop window she'd smashed in the village, and had muttered something about how he now understood how being in love made people do things they'd never once have been able to imagine.

Dash crawled out from under the table and pricked up his ears.

'That's barking. It must be the Duchess. Stig is here,' said Emma.

The doorbell rang.

'Could you answer that, Bligh, and I'll take Mum out to the yard. If you could send Stig around the side of the farmhouse…'

The back door creaked as Emma led Gail outside, Dash charging ahead to meet his friend. Stig appeared with Bligh following him. A white bandage was wrapped around his head and he wore a camouflage T-shirt. Emma had seen him first thing when he'd dropped by the pet shop to pick up his dog. The hospital had given him some clean clothes. Due to the surgical dressing, he couldn't wear his woolly hat.

'Where's Tilly?' she said.

Stig exhaled. 'She's done a runner. I went up to the station. Nothing. She must have been worried that one of us was going to report her.'

Emma's shoulders sank. 'And Rita?'

'I've just seen her – she sends her best. The fire last night… it hit her hard. Made her think about her family. She's going back to the city to pay her parents a visit.'

'What's all that barking?' called a distant voice, and Andrea appeared with a small shovel in her hand. Gail was sitting in her rocking chair, flicking through the curtain sample book.

Emma was just about to introduce Stig when Gail looked up and gasped. She got to her feet. Tears had sprung to her eyes. Her bottom lip trembled.

'You're back! You're back! I've missed you so much,' she said eventually, and made her way forward.

Stig looked at Emma, who turned to Andrea. She shrugged and shook her head.

'I knew that knock on the door with bad news was wrong.' Gail wrapped her arms around Stig. 'No one believed me when I said you were still alive.' Her face broke into a smile and she looked at the others. 'Uncle Paul is the strongest swimmer I know. And the best cake-maker. Dad's going to be so happy he's home.'

Chapter 16

Andrea bustled forward. 'I must apologise,' she said, gently removing Gail's arms from around Stig. 'My mother's a bit…'

Gail glared and hugged Stig again. 'You're just jealous because me and Uncle Paul are so close. All those weekends he visited and I learnt how to make Victoria sponge and shortbread.' She beamed at Stig. 'Remember that cross-stitch certificate I made you once? Dad helped me spell out the words to say you were the best navy chef ever.'

Andrea reached out again but Stig patted Gail's arms. 'And you were the best cookery student,' he said.

Emma's throat hurt. Gail looked the happiest she'd been since her return.

'What a lovely necklace,' he said, and slowly extricated himself from her embrace.

Gail blushed. 'Princess Diana gave it to me,' she whispered. 'I met her years ago. We were good friends. But don't tell anyone.' She jerked her head towards Emma. 'The woman who talks too much might steal it. I used to have lots of lovely necklaces. Now I can't find any of them.'

Stig removed her arms, which had once again wrapped around him. 'I need a shower before anyone gets that close.'

Gail pulled a face. 'Yes. You do smell a bit. And your nails need a clean. What happened to your head?'

'How about we chat to Uncle Paul later?' said Andrea. 'He must be tired. And it's time for your tea.'

Gail stared for a moment and then her expression became vacant. 'Yes. Yes, it's time for tea.'

Bligh took her into the kitchen.

'And this was exactly what I wanted to avoid,' said Andrea, and frowned. 'New people confuse her. We're very lucky she didn't get upset instead.' She glanced at Stig. 'But thank you for playing along. It's the kindest way.'

'No problem. Me and Emma have seen it all on the streets. Eventually you learn just to roll with it.'

People like Mad Hatter Holly. Or Tony, with his depression. Smelly Stan from under the bridge who couldn't remember where he grew up, or Big John who swore he was related to Bruno Mars.

He raised an eyebrow. 'I take it her uncle died whilst serving in the Royal Navy?'

'The Falklands,' said Andrea. 'He was on HMS *Sheffield*.'

'It got sunk?' asked Stig.

Both sisters nodded. Gail had talked about her uncle Paul a lot over the years. He'd never got married, nor had kids, and had seen her more as a daughter than a niece.

'I can see why she made the mistake,' said Andrea. 'I've seen photos and Uncle Paul had thick brown hair like yours. Plus he loved dogs.'

'Perhaps I should go.' Stig bent down to stroke the Duchess. 'I don't want to make things worse.'

She paused. 'No... no, it's all right. You're only going to be here a couple of hours. You can have a wash in the barn if you like. Emma can get you a towel. Right. I'd

165

better get Mum's tea on. There's lemonade in the fridge,' she added abruptly and headed back inside before either of them could thank her.

Emma proceeded to give Stig a tour, though her thoughts soon strayed. Bligh had seemed upset about her pregnancy. Was it possible that he still cared? And did Mum's comment about her stealing the necklace mean that Gail was beginning to make a connection between the woman who talked too much and the old version of her younger daughter?

Stig petted the rabbits and lifted the mended trampoline into the goats' enclosure. Both he and Emma laughed as the animals jumped on and off it. He helped feed the chickens and marvelled at the tranquillity as they sat under the weeping willow.

'It's beautiful here,' he said as they returned to the barn. They sat in the deckchairs outside, eating cheese and tomato sandwiches.

'I know, and I never appreciated it before, believing a more glamorous setting would somehow make me a better, more attractive person.' Emma didn't realise back then that it was the internal scenery that counted most.

They sat, mesmerised, as the sun sank and tangerine stripes spread across the sky. Andrea had put an exhausted Gail to bed.

'How about a hot chocolate before you head off?' Emma asked. 'It's quite my favourite drink these days.'

'Thanks, sounds great.' He eyed her curiously. 'So you don't ever miss your old habits?'

She picked up his plate. 'I used to think people were lying when they said they didn't. But now? Me get back on that emotional see-saw? No thanks. Never again.'

She went towards the kitchen, leaving Stig with Dash and the Duchess, who were lying next to each other. It had just gone nine. Bats swooped over the barn. A hedgehog ambled across the yard. In the distance, an owl hooted. She opened the back door to find Andrea holding a pile of brochures.

'What are those?'

'Sheets of dreams I can no longer afford.' She pushed past. Emma went inside. Bligh sat at the kitchen table in front of an empty mug.

'What's Andrea doing?'

'Throwing away her travel brochures. She's collected them over the years to do her drawings from. And she hoped she might need them one day to plan an amazing trip, but now, with the boiler on its last legs, I think she's finally decided she's never going to see further than Manchester.'

Emma's stomach twisted as she put down the crockery and took the hot chocolate powder out of the cupboard. 'This is my fault.'

'Whether you were here or not, she'd never have left with Gail being ill.'

Emma made the drinks while Bligh took a last look at the boiler. When she went outside, Andrea was sitting chatting to Stig. They were flicking through the brochures. Emma put his mug down.

'Do you want one, Andrea?'

'Why not,' she said.

Emma gave her the other mug. She couldn't believe how much brighter Andrea looked gazing at the exotic photos.

'India was great,' said Stig. 'I went there during a gap year and volunteered.'

'I've always wanted to do that,' said Andrea. 'Where else have you been?'

'The Peruvian Amazon with university… we monitored insect life and helped look after abused spectacled bears. The colours of the rainforest were magnificent. Vibrant. Clean. Unforgettable.'

'Mum would have loved doing something like that.' Andrea undid her ponytail. 'We used to tease her that this farm was more of a centre for waifs and strays, as she was always taking in neglected or abandoned animals.'

'I still can't get used to seeing her eat meat,' said Emma. She strained her ears. Was that the front doorbell?

Andrea picked up a brochure with the Eiffel Tower on the front. 'I haven't even been to Europe. In fact I've never been out of England.'

'Where has your wanderlust come from? I mean…' Stig smiled, 'this is one big pile of brochures.'

'We used to live in London. I was old enough to remember what that was like – and what a contrast it was moving to somewhere like this. It made me wonder what else I was missing around the world. I used to love living in the capital, with its impressive skyline and its parks and the whoosh of the underground. I thought that was all there was. I'd sketch all the well-known buildings – Big Ben, the Houses of Parliament… and then we moved here and I felt inspired by the natural beauty of the Peak District.'

'Do you still draw? I'd love to see your work,' said Stig.

'No. Not any more.' Her face hardened.

'I grew up in Blackpool and never thought I'd want to leave,' said Stig. 'What with the arcades and the rides, it felt magical as a child. And there was the sea… But then I went on a school trip to Switzerland. It was the second year at high school and I came back determined to choose geography for GCSE. Mum and Dad laughed at my non-stop chat about the food and the mountain scenes. I couldn't believe the Swiss had four national languages. Suddenly Blackpool seemed so small.'

Emma couldn't bear to look at Andrea's wistful face any more. All these years she'd wanted to travel. Because of Emma, she hadn't. She went inside and up to Gail's room, mindful of her mum's comment about missing her necklaces. The one she'd worn today had kept her hands busy. Perhaps it would offer some comfort if she wore something around her neck more often. She used to have an especially favourite one her daughters had discovered in Afflecks in Manchester. It was silver-painted and bore large charms to do with sewing: a thimble and a large needle, a pin and a silver measuring tape, along with a pin cushion. They were bulky enough not to be broken by her fiddling.

Because her mum was asleep Emma opened all the drawers as quietly as she could and then looked under the bed and finally in the wardrobe. Perhaps it was in the wooden chest. She lifted it out and carried it downstairs. Her friend Beth had taught her many tricks, one of which was picking locks. She'd check with Andrea first. She headed outside and explained.

Andrea looked up from the brochures and shrugged. 'I don't see why not. I'd forgotten about that old box.'

At that moment, Bligh appeared, closely followed by...

'Ted?' Andrea stood up.

'Sorry. I'm sorry for calling so late. But...' he looked at Emma and Stig, 'the police have been questioning me all day.'

'I heard about last night,' Andrea said. 'Is everyone all right? I'm so glad you got out.'

'Yes. Thanks to Emma and her friends.'

'Coffee?' said Bligh.

'I don't want to disturb you. I've just come to say… Well, the police and fire officers wanted to know if there was anyone with a grievance against me.' He stared at Stig.

Chapter 17

No one said anything for a moment.

'Milk?' asked Bligh.

'Please. And you'd better make that two sugars.'

'Take a seat,' said Andrea and motioned to the rocking chair.

'Bligh popped into the Badger Inn at lunchtime – you're staying there?' asked Andrea, sitting down again. Stig stood up to give Emma his seat, but she insisted on sitting on the ground.

'Polly and Alan have been really decent,' said Ted. 'I tried to pay but they wouldn't hear of it. We've got a family room. Neighbours offered to put us up, but there's more space at the pub. My son's contract in Scotland finishes at the end of the week. Then we can all move into his. He wanted to drive back straight away, but we've reassured him the kids are okay. His place is only ten miles away, so I can commute back to the shop for as long as I have to – but right at the moment, it suits me to be on hand.' He sighed. 'Although God knows how long it will take before I'm up and running again. The way business has waned, I did wonder if it's worth it. But that shop is all I've ever known, and I'll be darned if I let that supermarket win.'

'So what was the cause of the fire? Do you know yet?' asked Emma. Surely Ted couldn't believe that the rough sleepers had been responsible.

Bligh came out and handed Ted a coffee.

'Initially the police suspected it might have been arson. They wanted to know if I could think of anyone who'd want to harm my family.' Ted shrugged. 'I'm a businessman. In debt. I've had to make unpopular decisions with suppliers and competitors to stay afloat. And... well...' He cleared his throat. 'The whole village knows about my plan to move the homeless on. It didn't take long for the police to hear about that and ask about my opponents.'

Andrea glanced at Emma and a look of surprise crossed her face. Emma caught her eye. Perhaps she'd been expecting a burst of expletives at the mere idea that Stig could have been involved.

'But they're the very people who saved your lives,' said Bligh, red in the face. 'Emma included.'

'And I just wanted Stig and Emma to know that I told the police in no uncertain terms that the rough sleepers weren't to blame. I wanted to come and thank you again, Emma – and everyone else. I wouldn't be able to sleep tonight unless I'd done that. I looked for you, Stig. I couldn't find the woman with the wacky haircut either, but I managed to say a proper thanks to most of the others.' His voice wavered. 'If it wasn't for you...'

'Best not to think about the what ifs,' said Andrea gently. 'So what *was* the cause?'

'A faulty tumble dryer, they think. I've been busy with the insurers all day. I'll have to start getting quotes for the building work.'

'My dad was a painter and decorator,' said Stig. 'If you need a hand with anything, I'm happy to help.'

Ted put down his drink and stared. 'After everything I've said?'

'Let's just say I know a thing or two about stress.'

Ted nodded. 'It must be hard constantly wondering where your next meal is coming from and trying to keep safe. I've never really thought about it before. And it didn't feel right, last night, the village pulling together to give my family a bed when the heroes would be sleeping on the pavement.'

'No, not so much my life now,' said Stig. 'All I meant was… I've seen how you and the other shop owners are struggling to make ends meet. When I was a teacher, the pressure was enormous. I couldn't see a way out. I just wanted to quit and take on a simple nine-to-five job, but I had a mortgage to pay, bills and debts, so there was no way I could leave for a position that paid less. The stress made me behave in ways I wouldn't normally.'

'Tell me about it,' said Andrea. 'Last year I thought the gas company would cut us off. I was always making payments late. It's the constant worry, isn't it? Eating away at your perspective. Sometimes it's as if the world's a spinning top – I just wanted to get off for a few seconds. I still feel like that now.' She glanced at the brochures.

'That's just how I felt, what with growing class sizes, the close monitoring from Ofsted and a sixty-hour week… I just couldn't take it any more.'

Andrea picked up a holiday brochure for Japan. 'I'd have been sorely tempted to take off – with Bligh's blessing – if it wasn't for Mum.'

Ted leant forward. 'I went to the doctor's a couple of weeks ago. My blood pressure's sky high.'

'I had a panic attack in the spring,' said Andrea quietly, 'and I get terrible headaches.'

'It's bad enough for me, and I don't even have my own business,' said Bligh. 'At least my insomnia has improved after I finally paid back some money I owed.'

Emma sat quietly and stared at the ground. Andrea – and Bligh – had done so well, shouldering all the responsibility of keeping the farm afloat.

They chatted a while longer about how the local economy could survive. Ted suggested that he still hold the next village meeting but change the agenda from getting rid of the homeless to how the community could pull together to tackle the competition.

'I never realised just how bad things have been,' Emma said to Andrea. The two sisters were in the kitchen. Emma was packing a bag of chopped ham and chicken for the Duchess before walking back to Phil's accompanied by Stig and Ted.

Andrea wiped down the units vigorously. 'It's close to the point where Mum's going to need residential care. Bligh and I just can't safely look after her any more. Her wandering off and eating those berries proved that.'

'But I can help. Let me stay longer. Me and Mum are getting on great and I'll be out of your way at Phil's in the evenings.'

She stopped wiping but didn't look up. 'What's the point? You'll be moving on eventually. I give it another week – maybe a month – before you get bored of Healdbury. Especially now you've got Aunt Thelma's money. I'm right, aren't I?'

Andrea waited. Emma so wanted to fill the silence with remonstrations – an insistence that she'd stay around for as long as she could. She wanted to shout how much the farm meant to her – the animals, the weeping willow, the flowers. The smells and sounds she'd never appreciated before. Above all, how much it meant to be close to family again, despite the emotional distance.

But she couldn't do that. Not now. Not after last night and once again seeing Polly and Alan at close quarters. She couldn't avoid them forever and she knew that the time was nearing for her to face her past recklessness and talk to the police.

She felt sick every time she thought about prison, but she couldn't just change her life on the surface. It had to go deeper, otherwise she'd be living a lie. She had to start putting others first, and for her own sake she had to take responsibility for her actions.

So she kept quiet and carried on chopping meat. And with even more vigorous arm movements, Andrea went back to her cleaning.

Before she left for Phil's, Emma rummaged in the kitchen drawer and managed to find a hairpin. Everyone else was outside talking, apart from Andrea, who'd been to check on Gail. She came downstairs with their mum's small sherry glass, washed it up and joined the men. Emma sat at the table and jiggled the pin for a few minutes. It wasn't as easy as she remembered. She was about to give up when with one final tweak the lock sprung open. Gingerly she lifted the lid.

A lump rose to her throat. Inside were Christmas cards the two sisters had made Gail, and their baby scan photos. There was a tiny pair of gloves with teddy bear ears that Emma had insisted on wearing all one winter – even indoors – and a certificate from school when Andrea had won a chess tournament. She took out these treasures and a triumphant smile crossed her face as underneath she saw the necklace. It lay next to her mum's collection of thimbles made from different-coloured metals.

Stig's head appeared around the back door. 'You ready to leave?'

'Just coming.'

She was about to close the lid when a pile of envelopes caught her eye. She lifted them out. They smelt musty. Her brow knotted as she sifted through and counted. Eighteen. All different colours and sizes. The white ones had browned with age. Each was addressed to her mum. She studied the writing. Perhaps they were from an old boyfriend. But as far as she knew, Mum had never met anyone after her dad. At one point Emma had teased that she was getting close to Bligh's father, but Gail had made it clear that she was steering clear of men in future – and as far as Emma knew, she had.

With a shrug, she shoved the envelopes into her rucksack. It was getting late. She'd take a proper look later.

6 months before going back

As Christmas approached, Emma found it increasingly difficult not to think about Ned. She hadn't confided in Rachel. The recovery programme was hard enough without taking on board someone else's problems.

She wasn't used to putting other people's feelings first.

She lay on her bed next to her friend as they chatted about Christmases past. Thinking about Ned had all become too much last week. She couldn't control the voice that used to tell her she was a bad person. So she'd asked for a one-to-one with Tess, and Emma had hinted that there was a chance she might have caused someone's death.

Tess said she should speak to the relevant authorities – perhaps seeking legal advice first. She didn't press for details. If Emma told her everything, no doubt she'd be duty-bound to contact the police herself. But she did reassure Emma that this week would help because they were doing Step Nine.

This step was all about making amends to the people who'd been hurt – for their sake and that of the addict, whose recovery might otherwise be eaten away by guilt and remorse. Everyone had to make three lists: the people they'd say sorry to now; the one-day maybes; and those who – for their own good – would be best left forever because further contact would cause upset.

The home drinkers' lists weren't very long, whereas Emma and Rachel's... Neither of them was sure where to start. Emma practically ran out of paper, what with Mum, Andrea and Bligh... Polly and Alan... the pub's customers, other villagers, and old school friends she'd shouted abuse at. Not to mention the complete strangers she'd insulted. Plus there were those she owed money to.

Rachel adjusted the pillow behind her neck. 'And then there was the Christmas I threw up over Mum's new cream dress. She'd saved for weeks to buy it and actually cried. The stains never came out. She didn't speak to me for a week.' She bit her lip. 'Making amends isn't going to be easy.'

'I've decided to start with Andrea,' said Emma. 'I've written a letter that I'll post tonight. I feel a bit better already.'

'Why not phone?'

'This way I can set my thoughts out properly. If we have an actual conversation, I might react to things she says in the heat of the moment, and vice versa. I think my initial approach needs to be scripted. It isn't long – there's just too much to say sorry for in one go.'

Rachel groaned. 'I hear you. I can't remember the last time Mum and I actually spoke instead of shouting. Although I can see now that was usually because I'd had a drink.'

'Have you thought any more about getting in touch?'

Rachel rested her head against Emma's shoulder. 'Yes. Well, you've heard me in class. I can see now that things were difficult for her. She just did the best she could. But she's not a letter person. Doesn't even read books. So I'm going to ring her when I've completed the whole programme.'

'Do you think Tess is right? That making amends won't necessarily bring forgiveness, and we have to accept that?'

She felt Rachel's head nod. 'Yup. We're having weeks of expert help to deal with our feelings, whereas the people we say sorry to might still be full of anger towards us and not know how to deal with that.'

But Emma hadn't drunk for almost six months now. Surely she'd find forgiveness when Andrea, Bligh and Mum knew how much she'd changed?

'Your mum won't recognise you,' she said. 'How much weight have you lost?'

Rachel sat up and smiled. 'No idea, but it's a good thing we were allowed out for an afternoon's shopping today. My old trousers were practically falling off.'

They'd visited the local charity shops. It felt exciting to care about their appearance again. Rachel had helped Emma choose a new coat. Emma managed not to spend too much time looking at baby clothes that might have suited Josephine.

Rachel reached for her work booklet while Emma got off the bed and settled at her small desk. Andrea's letter was waiting there, almost daring her to post it. She opened it up and read through every word. Then again. And once more. Finally she folded it and slid it into an envelope. She sealed it, stuck on a stamp and then kissed the front. Rachel caught her eye and winked.

> *Dear Andrea,*
>
> *Hi. I hope you and Mum are well – and that you have a good Christmas.*
>
> *I'm writing to let you know that I've got into treatment.*
>
> *What I'm really writing to say, though, is that I'm so sorry. For everything. All the trouble I caused. The money you had to spend to bail me out. The names I called you. The lying. The stealing. Me and my problems taking up so much of your time.*
>
> *You had every right to be angry. Looking back, I'm surprised you put up with me for so long. We're sisters, but that doesn't entitle me to your unconditional love. I took you for granted.*
>
> *We were close as children, weren't we? Like the time we both got tattoos. Mum went mad. We couldn't stop laughing, which made her even angrier when she found out they were fake. Plus now and then we'd speak in our GCSE French so that she couldn't understand. Sometimes we were proper little devils.*
>
> *I remember how we wanted to call our new home Forget-Me-Not Farm. Mum said it sounded silly. We thought it was cute.*

You'd help me with school projects and I taught you how to use contouring kits, even though I was only fifteen and you were almost twenty. We used to walk around arm in arm. When did that stop? I reckoned you gave the best hugs. You thought me funny even without telling jokes. I liked that.

I'll never forget that cake we made Mum for her birthday – the one that was supposed to look like the farm. My marzipan pink pigs looked more like thumbs. Your marshmallow sheep fell off at the last minute.

You and me, Andrea, we've always been so different and yet that never seemed to matter. I love marmalade. You hate it. My music taste is eclectic. You only like big band and jazz. Your feet are a generous size seven, mine a diminutive four. Growing fruit and vegetables interests you. I prefer animals.

That person… the drunk… it was me but it wasn't. I was ill.

At the same time, that's no excuse – I take responsibility for my actions and I intend to apologise to everyone in the village.

I know it's asking a lot, but I'd like to visit. Will you just think about it? I'd be so grateful so that I could explain; try to make up for the past. My address and phone number are on the back of the envelope.

Please give my love to Mum.

Emma X

Emma sat in the Quaker meeting room. Every time the door opened, she looked up hoping it would be Rachel. Now that treatment was over, she missed a daily dose of her friend's humour. Rachel had temporarily gone back to work. Emma was in recovery services. They chatted on WhatsApp and met up when they could. A weekly definite was this evening's AA meeting.

She took off her hat and scarf and chatted briefly to her friend Bev. From across the room, Old Len gave a thumbs-up and Emma half-heartedly gave one back. She tried to remember what Len had said to her at her first meeting: *It doesn't get better, but you do.* In other words, life still happened – bereavement, fallings-out, divorce, illness – but AA seemed to give people a coping mechanism.

She would never forget her first ever meeting. It had taken place shortly after her detox. She'd stood outside the church door and wondered if she'd be sick, swearing inwardly at Dave from Listening EAR who'd pushed her to attend. Just the words Alcoholics Anonymous had brought to mind an image of men in dirty raincoats who slept on park benches. The irony wasn't lost on her that it wasn't so long since she'd been one of those rough sleepers.

She'd entered the room to a most unexpected tableau. Polished shoes. Clean clothes. Shaved faces. Bright eyes. All accompanied by friendly chat and the clink of mugs. Men had congregated on the far side, women nearby. They all exchanged hugs and passed around chocolate biscuits.

A woman called Julie had offered her a brew. 'Well done for getting here on your own. Someone had to bring me my first time.' She'd jerked her head to a nearby member. 'Bev, this is Emma. She's new too. Now, sit yourself down. My advice today is to just listen. Don't look for the differences in people's stories – just see if you can relate to their feelings.'

Bang on the hour, the man chosen to chair announced the start of the meeting. Someone read from the Big Book – whatever that was. The chairman welcomed Emma, Bev and another newcomer who was crying, then talked about his own drinking history and how AA made him better. Next, other people randomly shared, one at a time, airing problems or sharing their inspiring journeys.

'Just keep coming back,' Old Len had said at the end. He was one of the group's old-timers – twenty-three years sober. 'We're all here for you – we've been in your shoes. Take it one day at a time.' He'd pushed a newcomer's pack into her hands. It included a list of the region's meetings. Women gave Emma their phone numbers. She left as quickly as possible.

She came back to the present and smiled at the memory and her thoughts about Len. Poor bastard, she'd said to herself on the way home – fancy still attending meetings after all that time. She'd never go back. It just wasn't for her. Except that she couldn't stop thinking about how content everyone had seemed. She'd expected people to be glumly sitting on their hands, desperate for a drink. Instead they'd spoken cheerily about grandkids, holidays, last night's telly…

She looked up. Rachel hugged several people and took off her duffel coat. Then she grabbed a coffee, sat down next to Emma and yawned.

'Hard day at the office?' said Emma in a bright voice.

'It's tiring combining the job with the rehab training course. I can't wait to jack in the web designing. But until then, some of us have to work to support the economy. From what you say, recovery services is all about meditation, gardening and aromatherapy.'

Emma punched her arm playfully. 'This week we're also doing a course on anger management. It's great picking up new friends and hobbies – makes me realise how much I used to isolate.'

'Talking of new beginnings…' Rachel cleared her throat. 'You're looking at the proud owner of a gorgeous tabby cat.'

'What?'

Rachel laughed. 'I know – I can't believe I've taken responsibility for another living being. He belonged to my neighbours, who are moving abroad. They were so worried about leaving him behind, and he does have an irresistible purr. I've renamed him Idris, after the gorgeous Mr Elba. My feline friend is so handsome.' She took out her phone and showed Emma a photo. 'I always wanted a cat when I was little, but it wouldn't have worked in a tower block and Mum said the last thing we needed was another mouth to feed. But I looked after the hamsters at school and eventually persuaded Mum that a goldfish would be cheap enough. I used to feed it biscuit crumbs on the sly. The water was always slightly cloudy. Perhaps that was why. Mum always said it was perfect company for a chatterbox like me, though she didn't like the tank's smell. I was heartbroken when she gave Bubbles away without me knowing.' She squeezed Emma's hand. 'But what about you? How's today been?'

'Okay.' Emma couldn't face talking about it.

Today was the twentieth of January – the hardest date ever. Her due date. The day when she would have finally met her baby. Would she have had Joe's dirty-blonde hair or Emma's small feet? She passed one hand across her stomach. *I still think of you, little Josephine.*

She sipped her coffee. 'I told you about Andrea?'

'I was sorry she sent your letter back unopened. Will you write to her again?'

'There's no point. I'll leave it now until I'm feeling stronger, and then I'll go back. Apologise face to face. What about your mum?'

'We've agreed to meet up next week.'

'That's great.'

'I hope so. She sounded so bitter. We'll see.'

The meeting started and both of them listened. Emma didn't share, even though she really should have got her feelings out into the open. Instead, her mind kept drifting… Today she might have been in hospital, cradling her daughter, learning how to feed her and change nappies.

All week, as the twentieth approached, discontent had fluttered in her stomach. Talking would have helped to put it in perspective. Talking would have stopped it leading to negative thoughts about Bligh's dad and Ned, about Andrea sending back the letter and how that proved Emma must still be a bad person.

On the way home, she stopped outside a baby store and stared at the toys and buggies. The shop next door was an off-licence, and for just the briefest of moments Emma glanced inside.

Just one glass won't hurt, said the voice on her shoulder that she hadn't heard for a long time.

Chapter 18

The farm fell into a different routine over the next fort-night. Stig started to visit every day. The shed needed a makeover inside due to holes in the roof and mouldy walls. He did the necessary work in return for food. Once his bandage came off, Gail stopped calling him Uncle Paul.

He started to stay longer and grab a wash and a late snack after work. Conversation between Emma and Bligh became easier. Nothing changed between her and Andrea, but now and again something about her older sister softened. Emma heard her briefly whistle, and Andrea didn't snap when she forgot to mention that the bank had rung.

It was Thursday, and they were almost at the end of a long, humid week. Emma had forgotten how busy the summer got. She fell straight asleep most evenings when she went back to Phil's. She hadn't even opened those envelopes that she'd found – in fact she hadn't yet decided whether she should, so they'd remained stashed in her bedside drawer.

Following an afternoon spent digging potatoes, Stig had cleaned up, and Emma had given his clothes a quick wash. Dash and the Duchess lay in the yard, panting by a large bowl of water. Gail sat in the rocking chair, fiddling with her sewing-themed necklace. Stig had found an old bench in the shed, rubbed it down and repainted it. Now there were ample seats for everyone.

Emma looked around. Her chest glowed at the familiarity.

'It was good of Ted to bring us those chocolates. You should have seen his grandchildren petting the rabbits this morning,' she said as Bligh joined them. Stig and Andrea were sitting on the bench chatting about their favourite David Attenborough programmes.

He dropped into the deckchair next to Emma's. 'They're good kids. Didn't they clean out the hutch?'

She nodded.

'How did Ted's meeting go? You seemed to be gone for most of the afternoon.'

Stig and Andrea stopped talking.

Emma sipped her lemonade. 'Yes, I only got back an hour ago. It went well. Great, in fact. It didn't take long to persuade most people that the majority of rough sleepers aren't a problem — that the real threat is the big out-of-town retailers, and that should be their focus. A few spoke about appearances mattering and that the homeless would put off shoppers, but several others piped up and said that so far they'd not committed any crimes.'

'What about that bloke who's made camp by the taxi rank near the Red Lion?' said Bligh. 'I walked past last week and he was blind drunk and hurling abuse at people.'

'I spoke to him on Wednesday's soup run.'

'What did he say?'

She looked at Stig. She'd offered to take the man to AA, and he'd told her to eff off. Not so long ago, that had been her, full of resentments, denying her problems… This man hadn't hit his rock bottom yet.

'The police were at the meeting and are going to keep an eye out. You can't write off a whole bunch of people just because of one. I'll have another word with him on the soup run tomorrow night. You could tell that some people at the meeting weren't happy, but fortunately Ted had a master move up his sleeve.'

Bligh raised his eyebrows.

'You know the couple who've been begging outside the bank on Church Street? I told you they'd been in care? Well an older woman camps out with them now. Apparently she used to run her own coffee shop. Ted invited her to stand up and tell her story. Her business was doing okay until a well-known brand opened up opposite. She just couldn't compete with their exotic-sounding lattes and decadent interior. She ran into debt and lost everything.' Emma sipped her drink. 'You could tell the local entrepreneurs were really shocked at the thought that they could end up like her. Anyway, the upshot is that the meeting swiftly moved on to brainstorming how to boost the local economy.'

'What ideas did people come up with?' asked Andrea.

'Small ones to start, where businesses club together to bring in money. For example, the bookshop is going to try to get more signings and other events, and they'll get the teashop by the church to do the catering. But one standout idea was to run a Sunday market. Mrs Beatty visits them across the region and suggested Healdbury start its own, involving local farms and craftsmen. Each shop could run a stall. Foxglove Farm could sell its produce and hand out cards for the online vegetable delivery business. Ted would set up a cheese stall alongside the bakery, and they'd push each other's products by handing out sand-wich samples. Polly and Alan have got a popcorn and candy floss machine they found in the pub's cellar and have never used...'

Polly and Alan. It was becoming increasingly difficult to be in their presence, but in a way, this made Emma focus more fully on her future. She'd come to a decision. She'd accepted that she just wasn't academic enough to get the qualifications to be a vet, and anyway, she didn't need the ego boost of that status any more. But what about a veterinary nurse? Working at Foxglove Farm again had reignited her passion for animals. Maybe, if she ended up in prison, she'd be allowed to do some sort of distance learning course. That would give her a purpose. Perhaps make her sentence bearable – not that she'd deserve respite. An image of Ned's young face flashed into her mind. She felt sick and forced herself back to answering Andrea's question.

'... and the owner of the teashop thought they could sell takeaway drinks and cakes.' She put down her glass. 'Everyone was quite excited by the end. Even Phil thought he may as well try ordering in some new pet toys to sell. We could offer something more personal than the bigger brands and do really well at Christmas. Also, a resident who's retired here now and who used to be a journalist will help get some coverage in the local news-paper – a story with heart about locals doing their best to compete with the big boys of business. He reckoned the *Manchester Evening News* would definitely go for it, and...'

The Duchess got to her feet and ran across the yard, tail wagging.

Stig stood up, his brow knotted. 'That's usually how she greets a friend.'

Emma started to get up too, but Bligh raised his palm. 'I'm nearest. Someone must be lost.' He disappeared around to the front of the farmhouse.

Minutes later, angry shouting came from that direction. Dash joined the Duchess and both dogs started barking. Stig jumped up as Bligh and another man came into view, fighting. Bligh threw a punch and the smaller man landed on the gravel. Emma squinted in the late sunlight, trying to make out his face in between punches. It was clean-shaven and tanned. His blonde hair was shoulder length but styled. He wore pumps, skinny jeans and a tight-fitting T-shirt. He lunged at solid Bligh and head-butted him in the stomach.

Andrea shouted at them to stop, while Emma charged right in. Stig hauled her back and put himself between the two men.

'Violence isn't the answer,' he said, just as Bligh's fist accidentally hit him in the eye.

A wail came from Gail, who stood up and started to pull at her cardigan sleeve. Andrea hurried to her side.

'For God's sake!' shouted Emma as the Duchess snarled and took hold of Bligh's trouser leg. She grabbed the dog's collar and with all her strength pulled her away.

'Emma, it's me,' said a voice that made the hairs on her neck stand on end.

She stepped away from Bligh and stared at the man's face. Her knees buckled. 'Joe? *Joe?* Is that really you?'

'It's him, isn't it, the one who got you up the duff and then did a runner,' said Bligh.

Andrea's face paled.

Chapter 19

'You're *pregnant*?' said Andrea.

'Emma?' said Joe, and wiped his nose with his arm. She stared at the blood.

Bligh looked down at his fists. 'Sorry,' he said to Stig. 'I didn't mean for you to get in the way.'

Joe. Joe was really here. Emma walked up to him and scanned that familiar face, the expressive eyes, the sardonic mouth. A wave of pain washed through her chest. For a second, all the old feelings came back – the crisp agony that had cut through her when he left.

'Stig? Good to see you, mate,' said Joe in a daze. The two men hugged. He stared back at Emma. 'What's this about a baby?'

'I'd like to know that too,' said Andrea in a strained voice.

Gail was still pulling at her cardigan sleeve. 'Is this my fault?' she said. 'All this noise – am I in trouble?'

Andrea breathed in and put an arm around her mum's shoulders. 'Of course not. It's just the men being silly. Come on, let's get you something to eat, and then how about a nice relaxing bath?'

'We should give Emma and Joe some space,' said Stig, one hand over his face. He turned to Andrea. 'Thanks for today's work. I'll get going.'

'First you'll need a packet of frozen peas on that eye. And it's nice to have someone around here who knows how to behave.' Andrea glared at Bligh. 'Hold on a moment, Stig. I'll just sort Mum out.' She looked at Emma and opened her mouth, before changing her mind.

'Andrea, wait,' said Bligh, and followed her inside.

Emma led Joe past the animal pens. They reached the weeping willow. She looked him up and down. His arms slid around her. He felt sturdier than before. His embrace used to make her feel so safe.

They sat down on the bench. Complimented each other on their healthy appearance. Emma asked how he'd managed to track her down, given that he'd thrown away her address. Joe smiled. Said that Foxglove Farm, Broadgrass Hill, Healdbury wasn't exactly difficult to remember. He was staying at the Badger Inn, having finished work early. He lived in Blackpool now and was an assistant manager in one of the arcades.

'That's where Stig comes from,' said Emma. 'Sounds like you're doing well.'

'Management like my ability to deal with troublemakers. I never realised living on the streets would improve my CV.' He gave a wry smile. 'How come Stig's here?'

'Long story – rough sleepers have been moved out of the city. What made you think I'd come home? It was a bit of a gamble.'

'I figured that if you weren't here, your family might have had news.'

She asked about his own family. Now and again he contemplated contacting them, he said. That was a start.

'So why did you come to find me? I thought—'

'I think I get to ask the questions first.' His eyes fell to her stomach.

So Emma told him. She explained how she'd never got to use his tampons.

'And what did you do?' asked Joe 'Did you have the baby? Am I... Can I meet...?'

She had to turn away, unable to bear the note of excitement in his voice. He'd talked to her once about how difficult it had been for him to accept that he'd probably never have kids.

'Oh. Did... didn't you go through with the pregnancy? I mean...' his voice faltered, 'I wouldn't blame you. Of course I wouldn't. I understand. You and I had enough trouble looking after ourselves.'

Emma's vision blurred for a second. She explained what had happened. Gently Joe took her chin and moved her head to face him.

'The miscarriage was early, but I just got this feeling... I named her Josephine – after you.'

'I'm sorry I wasn't with you.'

'I wanted her so much,' she gulped.

'And you'd have been the best mum ever.'

'I hope so,' she said in a muffled voice. 'You know, the pregnancy prompted me to get treatment.'

They talked about rehab. Joe had finally got a detox in London and a case worker who understood him.

'What happened with you, Ems... it was a complete mind-fuck and made me realise I had to turn things around.'

'Honoured to be your rock bottom.'

'You get it, right?'

'Yes. Yes, I do. And you're near the top of my list of people to say sorry to. Even though for months I felt confused. For me... what we did felt right.'

'We were both off our heads. I cried afterwards, Emma. How could anything about that make you think it was meant to be? That I was happy with it?'

'I wasn't thinking about you. That's the whole point. I was selfish. I told myself I was capable of changing you.' Her heart pounded. 'I'm not proud.'

'You'd thought it through that much? I assumed you were just pissed.' He leant back.

'I *was*. The drink convinced me of ridiculous possibilities – told me things could be different. But that drunk Emma isn't around any more – she was an arrogant fantasist. Remember Big John, who insisted he was related to Bruno Mars?'

A muscle flickered in his cheek.

'Well, you were my Bruno. It was fiction, but what I thought we had – or could have had – kept me going.'

'It felt like such a betrayal. You knew I'd only just accepted that my years of saying I was bisexual were a lie. You knew how confused I'd been – how that... that fight for identity helped turn me to drugs. And then when *I* finally accepted I was gay, you wouldn't. You were supposed to be my friend.'

Her cheeks reddened.

'I'm gay, Emma.'

'I know.'

'Do you? I like men. One hundred per cent. Have you really accepted that?'

She put her hand on her heart. 'I promise. Yes. Everything's so clear now. But when you used to talk about the relationship you had with that woman called

Kelly, I… I thought that perhaps there was a chance for us.'

'I told you that was a mistake, me kidding myself I could take the more easily accepted road of getting married, having kids… But you thought you knew better.' His top lip curled with disgust.

Emma tried to explain that becoming homeless had made her feel as though she'd been stranded on an island, with no means of getting back out to sea. But then Joe had sailed in, like a lifeboat. All she'd really wanted was cuddles – that close human contact and comfort, on the most basic level – but her feelings had got out of hand. She'd started to imagine that the two of them could create their own perfect family.

'Christ, so you even completed the heterosexual package by getting pregnant.' He stood up and paced around. 'Did you have it all planned?'

His words punched the air out of her lungs and she gasped, jumping to her feet. She strode over to him, fists curled.

'Shit. Look, ignore me, Ems, I'm a dick and just in shock about the baby. I should never—'

'You think I got pregnant on purpose? It's not all my fault. How dare you take the moral high ground? I admit my part in it, but sometimes you kissed me first, and the sex… it wasn't all one-way. I couldn't have done it on my own. And you should have said something.' She pointed her finger at him. 'You ended up hurting me anyway. You used my friendship for your own ends and then just ditched me like everyone else.'

'No, Emma—'

'You think I tried to trap you? That the pregnancy was simply some sort of tactic?' She wouldn't have him talk about Josephine like that.

'I think it's time you left,' boomed a voice. Bligh appeared from the shadows.

'This is between me and Emma,' snapped Joe.

'Now!'

Chest heaving, Emma collapsed onto the bench. She bent her head and wiped her cheeks. When she looked up, Joe had gone and Bligh was sitting by her side. He waited until her shoulders stopped jerking and then draped his arm around her.

Emma groaned. 'I handled that badly. All the mental tools I've gained over the last year... where did they go?'

'I didn't like his tone, whatever was wrong. He had no right to speak to you like that.'

'I'll find him tomorrow. Talk properly. He's staying with Polly and Alan. He's just upset.' She closed her eyes tight for a second. 'How's Andrea?'

'I'm not sure. She didn't say much.'

Emma made her excuses to leave. She needed to clear her head. Bligh offered to drive her home, but she chose to walk instead. Stig was still inside with Andrea, and right now, Emma couldn't face her sister.

As she walked down Broadgrass Hill, she looked at the village ahead. Lights began to come on in the houses. As she passed the butcher's, barbecue smoke filled the air. She heard laughter and the clink of glasses. She wiped the back of her neck, which was sweaty from the summer air. With swollen eyes she stumbled into the pet shop. Phil was still up, at the kitchen table.

He pushed a piece of paper towards her. 'So, what do you think?' he said without looking up. 'Rubbish, isn't it?'

It was an advert for him to look after pets during the holidays.

'I like the way you've listed the rates in bold letters. It would put me off if I had to ask someone I knew what their prices were – I'd then feel kind of obliged. And the sketch of that dog is great.'

'You're not taking the piss?'

'No. Promise.' She tore off a square of kitchen roll. 'Let me know if you need a hand asking shopkeepers to pin them up in their windows.' She blew her nose.

Phil looked up. 'What's wrong? Hay fever? Or aren't you as tough as you like us all to think?'

She slumped at the table. Leant on her elbows. Rested her chin on her fists.

'The old Emma came out to play tonight. Even though she wasn't drinking, it wasn't a pretty sight.'

He paused. 'Ginger biscuit?'

Her chin quivered and all she could do was nod.

He stood up, switched on the kettle and passed her the tin.

Chapter 20

Emma overslept the next morning. Did Joe really think she'd tried to trap him? Why was Bligh so upset? Would Andrea have preferred to have known about the pregnancy at the time?

Determined to catch Joe, she skipped her morning routines, pulling on a pair of shorts and an old T-shirt from the day before. Without even brushing her hair, she rushed out of the pet shop. Stig was sitting on the pavement reading.

He looked up. 'You okay?'

'I've been better.' She sighed and knelt down. 'But what about your eye?'

'My whole face was numb by the time Andrea let me remove the bag of peas. She said I could sleep over in the barn, but…'

'You should have. The Duchess would have loved that.'

He stared at the page. Gently she nudged his shoulder and he looked up.

'I guess I'm not used to people being nice. It doesn't feel right, accepting her hospitality. I mean, I could be anyone. She should be more careful.'

'And the very fact that you think that proves that you're worthy of a bed for the night. She's not exactly offering you a room at the Ritz.'

They both smiled.

'Speak later, yes? I've got to hurry. I want to catch Joe at the Badger Inn.' Emma stood up and smoothed down her hair.

'I saw Bligh leaving there earlier this morning when me and my girl went for a walk. I was going to say hello but sensed he needed a bit of space.'

Emma's brow knotted.

'He pounded his fist into the palm of his other hand before getting in his car and speeding up Broadgrass Hill.'

Emma headed off to the pub. She pushed the door open and entered. A couple of guests were eating breakfast. Alan was wiping down tables. Polly stood at the coffee machine. Emma hesitated before approaching the bar. The room smelt of fried bacon and detergent.

Alan walked over and Polly turned her head to stare.

'Sorry for barging in, but a friend of mine is staying here... he's called Joe. Bligh might have visited him this morning.'

'The young man with the bruised face?' Alan shook his head.

'Is he still here?'

'I'm afraid you've just missed him,' said Polly. 'He left about twenty minutes ago, muttering something about a train.'

Emma exited the pub and broke into a jog down the high street and up towards the station. A couple of people who'd ignored her before the cheese shop fire smiled. Emma squinted in the sunshine as she left the narrow nettle-lined path that led to the station's approach. Heart thumping, she reached the pavement to the right of the huge automatic glass doors.

'Joe?' she said, out of breath. Thank God. He was sitting with a couple who'd recently turned up to her soup run. 'Can we talk?'

'I think Bligh's done your talking for you.'

'What did he say?'

'Said to leave Healdbury, that there was nothing here for me; said that you didn't need a man in your life right now – especially one who'd walk out on his own child.'

'*What?*' Bligh was *still* trying to be her fixer?

'He made it sound as if you really hated me…' His eyes shone, revealing shades of the old, vulnerable Joe.

'Of course I don't. Look, we need to chat.'

Joe stood and picked up his rucksack. Cautiously, Emma linked arms. He didn't pull away. She led him back to the narrow path that ran through a small grassy area. His rucksack slipped off and they sat down opposite each other, holding hands.

'Me first,' said Joe. 'I'm really sorry for what I said about you purposely getting pregnant. You know I'd never think that. I was just reeling from the news that I'd become a dad without even knowing it – and then hadn't.'

'And I shouldn't have lost my temper. The trouble is, now and then the miscarriage still feels raw. I had so many plans, you see.' Emma swallowed. 'The birth was going to be my new beginning and I felt so angry for her.' She rubbed her thumbs over his palms.

His head dropped for a moment and then he looked up. 'You were right, you know. It did take two. I shouldn't have blamed you, and I realised that during recovery, but seeing you yesterday brought everything back. I think we were just coming at our friendship from different angles. When we met, I was such a mess. You were a bit older, kind… it felt good to feel someone was looking out for me. We had so much in common. I felt a connection.'

'Whereas me, I saw a sweet-natured, pretty hot guy and my ego decided I could change your sexuality. Well, not even that – it just decided I could make you not care about it.' She let go of his hands and pulled at a sphere of clover. 'All your life you'd had people not accept you for who you were, and I was no better. But I've changed, Joe. Gained perspective. Everything's clearer. It's obvious to me now that you are – and always were – gay. The signs were there, but I ignored them. One thing I don't understand, though… why didn't you stop… you know… what happened that night, before things went too far? I honestly thought you'd enjoyed it, until I heard you crying afterwards. I'd have stopped straight away if I'd known it didn't feel right for you.'

'I… I know.'

'Now I can appreciate how much that night must have devastated you. But at the time, I just drank more and told myself you were simply having a bad day.'

'I was out of it. It all felt blurred, as if my body was on automatic. It was only when I came off that high that I realised we'd actually…'

'Please forgive me, Joe. I'm so sorry.'

'Only if you forgive me too.'

They both leant forward and hugged. For once, Emma broke contact first.

'Look at us,' she said, 'letting go of resentments. Our case workers would be proud.'

Joe swatted away a fly. 'So… I'm pretty hot, am I?'

'Remember, I used to have a crush on Piers Morgan, so some might say my hotness radar is off.'

He smiled, just a little.

'I've missed this, Joe – especially a few weeks into rehab, when I realised I'd never really been in love with you. It was all the illness. I knew that I'd ruined a special friendship. I was so angry with myself.'

'Don't relive it. We're in each other's lives again. That's all that matters.'

'And I'm here for you, Joe. Any time you need help, I've got your back. Promise.'

'Ditto.'

'Will you stay around for a while?'

'I'm visiting friends in Manchester tomorrow – perhaps we could meet up for a coffee during the day, if you've got the time. And there's this old movie being shown at the Printworks…'

They walked back into the village, bought sandwiches and went to Healdbury stream with Stig and the Duchess. Stig had been chatting to Ted, who'd accepted a quote for the shop to be repaired and wanted to learn from his expertise on interior decorating. Despite her advancing years, the dog retrieved sticks from the stream with gusto. She showered everyone when she shook herself dry, like a spinning brush in an automatic car wash – just like Dash used to. Emma felt happier than she had done in ages.

It felt grown up, saying sorry, accepting apologies, talking things through and reaching an understanding – being able to promise things you knew you would stick to. She felt more… solid, in a way she never had in the old days.

She could hardly believe it. Joe had forgiven her. Knowing that gave her the strength to head back to the farm. She went around to the back door and entered the kitchen. Andrea was washing strawberries.

'Where's Mum?'

'Taking a nap.'

Emma joined Andrea at the sink.

Andrea shook her head and took a sip from her mug of tea. 'I'm fine on my own. In fact, after last night I could do with some space.'

'I'm sorry for all the upset. I didn't know Joe was coming.'

'You think that's what I'm upset about? A couple of grown men acting like teenagers?'

'No… of course not. Look, the miscarriage – it happened at the end of my detox.'

Andrea stopped washing up and turned to face her. 'You didn't think to tell me when you found out you were pregnant? You didn't think I'd help?' she said in a flat voice.

'It was difficult.'

'You think me that bad a sister? I've been going over and over it in my mind. You really think that despite everything, I wouldn't have been there for you and my niece or nephew?'

'Of course I didn't think that, but—'

Andrea picked up a tea towel. 'This was a baby. Family.' Her voice trembled. 'Did you tell me about it in that letter?'

'No.'

'Why not?'

'I thought it would be shocking enough to hear from me after so long, let alone with the addition of that bomb-shell. And in a way… what was the point? The pregnancy was over.'

The towel missed the kitchen unit and landed on the floor as Andrea let it fall. She turned to go, but Emma held her arm. Andrea shook off her hand. 'You think you're the only one who's carried any guilt through all of this?'

'I used to think that,' Emma said, cheeks flaming. 'But then Bligh told me he felt he was to blame. Please don't tell me you felt like that as well. No one is responsible for my mess-ups apart from me.'

'Easy to say. You're not the one lying in bed at night asking yourself again and again whether it was something you did. I'm your big sister, for God's sake – have you any idea how it felt watching helplessly as you threw your life away? Was I too intolerant? Or should I have thrown you out earlier? Was it my fault we grew apart? Was I to blame for introducing you to alcohol when we used to drink cocktails in my room? Was it to do with your father? Was it somehow my fault he never hung around?' She leant against the sink for a moment. Eventually her shoulders sank. 'I'm going to check on Mum.'

Emma touched her arm. 'Please. It's so good to be talking honestly like this. Sit down. Let's sort this out once and for all.'

'You still don't understand. There is no once and for all.' Andrea's voice was a monotone. 'There's no solution. No answer. How can you expect that after everything you did? After the way you left?'

'But there *is*. I've learnt why all this happened. It's down to me – my character flaws. It's nothing to do with you or Bligh, or anyone else.'

'Then I guess you'll just have to work on forgiving yourself.'

'But I love you, Andrea. I do,' Emma said in a broken voice. 'I'm so sorry.'

Andrea's face crumpled. 'And I love you too. Always have. You're my little sister.'

'So why can't we try to resolve this?'

Clenching her hands together, she looked Emma straight in the eye. 'Because I can't ever forget.'

4 months before going back

Emma loved her new flat. It consisted of three basic rooms, it was on a main road, and she could have sworn it had tap dancers for neighbours. But it was hers, and it was safe. Slowly she personalised its blank canvas. Working in the charity shop gave her access to beautiful but affordable features, such as the tasselled Indian silk scarf she hung across the bed. In each room she placed a fragrant candle from the pound shop, including white musk in the bedroom.

Small things made a big difference.

White musk was supposed to smell sexy, she thought, walking home after her shift. Today was Valentine's Day and her thoughts strayed to Joe. She still missed his smile, which could warm up the frostiest winter day. She'd loved the banter between them. They used to laugh that they could read each other's minds. Was it any surprise that the old Emma had wanted more than he could provide?

Back at the flat, she switched on the kettle and sat on her small sofa in the dark. She had been the worst kind of friend to Joe. Heat swamped her neck as she recalled giving him a Valentine's Day card he hadn't wanted.

On the way home, she'd treated herself to a bar of chocolate – Beth's favourite Twix. Had Beth stayed sober? Was she back living with her kids? Emma drew the curtains and sat down again. The silence exacerbated the discontent she'd felt since her due date in January. She leant forward to the fake mahogany coffee table and turned on a small second-hand radio.

Her time at recovery services had ended now. The volunteering and AA were her lifelines – and her doctor. He'd agreed she wasn't quite ready to go back to work and had signed her off for a while longer.

A song came on. Emma stopped chewing. It was 'Crazy Little Thing Called Love' by Queen. That had been her and Bligh's song. A joke at first – he'd sing it affectionately. She recalled their first ever Valentine's Day together. He had taken her out for a romantic dinner in Manchester's Chinatown. He'd rung ahead to ask for red roses and candles. Bought her favourite perfume and written a poem inside her card. Emma bit into the chocolate bar again and thought back to that night of making love. She'd been drunk. Bligh had taken a glass of water to the bedroom for her. She'd given him his present – a humorous pair of furry handcuffs. Why hadn't she been more thoughtful?

Unable to finish the chocolate, she paced around the lounge with a growing sense of unease. She tried to meditate. Lit a joss stick. Skim-read part of the Big Book. Valentine's Day had raised all sorts of unsettling questions. Bligh… Joe… they were the two big loves of her life. But neither relationship had been real.

Her mind went into overdrive, playing over and over again the turning-point scenes from the last couple of years. Her first night on the streets, sleeping with Joe, losing Josephine… And she tried to block out memories of that morning she'd woken up in the luxury hotel. It would do no good remembering. Yet the scenes came back in minute detail. It was as if someone had Photoshopped her life from matt to glossy, with the room's plush decor. That was if you ignored the condoms on the carpet. She'd woken up on the freezing floor and had eventually seen the splats of latex, wet and sticky...

Her hand rose to her throat and she squeezed her eyes tight, hoping to somehow destroy the memories, but the dried blood stuck to her dress flashed into her mind and a wave of nausea rose up her throat as she recalled the panic. She had pulled the material away from her body. Had she been stabbed? No. Thank God. There was no wound. Did that mean she'd injured someone else?

The radio played another song and she returned to the present. She picked up the chocolate bar again, praying the past would stay where it was meant to. But it came back as she shivered, thinking back to the sickly fear that had crept over her as she'd sat in that hotel room, desperately trying to remember what had happened the night before. Eventually her mental fog had cleared. That was it – Bligh had asked her if she'd bothered buying Andrea and Mum a Christmas present. Of course, she hadn't, so to spite him, she had taken both of the debit cards from his wallet. She'd got all dressed up and driven the family car into Manchester, where she was due to meet friends for a bar crawl. She knew the PIN code of one card and had withdrawn cash up to its limit. The other card was contactless.

In the end, she'd decided to skip the shops and met her friends at the hotel instead. She'd insisted on buying all the drinks. What happened after last orders had been a blur, and when she'd woken on the floor, her mind was a blank. She'd gone to the window. It was still dark. Six o'clock. Ice everywhere. Someone had knocked sharply on the door. It was the assistant manager. She'd handed over a receipt.

'This is your bar bill. The security guard who escorted you back to your room said it fell out of your hand but you wouldn't take it back.'

Security guard? Bar bill? She'd studied the slip of paper and her legs felt shaky. 'Almost fifteen hundred pounds? That's not possible, just for one night.'

'Two,' the woman had said sharply.

That meant it was now Christmas Eve. Emma couldn't believe it.

'Your guests left in the early hours yesterday morning, and last night you were quiet,' the assistant manager said. 'Otherwise we'd have been forced to ask you to vacate too. We only let you stay on as a goodwill gesture, seeing as you… didn't feel well. But it's my duty to tell you that you aren't welcome here again – whoever your boss is. And I'd now ask you to leave within the next hour.'

Emma had slammed the door shut and headed straight for a half-full bottle of champagne. Her boss? What a joke. She wondered what else she'd made up.

She'd taken out her phone and, ignoring the texts from Andrea and Bligh, gone onto Instagram. Ah ha! There she was dancing. Taking selfies. People were using empty bottles as pretend microphones. It looked as if she'd had the best time ever. But then she watched the videos she hadn't posted.

Someone had knocked over the TV and tried to pick up the shards of glass. They'd cut their arm badly and fallen against her. That was where the blood had come from. The room had emptied apart from an older man and two young women on the bed who couldn't have been much more than eighteen. Disgust had lifted the champagne to her lips once more. Something about him had seemed familiar. She couldn't get a close look but reckoned he was old enough to be their grandad.

The screen then went black, but an hour later she'd recorded again. It was just her now... No, wait... another person was sitting on the bed. Legs with thread veins and saggy knees hurriedly pushed themselves into trousers. She couldn't see his face but sensed it was the familiar older man. She was shouting that she'd report him – that he'd lose everything. The screen had then gone dead again.

Buoyed by more champagne, Emma had shrugged off the confusion and sense of unease. She'd got dressed and sauntered through the lobby. Having already paid the huge bill she'd gone outside and withdrawn cash with Bligh's debit card again – well, she might need money for New Year's Eve. She'd climbed into the car. The dashboard said it was six forty-five and minus one outside. Somehow she left the crowded car park without scraping another vehicle and half an hour later was on the outskirts of Healdbury, listening to her music.

The road began to wind as she approached the Christmas tree farm. Humming, she opened the Instagram app on her phone and every now and again glanced across at her friends' photos. Suddenly her body was thrown forward as the car hit something and skidded. Emma struggled to keep control of the steering wheel, but at last the car slowed. She thought maybe she'd hit a fox or a badger – although it had felt heavier than that. Perhaps a big sheep.

When she reached Foxglove Farm, she cleaned the blood off the front headlight to avoid any boring questions, then opened the back door, hoping to go straight to bed.

She hadn't counted on the welcome party…

Emma jolted back to the present day and her flat. The chocolate bar had fallen from her hand. She felt sick. Afraid. Ashamed. Disgusted. Her pulse raced as she picked up her phone and clicked into WhatsApp.

Emma: Hello? Rachel? You there?

Rachel: Hi there! What are you up to?

Emma: Eating chocolate. You?

Rachel: I've had a knackering day at work, so me and Idris are spending the night together :)

Emma: :)

Rachel: You okay?

Emma: Yes. No. I don't know. Memories. Bad ones. They keep coming back. I just needed someone to chat to.

Rachel: Oh lovely, I understand. I'm here for you – I mean, you did listen to me for over an hour last week after I had that run-in with a client. Do you keep replaying the past?

Emma: Yes. Sometimes it just won't go away.

It made her want to drink. It did. There. She'd said it. Despite all her efforts to get sober. Despite how bad she knew life with alcohol used to be.

Rachel: I still have sleepless nights, you know, hating on myself for the things I've done.

Emma: You do?

Rachel: Of course. That's probably normal, don't you think? Now we've got perspective, it gives the past a whole different feel. But I reckon the horror will eventually pass.

Emma: It's just with it being Valentine's Day I can't help thinking about all the relationships I've messed up.

Just one glass would make her feel so much better. Take the edge off. Give life that warm glow it was currently missing.

Rachel: Oh dearie me – that's not a pity party you're holding, is it?

Emma: Why? Wanna come?

Rachel: No thanks! I'm perfectly happy.

Emma: Are you?

Rachel: Um, yes. I am actually. I've been meaning to tell you...

Emma: ??

Rachel: I... I've met someone. I was too scared to tell anyone in case I jinxed it. I haven't got the best track record either.

Emma: Right. Gosh. Congratulations.

Rachel: It's Rick. The guy from work I mentioned a few weeks ago, who's been really supportive. We've been out for a few coffees and started going to the gym together. He's given me some great tips on healthy eating. I wasn't sure at first, I mean – I'd forgotten what genuine attraction felt like. For the last few years I've always had my beer goggles on when going for the opposite sex. But he's really sweet, Emma – and clever. His edgy designs make mine look like doodles.

Emma: I'm sure that's not true. So you aren't out with him tonight?

Rachel: No. He'd arranged a couple of months ago to take his dad to a big band concert.

Emma: He sounds decent. So… have you and he… :)

Rachel: :):):)

Emma: !!

Rachel: Weird it was. Weird in a good way, but very different. Tess once talked about this – said it can be hard to get used to, getting naked without the drink fooling you you're a sex god. I felt so self-conscious about how I looked, how I sounded and whether Rick was having a good time. Awful to admit, but it's the first time in years I've thought about what my partner wanted.

Emma: So is sober sex to be recommended?

Rachel: Oh definitely. You know… I cried afterwards. I'd experienced such an emotional connection. I never knew that was possible.

Emma: <3 <3

Rachel: So yes. Go for it. When you meet the right person. And that's my last word on the matter. It wouldn't be fair on Rick to talk about our sex life again. Oh God. Listen to me. I've developed a sense of integrity :):)

Emma: We're changing – I think it's called growing up :)

213

Despite all the smiley faces, Emma still felt low hours later, as she got into bed. She was genuinely happy for Rachel, but her friend's news just added to her dwelling on how selfish she'd been with Bligh and Joe. She couldn't stop fidgeting. Didn't meditate; didn't fill in her gratitude journal or do her nightly reading. Didn't do any of the things that kept her safe.

She closed her eyes tight and threw off the covers as if to get up, but then pulled them back. There was one thing she hadn't told Rachel. On the way home today, she had stopped off at the off-licence. She hadn't meant to, but they'd had a three-for-two sale. She'd hovered outside for a while, the fuck-it button looming large and bright, then decided it wouldn't hurt just to go in and look. And now a bag by the front door contained a trio of white wine bottles calling her name.

3 months before going back

It was the end of March and Mother's Day. This date was always going to be a hard one. Emma wished she hadn't been rostered to go into work. The charity shop was humming with families who had been out for a celebratory lunch. Grandmas and daughters, grandkids in buggies…

Over the months, babies, prams had slowly become less prominent as she'd strolled around Manchester. The sharp yearning to have something of her own to look after had turned into a dull ache. She could appreciate now how tough it would have been to bring up a small child on her own during early sobriety – but none of that stopped today's what ifs and if onlys.

Josephine would have been two months old and smiling.

She took an afternoon break but couldn't manage a hot drink or a biscuit. All she could think about was those three bottles she still had at home, still unopened.

She said goodbye to her colleagues and hurried back to her flat with only one intention. She hardly felt the spray of water from a car speeding through a puddle near the kerb. When she got inside, she threw down her bag, shook off her jacket and went into her room. She pulled the bottles out from under the bed – proof that the old insanity had already started: where was the logic in hiding them from herself? She put two in the fridge and almost laughed at her sophistication. Then she grabbed a glass and put it, and the third bottle, on the coffee table. She sat on the sofa and stared at her two accomplices. The wine bottle winked.

Go on. Unscrew my top. You know you want to.

She leant forward, picked it up and ran her fingers down the smooth glass. Then she placed it back down on the table and put her head in her hands. That rambling narrative had already started in her head.

Go on, just have one, it really won't hurt. You can start your resolutions again tomorrow. Yes, but then I'll have lost all of these months' hard work. No you won't, it's just a slip. But then what does that say about the new person I'm becoming – has it all been a sham?

Cue the identity crisis she hadn't felt for a while. Who was she? Which was the real Emma – the drunk or the meditating charity worker?

A car backfired outside and she sat up. The bottle winked again and Emma began to unscrew the lid. She'd not gone to as many meetings recently, convinced that friends would see that she was almost tipping over the edge.

She twisted the lid shut again and put the bottle under the table, then jumped up and paced up and down. She knocked back a large glass of water. Flicked on the telly, then flicked it off. Ate a biscuit. Scanned a magazine. Finally she retrieved the bottle and carried it into the bedroom. The mattress creaked as she dropped onto the bed.

The bottle felt seductive. Inviting. Like an intimate friend. She crashed it down onto her bedside table and held her head in her hands again.

Fuck it. She deserved a drink for getting sober.

Tears trickled down her face as she acknowledged the insanity of that sentiment.

Teeth clenched, she grabbed her phone and went into WhatsApp.

Emma: Rachel?

Rachel: Hi, Emma? How are you doing?

How could she admit the truth?

Emma: You first. Things better today?

Rachel: A bit. Thanks again for the chat last night. You helped me realise that me and Rick splitting up… it's for the best. I should never have started a relationship until my recovery was really concrete.

Emma: You sure you're okay? How was it at work today? Was he still understanding about you needing to just focus on yourself?

Rachel: Awkward. He apologised. Said the last thing he'd want is to jeopardise my health. He didn't realise about all my routines. It's my fault I let them slip because of our relationship. I really like him still, Emma, but I can't afford to risk going back to old habits. Not when things are finally getting back on track with Mum.

Emma: How's that going?

Rachel: Not bad. We met up again yesterday. I've done my amends and she says she accepts them and even said sorry for a few things herself. Apparently she was always proud of my degree – just disappointed for me that I didn't do better. And so worried about my drinking. It made her feel guilty.

Emma: Why?

Rachel: Sometimes she felt selfish that she'd sent my father away. She said that at the time she hadn't been thinking about me – that I might have needed a father in my life and that he could have helped in so many ways. So when I almost flunked my degree, when I began drinking, she blamed herself. I've told her that's rubbish. We've talked it all through. We even hugged.

Emma: Oh Rachel, I'm so pleased.

Rachel: And to my amazement, she's even mooted the idea that I could track him down. She says he was a kind person. Even though it was a one-night stand, she'd known him at school.

Emma: That's fantastic. I'm so happy for you.

Rachel: He had ginger hair as well, just like Mum. Just like me... Anyway, how about you? Are you going to the meeting tomorrow night? You didn't go last week.

Rachel: Emma? Are you there?

Emma: I'm... It's nothing. I'm okay.

Rachel: Nothing is usually something. Spill.

Emma: I can't.

Rachel: You can. We know the worst of each other. I'm not going to judge. I'm here to help. You know that.

Emma: I'm sitting in front of a wine bottle.

Rachel: Is this some kind of joke?

Emma: No. Oh Rachel, I wish it was.

Rachel: Oh darling… have you started to drink?

Emma: Not yet.

But I will, she thought. I know it. I can't wait another minute.

Rachel: Well done. You don't need it.

Emma: I do. I'm fed up. Being sober is boring.

Rachel: What's so exciting about getting pissed? Blacking out? Waking up wishing you hadn't?

Emma: I could just drink for tonight. Take the edge off my feelings.

That sounded like a plan. How difficult could it be to stop after just one night, now that she'd learnt so much about recovery? It'd be easy, right?

Rachel: Take those bottles around to your neighbour, then come back to the phone.

Emma's grip tightened around the bottle's neck.

Emma: I… I don't want to. They could just stay under the bed. I'll take them back to the shop tomorrow. Get my money back.

Rachel: That's making excuses. We've all been there. You're kidding yourself and you know it.

Emma: She'll think I'm crazy.

Rachel: And if you start drinking, she'll meet the really crazy you. You don't want that – proved by the fact that you've opened this chat. Something is telling you not to pick up. Just tell her someone gave them to you as a gift but you don't like wine.

Emma: But I do like wine. A lot.

Rachel: No. You used to. Do you want me to come around? I can be there in less than an hour.

Rachel: Emma?

Rachel: EMMA? SPEAK TO ME. ARE YOU THERE?

Emma: Yes. Look, just forget I said anything. I shouldn't have bothered you. Don't worry, I know what I'm doing. I'll message you tomorrow.

Rachel: No! No you don't. You don't give up your sobriety like that. Remember who you're doing it for – who set you on this journey.

Emma: That's unfair.

Rachel: No it's not. You start drinking again, Emma, and you're letting not only yourself down, but Josephine as well.

A sob rose at the back of Emma's throat.

Rachel: Get around to your neighbour's.

Rachel: Emma?

Emma: I'm back.

Rachel: You've done it?

Emma: Yes.

Rachel: Honest?

Emma: Yes. Thanks so much. I can't believe I almost threw away everything I've achieved. I don't ever want to go back to being the person I used to be. And you were right. If I start drinking again, I'm breaking my promise to my little girl.

Emma wiped her eyes and her shoulders relaxed.

Emma: It was my neighbour's birthday, so good timing, I guess. What a relief.

Rachel: The first year is hideously difficult, everyone knows that. Do you remember Tess telling us the main reason people relapse?

Emma: They stopped drinking but didn't change their lives.

Rachel: Exactly. But look at you with your volunteering and your meditation...

Emma: I think I'll head out for a walk. The fresh air will do me good. Maybe I'll stop off somewhere and get a hot chocolate.

Rachel: Good idea – but ring me before you go to bed. Let me know you're still okay.

Emma: Thanks, Rachel. You're a star. Give Idris a tickle behind the ears from me.

Emma grabbed her jacket, her purse and her front door keys and headed outside into the brisk air, a renewed purpose in her stride. As she passed through the park gates, she took in the detail of a nearby tree, its branches outstretched as if welcoming the sky. Each leaf looked the same as the next, yet close up totally different. She inhaled the fresh scent of moist soil and the timber smell of a nearby log that had been cut up. Simple things that had been left unappreciated during her drinking years.

Thank God. Thank God she'd messaged Rachel.

She sat on a bench and studied the ground. A worm slunk past. A beetle shinier than patent leather tottered under the bench. Over the last years at Foxglove Farm, Emma had become so disconnected from nature, always looking to some imaginary future and never appreciating what was around her. Like the majestic weeping willow. The cacophony of croaks from the pond during mating season. The rich aroma of overripe tomatoes. The thud of goats' hooves as they played around. Little luxuries compared to life on the streets.

She bent down and picked a dandelion, and watched seeds drift through the air as she blew on its head. A young mother pushed her little girl on a swing. Every time she stopped and suggested it was time to go home for a bath, her daughter protested loudly, shouting, 'Again, again!' and giggling. Emma studied the cute pigtails and bright yellow wellington boots. The mother kissed the top of her head and they held hands tightly when they eventually left the play area.

It was scary how close Emma had come to betraying the memory of her own daughter. She felt sick at the thought of how just a few moments of madness could have undone months of hard work. Getting through those cravings, giving the wine away… that had made her feel so strong. Staying well meant that Josephine was still with her.

The GP had signed Emma off work for another two months. That took her to the beginning of June – almost one year exactly after she'd first approached addiction services.

It was fate, she decided. To celebrate that landmark, she'd take the next step forward. Nothing was going to make her slip back into old behaviours. When this last sick note ran out, it would be time to return to Foxglove Farm.

Chapter 21

After her talk – or was it an argument? – with Andrea, Emma headed back to the pet shop. She changed the hamsters' water, then took one out and stroked it for a few moments. Only two were left. Phil had actually sold three over the last couple of weeks. After replenishing their food bowl, she made herself a cup of tea and took it up to her room. Her bedside drawer was open, and as she went to shut it, she noticed an envelope stuffed underneath some socks. She took it out. It was the letter she'd sent to Andrea. The one her sister had returned without opening.

She reread it a few times. It had to be worth a last shot. The old Emma would have given up and sought refuge in a bottle. But things had changed. *She* had changed. She opened the drawer below and fished out a notebook and pen. She and Andrea didn't seem to be able to have a conversation. Her last hope was the written word. Her chest ached. Andrea felt so bad about the pregnancy. Emma hadn't wanted that.

She started to write, occasionally referring back to the original letter. Finally it was ready.

> *Dear Andrea,*
> *I know you didn't open the last one, but I really hope you read this. I know I've used up a million second chances. But hopefully by now you've seen*

that I'm sober. I miss you, Andrea. I want to help around the farm. I want to shoulder my share of the responsibilities that I dumped on you.

I am so sorry. For everything. All the trouble I caused. The money you had to spend, to bail me out of trouble. The names I called you. The lying. The stealing. Me and my problems taking up so much of your time. That thing with Dean...

You had every right to be angry. Looking back, I'm surprised you put up with me for so long. We're sisters, but that doesn't entitle me to your unconditional love, and I think – I know – I took you and Mum, Bligh, my home at Foxglove Farm for granted.

In the last letter, I wrote about how we were close and I lingered on happy memories from the past, but this time I'm focused on the now, on going forward. And I can still see what a wonderful person you are.

You'd have made a brilliant aunt. I know that. My big sister would have set a great example. I couldn't tell you about the pregnancy at the time: we weren't in touch and I was trying to stop drinking, trying to stop myself from ever hurting you or anyone else I loved again. But I wished I could have spoken to you. I still wonder if Josephine (that's what I called the baby) would have had your size sevens or my size fours. She'd have been very lucky to have you in her life. I reckon she would have loved Foxglove Farm.

That person – the drunk – it was me and it wasn't. I was ill.

> *At the same time, that's no excuse. I take responsibility for my actions and I am trying to make amends to people in the village.*
>
> *Please, Andrea, please don't ever blame yourself for what's happened. I've so much respect for the way you've coped — you've held everything together. Mum couldn't have managed without you.*
>
> *Again, I'm really, really sorry and will do whatever it takes to make things up to you both.*
>
> *Just tell me what I can do.*
>
> *With love,*
>
> *Emma X*

She slipped the piece of notepaper into an envelope, sealed it and wished it luck. Then she grabbed her rucksack. Clouds had come in, and for the first time in days, a shower threatened, so she packed her waterproof jacket and umbrella. She'd go back to Foxglove Farm and give Andrea the envelope, and then she needed to speak to Bligh.

All the way up Broadgrass Hill she thought about him, not noticing the spits of rain. How he'd marched around to the Badger Inn this morning and told Joe to get lost. He'd had no right to do that, yet part of her could harldy believe that he was still trying to protect her despite everything.

When she arrived at the farm, Gail was in the shop with Andrea. Dash barked his welcome and ran over. Emma knelt down and ruffled his neck. His fur was as wet as her hair.

Rather than hand the letter over and risk immediate rejection, she went into the farmhouse and up to Andrea's bedroom. She took the letter out of her dripping rucksack and stared at it for a few moments. Then she bent down and slipped it under the closed door.

Back downstairs, she heard a tap running in the kitchen. She walked through the lounge and around the corner to see Bligh washing his hands. He wore a short-sleeved checked T-shirt and tight navy jeans. He looked striking with his mariner's beard. He'd make a great partner for somebody – somebody else.

He glanced at her, then jerked his head towards a drawer. 'Could you pass me a tea towel – the other one is wet.'

She placed her rucksack on one of the kitchen chairs. 'Bligh… can we have a chat?'

He emptied the washing-up bowl and dried his hands. 'I've come in for lunch anyway.' He looked at his watch. 'We've got a while before the gas man calls.'

'Gas man?'

'The boiler's playing up again. I don't think it will be too long before we need that new one. Would you like a coffee?'

She shook her head, and drops of water flicked onto her cheeks. She took the tea towel and headed into the lounge, drying her hair. A few moments later, Bligh joined her. They both sat on the sofa. He put his drink on the coffee table. She stared at the watercolour of forget-me-nots and told Bligh that he shouldn't have visited Joe that morning. He turned red and asked if they were a couple.

'No. Joe's gay.'

Those words would have choked her while she was on the streets. Like the idea that she was just an ordinary person rather than a celebrity in the making. The drink had encouraged her ego to see the world as she wanted, not as it was.

Bligh's eyes widened. 'Gay? But… the pregnancy? How…?'

Emma did her best to explain. Life on the streets was chaotic.

'I'm my own person now, Bligh. I can sort out my own mess.'

'You can't, Emmie.'

She took a sharp intake of breath. He'd not called her that for so long.

'You never could manage,' he continued. 'You need me perhaps more than ever now. Look… you and me… we've a long way to go, but I reckon it could still work out. I'll help you move back. I'll talk to Andrea. Now that you're not drinking, we could go back to how things used to be.'

He wanted them to get back together? Emma sat dazed.

A few weeks ago, she'd have given anything to hear him call her by that pet name, but now it just represented the person she used to be. Bligh couldn't see that she'd changed.

'The thing is, Bligh, I'm not that person you knew before – not the drinking one, nor the girl you grew up with,' she said gently. 'It wasn't just the drink that was to blame for my flaws.'

He scratched his beard. 'I don't understand.'

She reminded him of their childhood. How sulky she'd get if they raced home from school and Bligh won. Eventually he always let her win because she became so stroppy. And how he'd do her homework for her because she wasn't good at maths. She was manipulating their friendship before she even discovered alcohol.

Bligh's brow furrowed. 'But we had fun, didn't we? You were a good friend. You shared treats. Visited me when I was off school ill. You thumped John Barton for calling me names when I wore braces.'

'But it wasn't an equal relationship. Not really. I took more than I gave. You must have felt that.'

He glanced away.

'The signs were always there indicating that one day I'd drink to cope with my character defects. I was broken, you know, at the end of my drinking – in pieces on the floor. Rehab helped me put those pieces back together, but in a different way.'

Bligh placed his hands on her shoulders. Told her to stop making things complicated. Yes, he admitted, it was a shock when she'd come back – he'd told himself that he never wanted to see her again. But now he wanted to give their relationship another go.

'Bligh. No.'

'But I still love you.' Apparently he'd never stopped. He had denied it for months. He explained how he'd hated himself for it after everything Emma had done. Yet for weeks and weeks, every time the phone rang he'd hoped it was her. 'We worked together, didn't we? In the old days.'

'No, we didn't. It was all about me falling apart and you trying to glue me back together.'

'And if I don't need to do that now, doesn't that simply mean things will be even better?' His hands dropped as she twisted her shoulders.

'So you'd feel exactly the same about me if I wasn't as needy?' Her voice softened. 'Wasn't that part of the attraction, Bligh? Be honest. Maybe our relationship was also connected to your self-esteem.'

His body stiffened.

'You always had to dig me out of a problem and – for a short while, at least – I'd be so grateful. Since I've got better, done volunteering, helped others, I get it – I understand how good that feels. But where do we go from here if I no longer need your help?'

'So now you're saying I'm some sort of misogynist who only wants a damsel in distress?'

'Of course not, but I know it hit you hard, your mum leaving. It's bound to have had an effect. You did everything for me, Bligh. Maybe it was because you were scared that I'd leave you too.'

He stared at the floor.

'My father going made me feel something was missing. You and I – we have a lot in common. We just dealt with our low self-esteem in different ways. I sought attention, whereas you gave it.'

He exhaled slowly. 'Or perhaps what all this boils down to is what I said before – you used me. On your part, it was never love.' To her surprise, his eyes welled up.

'Look at me.' She took his hand. 'Getting better – getting to know myself and coming back to Foxglove Farm – I've come to realise that I think you're right. I'm so sorry. I did my best. I thought I loved you, but I didn't.'

She'd only seen him cry once before, and that was when his dad was diagnosed with cancer. Poor, caring Bligh. How he must miss having his father to look after.

'Part of me did wonder if you and I would make up, but there's been Joe… the baby… My life's moved on in all sorts of ways since I left. We could never get back together. I can look after myself now. I want to. I need to, to stay well.' She needed to carry on being independent. She needed that self-respect. 'You know that quote Gail always used to laugh about, to do with Eric Morecambe playing the piano? How he was playing all the right notes but just not in the right order? Finally I've got things in order and found my priorities. But Bligh… you're still reading the old, muddled sheet music.'

He pulled his hand away.

'The drink just magnified what had already been going on in my head for years. Stopping drinking isn't enough. I have to work on how and what I think about everything and everyone – including you.'

He stood up. 'Analyse it as much as you want. The biggest surprise to me is that I think I preferred you drunk.'

Chapter 22

Bligh kept out of Emma's way for the rest of the day. She cleaned out the pigsty while Gail watched. Andrea didn't say a word as she ate her lunch and then returned to the shop. For the first time since coming back, Emma couldn't wait to leave the farm when early evening finally arrived. Birdsong accompanied her as she headed towards the village. She went into the pet shop. Phil was on the phone talking to someone about looking after their gerbils during the summer. She hurried up to her room and threw her rucksack down on the floor. It fell at an awkward angle, and where one side of the top hadn't fastened properly, an envelope jutted out.

Her pulse raced. Could Andrea have responded already to her letter? She knelt down and quickly undid the buckle and lifted back the top… It was the envelope she'd slipped under her sister's bedroom door – still unopened.

She got up and sat on the side of her bed. Her phone bleeped, but she ignored it. She lay down and stared at the ceiling. She used to spend hours like this in the squat, watching spiders make homes over nicotine stains.

Eventually she closed her eyes. Took stock of her return to Foxglove Farm. Her fantasy of slotting back into her old life was well and truly over.

Andrea's words, *the way you left*, echoed in her mind: her sister believed that the estrangement could not be sorted out. Emma would never forget her return to Foxglove Farm that fateful Christmas Eve; how she'd cleaned the blood off the car and then quietly opened the kitchen door…

She'd stopped dead and stared at Andrea and Bligh, sitting at the pine table, phones in their hands. Mum had been leaning against the kitchen unit.

'Where have you been?' she'd said. 'I hardly slept last night. You've done disappearing acts for twenty-four hours before, but two days? And with the car? Bligh told us you weren't in a fit state to drive. I've been worried sick.'

Emma had started rambling about shopping and wandering around the Christmas markets, but before she could finish, Gail had cut in.

'You always talk too much when confronted about your behaviour. Well, there's no wriggling out of this one. If you've been shopping, where are your bags? I'm not stupid, Emma. Even with my memory the way it is, it's obvious you've been out drinking.' She'd shaken her head. 'In any event, Bligh has the proof on… on that…'

Apparently Bligh had set up an Instagram account to keep track of Emma's antics.

'I don't understand. Why can't we just have a nice Christmas Eve?' Gail had busied herself with the kettle, which stood next to two jars with Post-it notes on them saying *Tea* and *Coffee*.

'How could you?' Andrea had whispered. 'You know she's not well.'

'She's fine. Stop treating her like a baby. Give her a party hat and a slice of Christmas pudding and she'll soon forget I've been out past my bedtime.' Emma burped.

'How dare you speak about her in that way? Who are you these days?'

'Who were those people in that hotel bedroom?' Bligh said, looking at his phone.

Emma wriggled out of her coat and let it drop to the floor.

'What the… where did that bloodstain come from?' Bligh took her elbow and led her into the lounge, where she collapsed onto the sofa.

Andrea had followed them in, and Emma explained that she wasn't injured. More details had come back to her as she'd driven home. The lecherous old guy in the video was one of her former lecturers from sixth-form college. That was why she'd thought she knew him. He was also a regular at the hotel and had smoothed things over with management before he left. Those young women must have been students. She was half tempted to report him.

Bligh asked who'd paid for the room. Slowly – very slowly – it came out how she'd *borrowed* his bank cards from his wallet. He pulled receipts out of her bag and looked at the amounts.

'Christ almighty.' He'd glanced at Andrea. 'All in all over two and a half thousand quid.' His head had snapped back to Emma. 'This is some kind of joke, right? Unless you're now doing drugs. How else is it possible to spend that much in two days?' He'd thrown the bag down on the floor as hard as he could. Explained how he'd saved that money to send his dad over to Germany. His dad had been researching a ground-breaking cure for his type of cancer and had found an expert offering treatment in Munich. He and Bligh had just about raised enough. Bligh was going to book the flight and hotel after Christmas. His dad only had six months left.

Bligh rarely got angry, but now he punched the wall. Emma had tried to approach him, but he'd backed away, shaking his grazed and bleeding knuckles. 'This is my dad's life we're talking about,' he'd shouted. 'You've taken away his last chance of survival for the sake of a good time. You should be up in court.'

She'd slurred her response. 'Please, Bligh, I'm sorry, I—'

'Have you any idea how long it took me to save that money?' he'd said. 'Weren't you curious as to why I sold my motorbike last month and started taking on odd jobs in the village during my spare time? No, of course you weren't, because you're incapable of thinking about anyone but yourself. Well, that's it. No more. You and me are over. I'm done. You've cheated on me. Lied. And now this – I can't take it any more.'

'But Bligh… listen…'

'You heard him,' Andrea had said, the pitch of her voice increasing. 'Just when I thought your behaviour couldn't get worse… this is the final straw. We've all had enough. As far as I'm concerned, you're no sister of mine. Get out now, or I'll call the police.'

Emma had wiped her eyes and become defiant. She'd charged upstairs and stuffed random clothes into a ruck-sack. Frantically she'd searched her usual hiding places, hoping to find some drink. Eventually she discovered a half-drunk bottle of vodka on top of her wardrobe – and next to it the pub's charity box. She must have stolen it during a blackout. She didn't remember. She shoved the charity box into her rucksack and went downstairs, pulling on her coat.

Ego bolstered by the vodka, she'd yanked open the kitchen door and glared at Mum. 'Andrea's always been

238

your favourite,' she'd said bitterly, before stumbling out into the courtyard.

'And don't come back,' Andrea had yelled as she walked unsteadily away…

Emma's stomach twisted now at the memories. She had stolen Bligh's money. Stolen the pub's collection which was for his dad as well. She'd discovered that later when she'd bothered reading a label on the box. Emma had stolen his dad's last chance of salvation. She got up and rummaged in her bedside drawer. She found her one-year sobriety coin and held it tight in her palm. *Thank you, thank you for my new life. The old one was a living hell.*

'Stig is here!' shouted Phil up the stairs.

Of course. The soup run. Emma had completely forgotten. She hadn't even made any sandwiches. It had felt like a long Friday, what with making things up with Joe and talking to Andrea and Bligh.

'I suppose you could prepare some basic food here,' said Phil gruffly when she came down and explained. She gave some cash to Stig, who charged off to the supermarket and came back with cling film, bread and ham.

'What's up?' he said as they buttered bread. After making them all a cup of tea, Phil had gone back to the shop to answer the phone. The animal boarding idea was really taking off. 'You seemed in such a good mood at lunchtime when we went to the stream with Joe.'

Emma grimaced. 'Not much to tell, apart from the fact that Andrea and Bligh both hate me more than ever.'

'C'mon, I'm sure that's not true.'

'You'd better believe it.' Emma proceeded to tell him about everything that had happened. 'They just can't see that I've truly changed, Stig. I've given them time, but it's

239

never going to happen. I… I don't blame them, but it's so frustrating.'

'You've still only been back a few weeks.'

'I know. I keep telling myself that. So, I've come to some decisions.'

'Are you leaving?'

Emma hoped not. She'd see when she spoke to the police about Ned.

'For the moment I'm going to continue living at Phil's and carry on helping out at the farm and with Mum.' Her shoulders dipped. 'But I have to change my goals. Making amends isn't all about getting forgiveness. I don't think I fully took that on board before.'

Stig put down his knife and squeezed her arm. 'I saw a meme on Facebook once, back in the day. It said that wisdom always comes at a price.'

Emma sighed. 'Very true. This last year I've learnt so much about the way the mind works. I've also learnt to accept things I can't change, and this is one of them. Things will never go back to how they were. I have to let go of the past. And I think that's Bligh's problem – he can't. He wants to return to how we were.'

'You're right, I think there is this expectation with forgiveness that things will go back to exactly how they used to be. With Olly, the kid from school, I soon realised that that was unrealistic. He was polite and still contributed well to the class. But he never joked around with me any more or asked for my help after lessons.' Stig looked at the kitchen clock. 'Come on. Let's finish up and go do our good deed for the day.'

Emma stared out of the kitchen window. Blue tits hopped around. She would put out the crusts before heading off.

'Just look at your life now – you're seeing your family, helping people like me, still not drinking. You've got new friends, and you've made things up with Joe. I'd say all of that was pretty great, wouldn't you?' said Stig gently.

'You're right. Compared to where I was last year it's… excuse my language, but it's a fucking miracle.'

–

Later that night, Emma strolled back to the pet shop with Phil. He'd come up to the station again, this time with some tins of dog food. Almost ten rough sleepers had turned up. The bakery's spare jam doughnuts had been a big hit. Stig had gone up to the farm. He'd decided Emma was right. He should accept Andrea's offer of sleeping in the barn for one night.

Emma didn't feel like chatting and went straight to her room. Her bedside drawer was jutting out. The envelopes from Gail's chest were visible on the left. She got changed into her pyjamas, cleaned her teeth and made herself comfortable on the bed. Perhaps it was time to look at her mum's letters.

She sifted through them, looking at the postmark dates, and decided to start with the earliest, sent eighteen years ago. It was the only one that had been opened. For the first time, she noticed that the postmarks and stamps were foreign. The envelopes dated longest ago had been sent to their old address in London. The rest had been forwarded to Foxglove Farm from there.

She was just about to pull out the envelope's contents when she hesitated. Having Alzheimer's didn't mean Gail had relinquished her right to privacy. Yet what if these were simply from a close friend she had lost touch with? Wouldn't they want to know if she was ill?

'I'll just look at one,' she told herself, knowing that thoughts of Andrea and Bligh would, in any event, keep her from sleep. She pulled out a card. A note fell onto the bed sheets.

Chapter 23

Emma picked up the note.

> Gail,
>
> Once again, I'm so sorry. I miss you and the girls but understand why we can no longer live together.
>
> I have no right to ask, but I'd be so very grateful if you would show this card to little Emma when she is old enough to read.
>
> Sorry again. I hope one day you can forgive me.
>
> Jean-Claude

Emma sat bolt upright and studied the postmarks again. The colours of the room spun as if she were living in the centre of a kaleidoscope. The printed postmark writing on the front of the envelopes was in French. Why hadn't she noticed?

Her father had sent this.

But how was that possible? Mum never kept secrets from Emma. Emma never kept secrets from Mum. It was a pact Gail had made with both of her daughters.

Had it meant nothing?

She picked up the card. A large number 1 decorated the front. She opened it up.

Dear Emma,

> *Happy first birthday.*
> *I think of you often.*

Papa

But he'd dumped her, not cared, abandoned her a matter of months after she was born...

With shaking hands she picked up an envelope dated a few years later. This time there was no note to Gail.

> *My darling Emma,*
>
> *So now you are seven. I hope you are behaving well for your mother. I'm sure you are — you were always a content baby. From the short time we were together, I remember you didn't ask for much. Just a funny face would make you laugh. A big bottle of milk meant you slept through the night.*
>
> *The unusual colour of your eyes, green speckled with chocolate brown, is etched in my memory. That and your button nose come from my grandmother.*
>
> *Happy birthday.*

Papa

Feeling sick, Emma opened the one from her thirteenth year.

> *Dearest Emma,*
>
> *Enjoy teenagehood. It might be scary at times, but your mum will give you good advice, of that I am sure.*
>
> *I don't know if she is giving you these cards. If she is, I just want you to know I still think of you*

*every morning when I get up. I have not forgotten
you. Never will.*

*If she's isn't, I hope some day you get to read
this. Don't blame her. I used to be a difficult person
to live with.*

Happy birthday.

Papa

Emma stared at her bed sheets. All this time, she'd thought
she'd meant nothing to him. All that time, before treatment, she'd never felt good enough.

How could Gail not have not passed on these letters?
How could she have let Emma believe her father had
thrown her away like a dirty tissue? That there must
have been something wrong with her? That she wasn't
as worthy of fatherly love as Andrea or other children?

And yet… poor Mum. Things must have been so bad
for him to leave. What had he done? And these were just
words – he'd never actually bothered to come and visit his
daughter.

She pushed the envelopes away. Gail had provided
more than enough love. She didn't need a long-distance
father.

And yet… if Gail had given Emma these cards years
ago, she might have felt better about herself and been in
a good job now, or married with kids.

She closed her eyes, breathed deeply and tried to take
control of her indignant thoughts. Yet they continued to
buzz through her mind as if it housed a disturbed bees'
nest. All the questions friends had asked her at primary
school about her absent dad – with this contact at least she
could have talked about him living in France and sending
her cards.

An intensely hot sensation gushed into her chest and her face screwed up as she skipped ahead to the last card. Inside this one was a letter – addressed to Emma *and* Gail.

Emma – I feel I should explain why I left and why I have never come back to England. When I knew your mother, I had a lot of… anger problems. I wasn't a well man. My own childhood had been difficult. My father treated me and my siblings badly. Yet that is no excuse for the way I treated Gail. If things didn't go my way, I am ashamed to say I coped by using my fists. I feel you need to know this so that you understand why your mother sent me away. I hit her, you see, and… I even hit Andrea once. On that occasion Gail said if I didn't move out of your lives immediately, she would call the police.

I was a coward – instead of taking my punishment; instead of getting help and trying to work things out, I took the first plane to Paris. But I never got over losing you, Emma. Not seeing you grow up eventually pushed me to get help.

Gail – I loved you. You deserved better. I hope you are happy now.

After treatment I met a kind woman – Michelle – and we have a son. He knows about you, Emma. Like me, one day he hopes you will get in touch.

As always, I have put my address above, but no pressure. The most important thing is that you do what is best for yourself.

Happy eighteenth. I have no doubt that, growing up under Gail's care, you have matured into a wonderful woman.

Good luck with your life.
And never forget, the past doesn't have to define
the future.

Papa/Jean-Claude

A solitary tear rolled down Emma's cheek and she sat in silence with her thoughts. Before long, plump globules of bitterness streamed down her face. She threw away the note. It landed on the floor. Eighteen envelopes. That was all she had to show for a father.

As for what he'd done... She'd always known her mum was strong, but this... Her fists curled. And how could he have hit Andrea?

She went downstairs and made a hot chocolate but ended up pouring it down the sink. She switched on the TV but couldn't concentrate on anything. She threw on her anorak and headed outside.

It felt strange not to see Stig and the Duchess asleep on the pavement. She breathed in the cool night air, took it down into her lungs, but it didn't extinguish the anger that had flooded her chest. Anger at Jean-Claude and, even though she tried to fight it, anger rising again at Gail for hiding his contact. She slumped to the ground.

Every year, on Emma's birthday, Mum had received one of these cards but had said nothing. She must have raced to the letter box after the postman visited and dashed upstairs to hide it.

All along, Emma had had a father who'd cared. So, he'd made mistakes... but who hadn't?

Mistakes? He physically abused your mum. And hit your sister.

But why hadn't they ever told her about his violence?

On the one hand, he was even worse than she'd imagined. Not only had he deserted a newborn child and her mother, he was also a wife- and child-beater. Yet the cards suggested he'd turned his life around. He was sorry. Had met another woman. Brought up a son who wanted to meet Emma.

A whole gamut of emotions played her body like an out-of-tune fiddle.

She went back indoors and up to her room. She shoved the envelopes into her rucksack, turned out the light and lay on her front. Perhaps darkness would take the discontent away. Yet hours passed without a minute of sleep. She had so many questions. How had her parents met? When exactly had things started to go wrong? Was the pregnancy planned? Had he been happy when he heard the news? Was Mum worried that Emma would head over to France and leave her if she found out where he was? Or were the memories too raw to talk about, so hiding all contact made things easier?

Eventually she nodded off, eyes red, her last thoughts flirting with the idea that maybe it wouldn't hurt to have a small drink tomorrow. That maybe she deserved one. Just for the shock.

Chapter 24

Emma left the pet shop early the next day. On her way up Broadgrass Hill, she didn't admire the cerulean sky. The morning chorus annoyed her, and she pulled a face at the pungent smell of manure. With irritation she batted away an errant bumblebee. As she walked up the drive to the farm, she kicked a lump of apple no doubt dropped by a bird. She headed straight past Stig with the merest nod of greeting, and set about cleaning the outside of the greenhouse.

Andrea and Bligh went about their business without talking to her, and for once she was glad. After a couple of hours, Stig brought her a cup of tea, and she grunted her thanks before returning to the job in hand. After she'd finished and had a wash, Andrea asked if she could look after Gail for a few hours. She and Bligh had some work to do on the farm's website – something about a glitch with the payment system. Emma gave an abrupt up and down of her head.

Baking always made things better, so she decided she and Gail would make cookies. She started off creaming the sugar and butter and then let Gail take over when the mixture felt light. Humming, her mum didn't seem aware of her daughter's silence. Andrea, however, left the dining room and came into the kitchen with a quizzical look on her face.

'You know Mum needs the stimulation of conversation.'

'I'm just tired,' said Emma. 'She seems happy enough.'

Andrea raised a disapproving eyebrow and disappeared.

Why not find something I'm doing right, for a change? thought Emma. Her insides twisted as she wondered if her sister had replaced the sherry under the sink. It wouldn't hurt to look. It didn't mean anything. Cautiously she opened the cupboard as if expecting a jack-in-the-box to spring out.

'Lost something?' said Bligh. He stood in the doorway, arms folded.

'Just looking for a new washing-up sponge,' Emma replied. Mentally she told him to fuck right off. Perhaps he heard, because he headed straight back into the dining room.

Come on, Emma. Get a grip. Andrea and Bligh's voices could be heard talking urgently. The words *relapse* and *sherry* wafted through to the kitchen.

Let them think the worst, she thought, and pulled off her apron. 'I can't do this today,' she called. 'I need some fresh air. You'll have to look after Mum.'

Without waiting for a reply, she hurried out of the back door. Dash barked as she appeared in the yard. She and the dog crossed to the greenhouse and Emma shut the door behind them. Dash lay on the ground and she sat cross-legged next to him. The beefy aroma of overripe tomatoes filled the air. Emma bowed her head. Took a deep breath. Did what she hadn't had to do for months and sat through the cravings. She tuned herself into the present and focused on the sounds around her. The squawk of a crow. Dash's snuffly nose. The distant rumble of the motorway. A sheep's baa. The hard ground felt familiar. She wondered who had claimed her patch outside Primark.

She stroked Dash's back and looked up as the door opened. Andrea came in and actually made eye contact. She sat down opposite. Emma felt as if they were children again.

'What's going on?' she said.

'Just a bad day. Sorry about before.'

'Are you drinking again?'

'No.'

Andrea pursed her lips. 'I knew this new version of you wouldn't last.'

It took all of Emma's strength not to snap.

'I've just had a shock, that's all.'

'Has Mum upset you? You've hardly spoken to her this morning. I know it's hard, but she is ill. We have to make allowances.'

Emma clenched her teeth.

'You've looked after her for a few weeks – imagine the patience I've needed for a couple of years. But she's our mother. She changed our nappies, listened to our problems and tended to our physical and emotional wounds for years. The least we can do is keep her happy until… until a more intensive kind of care is required.' Andrea sighed and got up to leave, but Emma pulled her back down.

'Did you know? About those envelopes in Mum's chest?'

'What?'

'I was going to ask you before opening them, but… they were from my father. Every birthday for eighteen years he sent me a card. Mum never passed them on. How could she deny me that contact?'

'Your dad?' Andrea frowned. 'What are you talking about?'

'I found a bunch of cards hidden in Mum's chest. In them he explains everything – the reason he left, the violence. Did you know? Did you? Why wasn't I told?'

Andrea's face flushed and without thinking her hand brushed her top lip.

'That scar…' Emma stared at it. 'Did he do that?'

Her hand dropped. 'Look, it was all a long time ago, there's no point in—'

Emma gasped.

'We never wanted to tell you – figured it was bad enough him leaving without you knowing the sordid details.' Andrea picked up a squashed tomato and brushed a finger over a patch of intact red skin. 'He slapped me across the face. His ring cut my mouth.'

'Oh, Andrea.'

'I don't remember much else. Mum told me little things over the years.' Andrea went on to explain how Jean-Claude had become increasingly controlling about what Gail wore and her choice of friends. How the violence had started slowly. A tap on the arm. An over-enthusiastic ruffle of her hair. The first time he really hurt her was a punch to her stomach. Mum was so shocked and he was so apologetic, she gave him another chance. Over time, she started to believe him when he told her it was her fault – that she made him do it. But apparently he hit Andrea because she wouldn't stop laughing over a joke. When he said the little girl had pushed him to lash out, Gail realised his standpoint had no logic – and that a baby screaming for a feed might be his next target.

'But didn't I still have a right to know he wanted to get in touch – whether I acted on that information or not?' said Emma eventually.

'Mum never got rid of those cards – perhaps she left them for you to find one day.'

'But I don't need them *now*. I needed them when I was a little girl, feeling I was less valuable than every other child.'

Andrea got to her feet again. 'No one has a perfect life, Emma. And I'm genuinely sorry about your dad, but mine actually died. There's no hope of me ever seeing him again – at least you have that chance if you want it.'

'I… I know, and I'm sorry, I didn't mean—'

'In any case, you had me and Mum. Bligh adored you. Mum worked bloody hard to give us a great childhood – and now she needs us to take care of her. Surely you aren't going to hold this against her?'

Emma scrambled to her feet as well. She threw her arms in the air. 'Since I opened those envelopes last night, I just feel so betrayed. I can't help it. Mum must have known how badly I needed the validation of knowing I had a father who cared, or at least acknowledged my existence. And all these years she's been carrying this secret.'

'Then now you know how Bligh and I feel,' Andrea said in a measured voice. 'Forgiving isn't so easy, is it? You've waltzed back into our lives expecting us to say that we understand. That we'll forget what happened in the past. Now you know what it feels like to be hurt irrevocably by someone you love. How difficult it is to understand how they could do that.'

Emma didn't blink. Hardly breathed. Stood completely still.

Her sister was right.

The lack of eye contact from Andrea, the rage simmering still in Bligh, the perpetual distance of some people in the village, all despite Emma's new outlook and lifestyle…

Finally she understood.

Chapter 25

A week later, Emma had upped her daily readings and meditation and fitted in two meetings. Yet she'd started to isolate. Hardly chatted to Stig. Avoided eating with Phil.

She had spent so many years hating her dad, and now she felt confused. She almost said no when Rachel texted her early on Saturday asking if she wanted to meet in Manchester for afternoon tea. But she could tell her friend needed to talk, and so reluctantly she agreed, though not before checking with Andrea, half hoping there would be some urgent job that needed doing on the farm.

'We can manage,' said Andrea, and gave her a curious look. 'Polly's coming over to spend some time with Mum.'

So at three o'clock, Emma and Rachel met in the popular Northern Quarter. They chose an unobtrusive café famous for its old-school decor. The furniture was worn, with holes in the upholstery and scratches on the tables. The staff wore uniforms and wrote down orders using pens rather than digital keypads. The smell of toasted teacakes hung in the air. Couples flirtatiously shared cake and children slurped from straws. Delicate floral crockery enhanced the vintage feel.

'Just look at the size of these teacups,' said Rachel. 'My gran has some like this. They provide only a mouthful compared to a Starbucks grande.'

A young waitress arrived with a three-tiered silver cake stand loaded with crustless ham and cheese finger sandwiches, scones bursting with cherries and an array of sponges.

'Well that's today's healthy eating out the window,' said Rachel, and grinned.

'You look really great. You put me to shame with your jogging.'

'It's more like fast walking at the moment.'

Emma managed a smile.

'After you.' Rachel jerked her head towards the food.

'I'm not really hungry,' said Emma. Reluctantly she took a cheese sandwich.

'Everything okay?'

'My appetite's just off. So, why did you want to meet up? It's lovely to see you, of course, but I sense there's a reason.'

'Nothing gets past you. It's this coming Monday... I'm a bit – read that as *a lot* – nervous.'

'Starting a new job is massive. I think it's brilliant you taking a pay cut to do something so worthwhile. Don't a lot of people drop out of the course?'

'Yes. It's certainly been challenging. I've studied motivational interviewing, restorative practice, boundaries and safeguarding, and I'm a walking dictionary when it comes to drugs...' Eyes shining, Rachel carried on talking for a few moments.

'So what's the problem?' said Emma, her eyes convincing her stomach that she wanted one of the plump scones. Against Cornish rules, she slathered it with clotted cream first and jam second.

'What if I'm rubbish? Web design's my thing. What if I can't be tough or kind enough? What if the people I deal with don't get any better? What if they relapse? I'll feel guilty. I messed up my degree – what if I mess this up?'

'Whoa! What if? What if? Hold on there. Talk about negative thinking. And you were drinking at university – you're sober now.'

Rachel looked sheepish. 'I know. I keep telling myself that I wouldn't have qualified if I wasn't up to the job.'

'And you don't need a qualification to prove you can do it,' said Emma. 'The way you've helped me says it all. Remember in the early days, whenever I thought about picking up, you weren't afraid to remind me that I'd be letting Josephine down?'

Her stomach clenched. This last week she hadn't thought much about her daughter.

'Then that weird week of nightmares I had. Dreams about running after Andrea and Mum and never being able to catch them up? You insisted on sleeping in my room, and when I woke up in the night, you were there with your kettle.' Emma smiled. 'You'll be perfect. Honestly. You know when to be kind and when to be firm. Anyone would be lucky to have you help them turn their life around.'

Rachel straightened up. 'You really think I can do it?'

'One hundred per cent,' said Emma in between crumbling mouthfuls of scone. 'And as for feeling guilty if others fail, remember what we've learnt – nothing and no one is to blame for someone's behaviour apart from themselves.'

Heat swept up Emma's neck as she recalled the past seven days of secretly blaming Gail for the way her life had developed. Poor Gail, who'd been stuck in an abusive relationship yet found her way out.

Rachel's face lit up, and she bit into a slice of chocolate sponge. 'Thanks. I feel so much better. It's just that when it comes to work, I've stayed in my comfort zone for so long.'

'Nothing can be more uncomfortable than sharing your most private feelings with strangers like we had to – I bet Monday will seem like a doddle.'

'And talking of comfort, how are things at the farm? Are you more at ease there now?'

Emma stared into her cup.

'What's wrong?' Rachel said gently.

Emma hesitated before blurting out the whole story, finishing with, '… and all this time Mum kept his contact from me.'

'You know I can relate to that,' Rachel said. 'All those years Mum refused to even tell me my dad's surname. But we have to remember Step Four and the inventories we drew up. All that letting go of resentments against people. Don't those words actually just mean forgiving them?'

Emma thought for a moment. Yes, that was true. And it was also true that she had expected everyone to let go of their resentments against her, yet when it came to Gail, she was finding it oh so hard.

'How about putting yourself in the other person's position?' said Rachel. 'It can't have been easy for Gail, carrying this secret, but what else could she have done? Did you say your father got help when he returned to France; that losing you finally made him face up to his behaviour?'

Emma nodded.

'Who does that remind you of?'

She thought for a moment. 'I don't know.'

'Yes you do.'

Emma's brow furrowed. 'You mean... me?' Of course. Losing Josephine was what had made her determined to see the treatment through.

'Maybe your mum had no choice. Maybe she knew your dad had to hit his rock bottom before he could change. If he'd stayed, the odds are his violence would have continued. She was protecting you, Emma.'

'But he *has* changed. Don't get me wrong – part of me hates him for what he did to my family, and if he wasn't remorseful, I wouldn't care how many cards he sent. But if his words are to be believed, he's a different man now. God knows I can't judge anyone who has made mistakes and got better.'

'But how was your mum to know for sure? Why would she risk letting an abusive partner back into all your lives again? And weren't your problems starting to get bad by the time you were eighteen? How could she have dropped this bombshell about your dad when you were so out of control?'

Emma stared into her lap. 'But I can't help thinking that if I'd seen those cards, I would never have ended up on the streets.'

'What were we just saying? No one is to blame for their addiction but themselves. Your self-esteem has been okay these last few months, yes?'

'Better than for a long time.'

'Right, but when you found out about these cards, be honest, was your first instinct to use?'

'I... I have had thoughts about drinking.'

'Even though those cards were effectively good news – that your father *did* care about you?'

Emma swallowed as she faced the truth that she'd ignored lately and that had been drilled into them during treatment – people like her were wired to use, whatever happened, good or bad.

'That devious inner voice will search for any reason to get you to pick up.' Rachel drained her cup. 'That's why we can never afford to be off our guard. And we can't mind-read… Who's to say that either of our lives would have been better with our fathers in them?'

Emma nodded. As a child, one reason she'd loved baking was because the cakes made her feel good inside after an argument with a friend or a tough exam at school. Or they seemed like the perfect way to celebrate after a good essay grade or a successful livestock birth. Even back then she was associating a substance with feelings. Whereas now – oh, she still loved baking, but in moderation and along with healthier coping mechanisms like talking to friends and meditation.

Andrea was right. Really, Emma had enjoyed a pretty idyllic childhood. She just couldn't see it at the time.

The conversation moved on to easier subjects, such as the weather and the books they were reading. Rachel mentioned how her mum had recently explained that all those years ago she hadn't simply given her daughter's goldfish away. Apparently it had died, but she hadn't wanted Rachel to be upset so had buried it in the local park and then pretended it had gone to a good home. Emma's shoulders relaxed. For the first time in days, the frantic buzz in her mind eased. Letting go of resentments, not thinking the worst of people, seeing things from their point of view – it was like a magic panacea.

When she came out of the café, she hugged Rachel goodbye. 'Thanks for helping me talk it through.'

'You're doing great,' said Rachel. 'Just keep on going, one day at a time. Forget about the what ifs… there's no point. And thanks again for helping me too.'

Emma stood for a moment, alone in a warm summer shower, and looked up to the sky. Drops of water landed on her cheeks. She closed her eyes and smiled, feeling lighter than she had in days, grateful for a friend to nudge her back onto the right track.

Thankful for rehab. For a roof over her head. For food. A purpose.

For a mother who'd always done her utmost to keep her safe.

The restlessness inside her dissipated and she went back inside the café to buy cherry scones for Stig, Bligh, Andrea and Mum.

On the way back to catch the train, she passed Primark. Outside, on her old patch, a young man sat behind a Starbucks cup. Emma stopped to put in change. He was called Abdul. His cheeks looked concave and spotty, just like Joe's used to. She told him she'd been where he was. Words slurring, he told her he had come out of care a year ago. Couldn't get a job. Emma bought him a sandwich and a latte and placed them on the ground next to him as his eyes closed. Then she delved into her bag, found a tissue and scribbled her case worker's number on it. Before walking up the street to Piccadilly station, she tucked it into his anorak pocket.

Back at Phil's, she wrote Andrea a different kind of letter. It was time to start accepting the new status quo and realising that relationships could not be rekindled exactly as they had been before – that some types of pain were not for healing.

This time she didn't put her letter in an envelope. That way it had to be read.

Dear Andrea,

I just wanted to say, if it's okay with you, that I'm keeping with what I said and will be sticking around for a while. I'll stay at Phil's. He's agreed to reduce the rent if I help him with a new venture. I will carry on with the soup run. But primarily I'm here to support you with Mum and help out on the farm. I'll do my best to work everything else around that — if you'll allow it, despite the pregnancy shock. I'm sorry you're upset.

I'll stop pressing for some sort of reconciliation. I think I understand now why you can't forget everything that has happened. So this is now about us all moving forward, if we can — on your terms.

Attached is a cheque for the boiler. Please take it, if not for you, then for Mum. Winter will be here before you know it and she'll need to keep warm. It's the least I can do.

I've got some ideas for the online shop, if you and Bligh are interested.

I understand why Gail never told me about my dad. It still hurts, the years I missed out on with him, but I love and respect Mum for protecting us. She did what she thought was best. I can see that.

See you tomorrow.

With love,

Emma X

PS You've always been the best sister and daughter.

As Saturday evening drew in, Emma hurried up Broadgrass Hill to the farm. She left the letter in the bag of scones in the kitchen. She grabbed some strawberry leaves for the rabbits and scratched the goats' chins. She surveyed the farm, full of gratitude for the life she was leading now. Under the gaze of Andrea and Polly, she gave Gail a quick hug before walking back down to the village.

Chapter 26

A few weeks later, and Emma's comfortable routine had been restored. Comfortable, that was, despite Bligh's frostiness and Andrea's continuing distance. But that was okay. Emma handed over a cheque for the boiler. It wasn't questioned, so her sister must have read the letter.

Day by day the tender affection she felt for her mum strengthened. She no longer felt anger, just a sense of sadness for what Gail must have endured. Yes, she would always believe that her mum had been wrong. Emma had a right to know that her father hadn't completely abandoned her. But what helped her deal with her sense of indignation was accepting that Gail's intentions had come from the heart. Emma didn't need the explanation she'd now never get from her mother. Every one of her youngest daughter's birthdays must have been so hard for her.

The rooms of AA were full of previously abused partners. Emma knew how difficult it was to prise oneself out of those situations. Gail had succeeded. Emma's sense of affection for her held hands with admiration. Part of Emma's problem in the past had been that she always believed that life could be better elsewhere. A yearning for status and validation had led her away from the things and people that really mattered. Rachel was right – who was to say that getting to know her father would have made her feel whole?

Crops ripened. Their respective pickles and jams stocked the shop. A chill descended into the evenings. Emma swore autumn started in the second half of August now. And with the hint of a change of season, Andrea suggested that Stig and the Duchess move permanently into the barn. She provided him with towels, bedding for an old mattress, Gail's unused alarm clock and a stack of her own favourite novels. Bligh gave him clothes he no longer wore and shared toiletries if he saw a two-for-one offer. Dash slept in the barn too, his new canine friend now owning a slice of the affection he had once felt only for humans.

Emma wondered if her sister realised what a support she'd been to Stig. She never asked questions about his past or future. Her matter-of-fact manner meant there was no embarrassment about money. Stig was more transparent and made it clear how he felt without actually saying it. If he and Andrea shared a joke, the humour would prop up his face for hours. When he sensed she was tired, he always said the same thing, in a jokey tone – 'One lump or two?' – knowing that the reply was neither. Then, after handing her a mug of tea, he'd insist on taking over her task. And she let him. Independent Andrea never did that. Perhaps that was her only tell.

Gail had started to obsess about the summer barbecues she'd once loved. Emma could picture them now. Her mum had become expert at making vegetable burgers, using chickpeas and peppers, with mozzarella running through the middle. She'd provided meat for her daughters and their friends, but it had to be free range, and in her recipe book she listed various marinades. She'd thrown together bowls of colourful salad made with their own fresh produce.

It was strange. As the weeks passed, Emma no longer remembered just the bad times. Like the barbecue when she'd had too much Pimm's and knocked into a trestle table. A large trifle had fallen to the floor, jelly, custard and cream splattering across the concrete, laced with fragments of glass. Mum had been so embarrassed.

Instead her memory's go-to was now happier times, like the year a young Emma and Bligh had been allowed to stay up late and barbecue marshmallows in the dark. They'd snuck around to the bench in front of the weeping willow and contemplated life and its meaning. Bligh insisted aliens lived on the moon and ran life on earth using powerful remote controls. Whereas Emma reckoned its inhabitants were dead spirits and that she would prove this when she and Bligh ended up there one day. Either way, both wanted to visit and swore they'd become astronauts.

Emma suggested they hold a barbecue to see if it spiked her mum's interest. It could take place during the bank holiday weekend right at the end of August.

'Fine, but I've no time to spare,' Andrea said. 'If you're prepared to sort out the food, go ahead – as long as the guest list is short.' She gave Emma a sideways glance. 'And don't include some dramatic invite to your father. For a start, it wouldn't be fair on Mum.'

'You honestly think I'd do that?'

Andrea's cheeks tinged pink but still she persevered. 'Are you going to contact him?'

'I'd be lying if I said it hadn't crossed my mind,' Emma replied. 'But no. Not at the moment. I'm still getting my head around finding those envelopes. This whole thing…

it's huge. Actually, I'm not sure I ever will get in touch. A few cards don't compare to everything Mum's done. And I believe you're right – Mum wanted me to find them when… when she was gone. I'll respect that wish and shelve any decisions about contact until the future. It's not about me at the moment. It's about Mum. Her wishes. Her health. Her happiness.'

Andrea stared as if briefly recognising a person from the distant past that she used to know.

After breakfast one morning, Emma sat down with her mum outside the barn. Gail got tired in the afternoons, so it was better to discuss the arrangements before lunch. As she rocked to and fro in her chair, fiddling with the sewing-themed necklace, she was quite definite about who the guests should be. She swore she'd never liked the vet, even though she knew him well and they used to often meet for a drink. But she insisted on inviting a one-time acquaintance, Joe, otherwise known as *the man who can head-butt.*

The guest list, dictated specifically by Gail, comprised:

- Andrea
- Bligh
- Polly and Alan and thingamabob
- The woman who talks too much
- Pet shop Phil
- The man who smells (Stig) (she no longer thought of him as Uncle Paul)
- The cheese man and his grandkids
- The man who can head-butt

The barbecue would take place on the bank holiday Monday afternoon. The villagers had wanted to hold the inaugural Sunday market the day before, but it was taking longer than anyone had anticipated to get the agreement of the council and trading licenses sorted. Still, the local papers had already featured the story and the delay had given people time to really think through their products.

As for food, Emma took ideas from her mum's old recipe book. Gail flicked through it, smiling now and again. Emma took her cue from the pictures her mum stared at most and concentrated on keeping things simple.

- Chicken breasts with tikka masala marinade
- Pork chops with rosemary and garlic
- Cheese and caramelised onion quiche
- Rice salad
- Potato wedges
- Coleslaw
- White and brown rolls
- Chocolate anything
- (Fish and chips – hopefully Gail would forget about this)

As the days passed, they refined the menu. They decided on chocolate tart and mocha muffins for dessert. Emma was thrilled that Joe would be able to come. In fact everyone on the list could make it apart from *thingamabob*.

Ever since the list had been compiled, Emma had found it increasingly difficult to get Ned out of her head. As her father slowly exited the darkest spot in her mind, Polly and Alan's son crept back in to fill it. At night she started to suffer nightmares like the ones she'd had in rehab. In them she relived the crash – hitting something and not knowing what it was. Except that when she pulled up at Foxglove Farm, on top of the bonnet was a mangled bike and a pile of bloodied newspapers.

Chapter 27

Gail was taking her usual late-afternoon nap. It was a cloudy day but still warm. Emma told Andrea she wouldn't be long. Her sister was cleaning out the chicken coop with the help of Stig. Bligh was on the computer designing labels for the new items they'd sell when the Sunday market was eventually up and running.

He'd done a lot of research and found sites where you could personalise items like cups and tea towels. Already thinking ahead to Christmas, he decided they needed to offer more gift options. So last night he, Andrea and Emma had brainstormed ideas such as reproducing photographs of Foxglove Farm onto a range of products. The name wouldn't be needed – it wasn't a well-known place – but scenic photos might help items sell. Andrea had asked ex-teacher Stig to share his views on what might appeal to younger customers. He came up with pens, notebooks and mouse mats bearing cute or funny photos of the farm's rescued animals.

Andrea's face practically split in two after the work was done and Stig instructed the Duchess to perform her two tricks – holding out her paw for a shake, and a rollover. Emma had forgotten how infectious her sister's laughter was – the way you could hear it rise from her belly and suddenly shoot out.

She set off down Broadgrass Hill. She had been unable to face lunch. Gail had managed a cheese and ham toastie followed by a small slice of the frosted carrot cake that she'd helped Emma make the day before. The recipe had come out of her scrapbook. Emma never tired of flicking through the pages and reminiscing over the meals the three of them used to make together. Vegetable hotpot – that was a favourite of Mum's. Parsnip mash, delicious with double cream and a pinch of nutmeg. And raspberry mousse, refreshing and light. On Sundays they'd really treat themselves, with a roast followed by cinnamon apple crumble.

The recipes she was adding at the back had already filled a lot of the spare pages. Stig had come up with ideas for the soup run, including potato and leek soup and a tomato relish his mum made every Christmas.

The new pages of the book represented the new story of her life.

She approached the village, but instead of continuing ahead, she turned right. The church stood behind the Tudor hall next to the butcher's. It was made up of grey stone, crumbling in parts, with a small spire above the belfry. The tiled roof was covered with intermittent moss. At the front was a clock that bore Roman numerals. The large oak door had two circular black handles. Sunlight illuminated the reds, yellows and purples of stained glass.

The graveyard extended the whole way round and was home to an array of headstones and sculptures. Emma's stomach rolled as she pushed open the little entrance gate. She wondered if Ned's stone carried his full name, and where to find it. But as she turned left and started to cut her way through patches of ragged grass, the answer was suddenly staring her straight in the face.

Polly and Alan were standing next to a white head-stone, accompanied by a big helium balloon bearing the number 18. Emma slipped behind a tall sculpture of an angel, feeling anything but angelic. The couple were smartly dressed, Alan in a suit, Polly wearing a tailored dress. Fresh flowers lay at their feet. They had their arms around each other's waists and were speaking to the stone. After a while, Alan took his phone out and fiddled with it. An Ed Sheeran song started to play, and Polly looked up at him. Emma could make out tears in the landlady's eyes.

She'd heard Polly talk about Ned once when she'd visited Andrea, saying that he was worth ten times the huge amount she and Alan had paid for fertility treatment. Ned must have been about fourteen at the time, and had spent the previous two days looking after Alan, who was ill with a bug, while Polly ran the pub. She'd described how he dashed home from school in his lunch hour and made soup. Then, at the end of the day, he'd read one of Alan's favourite books out loud and kept him supplied with fluids and cold flannels.

Emma looked back at the couple. The music had stopped. They stood wrapped up in each other, swaying gently as if it were still playing. Eventually Alan kissed his hand and placed it on the headstone, while Polly blew a kiss through the air. The balloon ducked backwards as if it had been hit.

She could hold off no longer. Tonight she would talk to Andrea and Bligh, before going to the police.

She slipped away and left the churchyard. The bench outside squeaked as she collapsed onto it. A trail of ants led into a crack in the bottom of the cobbled wall behind her, a kind of regimented form of chaos. Maybe that was what prison was like.

If Ned was alive, Polly and Alan would no doubt have been in the pub today, throwing a huge party for their son's eighteenth birthday. He'd probably have been preparing for university. Perhaps he'd have a girlfriend. Would he have been a doctor? A teacher? An entrepreneur? His parents would never know.

She got up and walked past the side of the church hall, turning right down the village's main street. She passed the butcher's and crossed the road at the Badger Inn. She wanted one last tour of the village to appreciate everything she used to take for granted.

To start with, she just stood outside the pub and breathed in the tobacco smoke from a nearby customer nursing a cigarette and a pint of beer. As a child, she'd had happy times here. The landlords before Polly and Alan had loved children and always put a straw and a cocktail umbrella in her orange juice. One Christmas, there had been a lock-in. She and Andrea had been so excited. The locals had played cards and darts and the landlords had made turkey sandwiches. Emma had felt so grown up drinking her fancy juice as the adults jokingly put fingers to their lips to keep everyone quiet.

She crossed the road and paused by the pet shop. Phil and Sheila had been good employers and given her a Christmas bonus. As her drinking got worse, they'd tried to be lenient when she turned up late or mischarged a customer. She'd loved that job. Often she'd stayed late to play with the hamsters or cuddle a new batch of rabbits. Some things didn't change.

'Coming in?' said a voice behind her.

Emma turned around.

Phil shrugged. 'Thought I'd try my hand at making a lasagne tonight. You can share the inevitable carnage if you want.'

'Tempting as that invitation is, I'll have to decline.'

'There's no pleasing some people,' he said, and they both smiled.

'I'm going for a walk, and then I've just got to pop back to the farm to see Andrea and Bligh.' Her voice thickened.

'Everything okay?'

'Yes. Yes, it's fine. I… I just wanted to say… thanks, Phil – thanks for taking me in. I'm so grateful. I don't know how I'd have managed without a room here.'

'What's brought this on? Had too much sun today?'

How Emma valued the gentle humour that was developing between them. If only she didn't have to leave, just when she was forging a new life in Healdbury.

She made her way down the street, past the estate agent's that used to be a sweet shop. Andrea would always choose toffees, Emma fruit bonbons. Mum gave them extra pocket money if they did one of the messier jobs, like mucking out the pigs. They'd go to the newsagent's and enjoy choosing magazines or new stationery. And then Andrea hit her teens and started to shop with friends instead. She always invited Emma, but it was a kind of unwritten rule that Emma would say no. Andrea would make it up to her by playing a favourite board game when she returned. Or baking together when Emma wasn't quite old enough to work the oven on her own.

'Beginning to take shape, isn't it?' said Ted, nodding towards his shop.

The blackened walls had been scrubbed and the windows cleaned. A joiner's van stood outside, along with an electrician's.

'That Stig's been a godsend. He wouldn't take payment for helping me redecorate upstairs, so I've promised him free cheese for life when we're up and running.'

'You might regret saying that. His dog is especially partial to a slice of Cheddar.'

'No regrets – I can never pay him back enough. Or any of you who got us out that night. When I think about what could have happened...' Ted's hand cupped his bald head. 'And remember, if you need any cheese for your soup run sandwiches, just call on me.'

Emma gave him a thumbs-up and moved on, spending time recalling past visits to the chemist, the hairdresser and the toy shop. Wrapped up in memories, she ended up at Healdbury stream. She took off her trainers and socks and paddled for a while, flexing her toes and inhaling sharply as the cool water washed over the top of her feet. She and Bligh would go there as children with brightly coloured nets to catch tiddlers. Gail always gave them strict instructions to throw back any fish straight away. Often they'd spot a majestic kingfisher, swooping across the water's surface. In the spring, nothing pleased them more than watching a string of baby ducks paddling furiously to keep up with their mother. And in winter, they'd dare each other to stand on the frozen stream's surface. Once it had cracked under Bligh's weight and his right leg got soaked to the knee. Their sides had ached with laughter.

With a heavy heart, she went back through the town and past the supermarket, where Rita used to sit. Emma wondered how she was doing. And Tilly. There was no way of knowing. She'd have to keep her eyes peeled next time she went into the city – whenever that might be.

As she made her way up Broadgrass Hill, she recalled running up there with Bligh after school. In the winter, as a treat on a Friday, they'd stop off at the teashop and walk back sipping takeaway hot chocolates. In the summer, ice creams would be the order of the day, if their pocket money allowed it.

When she walked around Healdbury now, faces and shop windows reminded her of the better times, when Mum was well and she and Andrea were best buddies. She passed the lamp post where Dash most liked to pee and carried on up to the farm.

1 month before going back

It had been a busy day at the charity shop, ending with Emma giving in her notice. She entered the Quaker meeting house. The door creaked its familiar welcome. The floorboards groaned their approval as she walked in. How frightened she'd been of this place the first time she'd turned up. Now it felt like a friend. Somewhere she'd shared the best and the worst of times. A building that kept her secrets.

She turned right and ran her hand along the sage-green wall as she entered the bright room. It was almost eight. Most of her friends here knew she wouldn't be attending meetings so regularly now – she would find somewhere closer to Healdbury – but she would always consider this her home group.

Old Len's face cracked into a smile. Pushing himself up, he got to his feet. They hugged. He adjusted his glasses.

'How are you today?'

'Not bad,' she said.

'You haven't drunk?' he said with a twinkle in his eye.

'No!'

'Then it's a great day, never forget that. And never forget to keep connected to these rooms.'

'You know me – like a bad penny, I keep turning up.' She smiled and gave a thumbs-up, then gazed around the circle of faces, warmth spreading through her chest. She loved how the older members looked after those in new sobriety. Len never failed to remind her to keep doing everything she needed to in order to keep well. One year dry seemed like a long time to her, but to the old-timers she was still in a raw, unpredictable place. She waved at a couple of people and got squashed between several more pairs of arms. She congratulated someone on getting their degree; asked another member if her longed-for divorce had finally been granted.

She helped herself to a cup of coffee from the trolley and took her usual seat next to Rachel. Julie was chosen to chair the meeting. On the hour, she asked for quiet. She asked if there were any newcomers or visitors, and then nodded at Rachel, who read out her favourite inspirational pages from the Big Book. Then Julie proceeded to share her story. About twenty minutes later, she opened the meeting. No one spoke for a few moments.

Emma cleared her throat. 'My name's Emma and I'm an alcoholic.'

'Hi, Emma,' said everyone as they looked at her and smiled.

'I'll keep it short – it's a big meeting tonight. It's just… well… firstly I wanted to express my gratitude. A couple of us are coming up to our first sobriety birthday next month.'

She glanced across the room at Bev, who winked.

Everyone murmured, 'Well done.'

'At one point I never believed that day would come. I thought stopping my bad behaviours was all there was to it, but I soon realised that staying stopped was the real challenge. I detoxed, had my treatment, but knew I would need something else to keep me on the straight and narrow – and that's been this fellowship. I certainly couldn't have done it on my own.

'That's not to say I didn't have my doubts about you all at the beginning. *The first drink's the worst?* What rubbish was that? And when you all said you never had drinking thoughts any more – I *knew* you were downright lying.'

A few people chuckled.

'But here I am, and… a few of you know this, but I'm going home in two weeks, to try and make amends. I'm nervous – a letter of apology I wrote has already been returned unopened – but I'm hoping my family will give me a chance when they see how much I've changed.

'On my way here tonight, I walked past a homeless man. He was out of it, an empty bottle by his side.' She looked at Bev, who nodded encouragingly. 'Some people are lucky and get here before having all the "yets". They haven't lost their partner yet. Their kids yet. Their job yet. I lost everything I had, but it's not the tangible things that unite people like us – it's the feelings we relate to.'

Grunts of agreement.

'Inside I'd hit my rock bottom and was hanging onto my sanity by a fraying rope. A rope I sometimes wished would curl around my neck. The only thing that kept me going was the whoosh of the first mouthful of drink that made me feel invincible.

'Nowadays I don't wake up to the crazy inner narrative. It's a Friday night and I'm glad to be sitting here, amongst you lot, instead of lying comatose on the street. You've all

277

helped me stick to the Twelve-Step Programme… being part of this group has given me continued strength and is one of the reasons I am able to try to put right the wrongs of my past. So thank you. I'll leave it there.'

'Thanks, Emma,' everyone chorused.

'Great share,' Rachel said an hour or so later after the meeting ended. People were clearing mugs and starting to put away the chairs.

'At least my body doesn't shake any more when I speak in front of everyone.'

Rachel hugged her. 'So… you're off soon. Best of luck. Keep me posted.'

Emma nodded.

'And remember – if things don't pan out as you expect…'

'I know. I have to accept the things I can't change.'

'It is the most challenging thing ever, to look back on our behaviour and acknowledge that we can't turn back the clock. I wish I could get back all the times I never gave Mum the benefit of the doubt, so easily casting her as the villain – but I can't.' She rummaged in her jeans pocket and pulled out a shiny gold metal disc. 'I got you a small gift.'

Emma's face flushed as she accepted the one-year sobriety coin.

'It's a little early, so put it away somewhere safe until your date arrives.' Rachel smiled. 'And don't forget what's written on the front.'

Emma didn't need to look. 'To Thine Own Self Be True,' she murmured.

'Yes. We don't need to impress or worry about fitting in any more, do we?'

'No, thank goodness. All I can do is be myself – I hadn't done that for a long time before I finally left Healdbury.'

'Whatever happens back at the farm, keep listening to your conscience that tells you the difference between right and wrong; the good voice you ignored before. As long as you keep that happy, then you'll be all right.'

'Simple, isn't it? But I could never have worked that out for myself.'

'Me neither.' Rachel slipped into her light jacket. 'You're a strong woman, Emma. I know that. Everything will work out. Take care, darling. I'm here for you, no matter what.'

'You too.'

A while back, Emma had told Rachel about the car accident and Ned. Her friend hadn't judged or acted shocked. Instead she'd sat quietly and let Emma talk through her concerns. They'd discussed how she could satisfy that voice of conscience and kept coming back to the same conclusion – she could no longer keep this secret.

Now Rachel looked at her watch. 'Idris will be waiting, and I'd better go or I'll miss Graham Norton on the telly.'

'Living life on the edge, eh?' said Emma, and smiled.

The two women looked at each other, and a lump formed in Emma's throat. Both knew how lucky they were to now be leading lives so ordinary.

Chapter 28

'Andrea? Bligh?' called Emma as she walked into the yard. No one was in the greenhouse. She scoured the animal pens and planted areas and looked in the shop. Stig came out of the barn, water on his face, a towel in his hands.

'Your sister and I have just finished cleaning out the chicken coop. She and Bligh are inside doing a stocktake.' He raised an eyebrow. 'Everything okay?'

'I just need a word with them.' Emma squeezed his arm before pushing open the back door and entering the kitchen. She downed a glass of water, then headed into the lounge, glancing at the forget-me-not watercolour.

Voices came from upstairs. She clasped her hands together and headed up to the bedrooms. Except hers wasn't for sleeping in any more. The door was wide open. Bligh and Andrea were counting jars of jam and pickles. Emma went in. Mum stood looking out of the window, fiddling with bubble wrap in her hands. The other two sat on the floor. It was strewn with paperwork.

Andrea looked up. 'We're in the middle of something.'

Emma sat down on a wooden chair. She looked around, her mind filling in the decor from her teenage years. The Rihanna poster... she used to drive her sister and Mum mad, every time it rained, by singing that 'Umbrella' number. Then there were the scented candles. The broad selection of DVDs.

'I… Could we just… You see…'

'What?' said Andrea, and sighed.

'It about something I did.'

Andrea's brow furrowed and she sat up straight. 'When? What's all this about?'

Emma's heartbeat pounded in her ears. 'I just saw Polly and Alan in the churchyard. They—'

'It's Ned's eighteenth today,' said Andrea. 'I know.'

'He died on the day I left.'

'It wasn't the best Christmas for the village for lots of reason,' said Bligh, and gave Emma a pointed look. He put down his calculator. 'The cold snap turned to torrential rain that week and floods hit the day after Boxing Day. The shops at the base of Healdbury stream were devastated.'

'It was icy that Christmas Eve,' said Emma, quietly. 'I had trouble steering straight.'

'And that had nothing to do with you enjoying too much champagne?' said Bligh, and shook his head. 'We examined the car. We know what you did.'

'You do?'

No. That wasn't possible. Surely they'd never have kept a secret like this?

'One of the headlights was cracked.' Andrea pursed her lips. 'How exactly did you do it? No surprises, you didn't stop.' She shook her head in disgust.

'I… But why haven't you told the police?' Emma's heart pounded louder.

'And spend our valuable time down at the station filling in forms over a scratched parked car they'd probably never find?' Bligh picked up his calculator again. 'Time was – still is – a luxury for us.'

Emma felt sick – with relief or disappointment, she wasn't sure. 'So you think I smashed into another car?'

'What else?' said Bligh. 'A bollard, perhaps? Don't tell us you crashed into a building.'

Andrea glanced at Gail, who was still distracted by the bubble wrap. She turned back to the stock. 'Look, we haven't got time for guessing games. Whatever it is, Emma, can't it wait?'

'No. I'm sorry, but I can't put it off any more. I've been wanting to tell you for ages, and Polly and Alan, but—'

'What have they got to do with it?' asked Andrea.

'It could… It might have been… You see… Oh God – I think I killed Ned.'

Silence hung in the air for a few moments.

'What do you mean?' Bligh looked at Andrea. 'Have you been drinking, because you aren't making any sense?'

'No, I don't drink any more. I've told you that.' Emma fiddled with the hem of her T-shirt. 'I didn't find out until rehab. My friend Rachel mentioned she'd been to Healdbury… the Badger Inn… She told me about Polly and Alan's loss. That morning Ned got hit, I was driving back from Manchester… the hotel…' Her cheeks blazed. 'I was looking at my phone. It was dark. I hit something just outside the Christmas tree farm – where Ned was found. Please believe me, I just didn't see and decided I must have hit… I don't know… a sheep or a deer. When I got back, there was blood on the front of the car and I wiped it off with hay.'

'You didn't stop?' said Andrea. 'Jesus, how much lower could you go?'

'But I never in a million years thought I'd hit a person.'

'So why tell us now?' said Bligh. He and Andrea looked at each other again.

'Because first thing tomorrow I'm going to talk to the police.'

'You're doing *what*?' Andrea's jaw dropped. 'You're confessing? Handing yourself in?'

'A hit-and-run... driving under the influence... manslaughter... you'd be looking at years behind bars,' said Bligh.

'I know. And it twists me up inside. I'm scared, but most of all I'm so sad that I can't stay here long term and help with the farm... help look after Mum.'

'Is that why you've never committed to staying here, every time I mentioned that no doubt you'd soon be moving on?' asked Andrea.

'Yes. I couldn't lie to you. I've stayed as long as I could to help out, but my conscience just won't let me rest any more. It's only fair to Ned – and Polly and Alan. They deserve some sort of closure. When I saw them at Ned's grave today...'

'But prison?' Andrea's eyes widened. 'You'd really take responsibility for your actions, even if that means being locked up? Last time you lived here, you wouldn't even admit to lying or finishing off a bottle of Mum's favourite sherry.'

'I'm going to miss her so much, but I've thought about it a lot. Since coming back, I realise that working with animals is all I want. I'd never get the grades to be a vet, but I'm hoping that I can at least do some reading in prison, or perhaps an online course, to help me eventually train as a veterinary nurse as close to Healdbury as possible – if the village will ever be able to stomach my return.'

'You really have considered what you're about to do...' said Bligh, and his voice petered away.

'I can't ever make up for what I did to your dad, Bligh. But I can do this for Ned and his parents.'

Andrea's shoulders bobbed up and down. 'Why come back to face the consequences? Why not just keep your mouth shut and go on the run?'

'Because I can't run away from *me*,' said Emma quietly. 'That's what the drinking was all about – trying to escape my messed-up thoughts and the problems they created. I don't do that any more. I do what it takes to keep my head straight.' She glanced at Gail. 'If I end up inside, I hope it doesn't have repercussions for you and Mum. I'm so sorry if it does.'

Andrea stood motionless.

'I just want you to know I won't ever come back unless you approve. I've embarrassed and let you down enough. All I ask is that now and again you give me updates on how Mum is. I'll give you the rest of my money from Aunt Thelma. It might help if Mum...' Her voice cracked. 'If she ever has to go into care.'

'Stop right there,' said Andrea. 'There's something you ought to know.'

'You didn't kill Ned,' said Bligh.

'What? But it was a hit-and-run. My whereabouts match the time and place, and—'

'Someone confessed six months later,' he continued. 'Didn't your friend know that?'

Emma stood up and wrung her hands. 'No... no, she didn't. But... are you sure? All this time I've—'

'No doubt about it,' said Andrea.

'I can't believe it.' Emma's voice choked up.

'It was a lorry driver,' said Bligh. 'He fell asleep at the wheel. The same thing happened to him six months later and he almost killed somebody else. He owned up to everything. That night, that Christmas Eve, he did stop and get out to look. He saw the mangled bike and Ned's body; the damage and blood on the front of his cab. It was at least some relief to Polly and Alan to find out that Ned didn't suffer – he was already dead when the driver got out of his cab.'

'He just panicked and drove away as quickly as he could,' said Andrea. 'Come to think of it, the police did find a dead deer nearby.'

'Perhaps that's what you hit,' said Bligh.

'So it wasn't me?' Emma gulped and covered her eyes with her hands. The sense of relief was almost too much. Her knees buckled.

Suddenly Gail was at her side, patting Emma's shoulder. 'You really do talk too much.'

Emma gave her mum the tightest hug, burrowing her face in Gail's shoulder.

'There, there…' said Gail, stroking her hair as if her daughter were Dash. 'How about some fish and chips?'

Chapter 29

Due to the soup run, Stig was now a dab hand in the kitchen and helped Emma prepare the food for the barbecue. For once, the bank holiday delivered the sunniest weather. Mrs Beatty had stopped crossing the road when they met, and gave Emma a discount on some pretty paper napkins and plates. Bill the butcher even gave her some discarded cuts to be cut up for the rough sleepers' dogs. In return, she gave them both some surplus fruit from the farm. All the village businesses had continued to help each other out. Emma could sense a common bond strengthening at the prospect of their first Sunday market in the autumn.

She had insisted on paying for the barbecue and reckoned Aunt Thelma would have approved. She'd been looking into veterinary nurse courses and it had helped that Phil had reduced her rent. She was going to help him with a business proposition he had for Andrea, to build proper animal kennels on part of the farm's unused land and run them. He was coming round tomorrow night with his plan. And eventually the international arts festival would be over and the rough sleepers would migrate back to the city. Her soup runs would be redundant. Perhaps then she could look for a part-time job to juggle alongside everything else.

At the back of Gail's recipe book the wad of blank pages continued to rapidly diminish. Instead of Andrea illustrating, Emma took a photo of every finished dish, printed it off and stuck it in. The barbecue provided the perfect opportunity to be creative, and she veered slightly from Gail's menu. She made a large raspberry tart with lemon drizzle over the top, as well as the chocolate one and the mocha muffins. Stig put his mind to making the cheese and caramelised onion quiche. Gail carried out the safe tasks like washing tomatoes. She also enjoyed folding the paper napkins several times over.

Stig set up a couple of trestle tables in front of the barn, and found as many chairs as he could – Andrea had invited a couple of extra friends, such as the chemist, who was very informative explaining Gail's various tablets. Stig lit the coals and set out the meat. Soon smoke wafted into the air.

Emma looked at her watch. Quarter to three. Joe had already arrived, and after a catch-up had headed over to Stig to help with the grilling. The remaining guests would be here any minute. They were lucky with the weather, which offered that perfect combination of blue skies and a pleasant breeze.

The first car to pull up belonged to Bligh. They hadn't seen him for a week. He'd announced he needed a break. In his absence, Stig had been a godsend. He'd helped with the heavy manual tasks and lightened the evening atmosphere with his tales about travel. He would some-times read to Gail in front of the barn. He and Emma had picked up a load of animal stories he thought suitable from the charity shop. They were never sure if she took them in, but the steady sound of his voice seemed to calm her before bed.

'Looks good,' Bligh said to Emma as he walked past the trestle tables. Dash ran around barking, the Duchess trying to keep up. 'How have things been?'

'Fine. Stig's got stuck in with the harvesting and has learnt how to make jam.'

'Great, because I've come back with some fresh ideas on how we can expand our range of online products, so it might mean that for the foreseeable future I'll be working at the computer. Perhaps you, Andrea and I could have a meeting in the next day or two. We can discuss the plans you had about introducing seasonal ranges for Easter and Christmas, and widening the sweet range, such as making fruit biscuits. I think you may be onto something there.' His voice sounded business-like.

He jerked his head and they moved away from everyone else.

'I've thought about things, and firstly, I want to apologise for that time I said I preferred you drunk. I wasn't myself. You coming back… it's taken a bit of getting used to.'

'You don't need to—'

'Please. Let me finish. I feel you should know… the so-called cancer specialist in Germany – it turned out to be a scam. We found out after Dad passed away. So even if we'd got him over there, in the end it wouldn't have made any difference.'

Emma put a hand to her throat. So she hadn't been involved in *anyone's* death.

'I probably should have told you sooner,' he said in a strained voice, 'but you still took away his hope, and mine, during those last days.'

He gave her a hard stare before heading inside to take a look at the new boiler that had been fitted while he was away.

'Are the guests arriving soon?' asked Gail, who was standing nearby fiddling with a chocolate wrapper.

'Yes. Any minute now,' said Emma. Her voice wavered. She pulled a tissue out of her trouser pocket and dabbed her eyes.

Gail tilted her head and studied Emma's face. 'You're a good girl – even with all that talking.'

Their eyes locked. Emma took her mum's hand, blinked away tears and lightly squeezed.

Andrea came outside. 'Did you remember to make ice cubes?' she asked sharply. 'I'll bring the lemonade out in a minute.'

'Yes,' replied Emma. 'Three trayfuls. Hopefully that will be enough.'

Andrea nodded. 'Mum's got a slight sniffle. Polly wants me to go to the cinema with her tonight, but I'm not sure.'

'Go, Andrea. You said yourself it's months since you last saw a film. If anything happens, I'll text you immediately. I can stay here as late as you want, and I was going to get that ironing done anyway.'

'I'll decide later,' Andrea said. Her jaw set in a determined line.

Ted arrived with his wife and grandkids, who immediately headed off to pet the rabbits. Polly and Alan were next. Alan marched straight past, but Polly stopped.

'Your sister told me you were pregnant but...'

Emma nodded.

'Losing a child – it gets marginally easier as time passes,' she said curtly.

Emma's eyelids pricked. 'Thanks, Polly, I—'

But the landlady had already walked away.

Phil arrived. He said hello and then headed over to see how the meat was doing. These days he looked ten years younger. He'd even started cycling and cooking again – last night, he'd made the two of them a stir-fry. He'd laughed when Emma said he should try online dating, but later that evening she found him absorbed with his laptop screen.

Her attention turned to Joe. She thought back to her neediness in the squat. The times she'd told passers-by to eff off. How she'd gone days without washing and ended the night by throwing up. She remembered the desperate Emma sobbing in front of assessment officer Ben.

That person seemed so alien to her now. She recalled a young Bligh's insistence that life on earth was directed by aliens on the moon. If so, the master of her journey must have changed hands, and she'd be forever grateful.

She ran a hand through her hair and walked out of sight, around the corner of the farmhouse. Some people could accept apologies, others couldn't. She had chased forgiveness so hard, but perhaps in the end it didn't really matter. The important things were kindness and trying to be a better person. She considered the guests connected to Foxglove Farm – orphaned Bligh, depressed Stig, divorced Phil, grieving Polly and Alan – and decided the place really had turned out to be a haven for waifs and strays. The old Gail would have been proud.

She passed the front door, where she'd stood cautiously knocking a couple of months earlier. The tall sunflower was in glorious bloom now. She went to the kissing gate, rested on the fence and gazed at the rows of pink foxgloves, recalling how they'd seemed to trumpet their welcome.

Stig appeared, carrying two slices of quiche. 'I've left Phil and Joe in charge. They're politely disagreeing over the best grilling technique.'

Emma turned around.

'You all right?'

'Yes, I'm good. Just taking a moment out. Things haven't quite worked out as I planned.'

'What, coming back?' He handed her a slice.

'I've made a little headway with Bligh, but he and Andrea are still so angry, and even worse, in part they're blaming themselves. I just want a bit of peace for them. They deserve that. I'd hoped me trying to make amends would heal the rift, for their sake as much as mine.' She sat down on the grass. Stig joined her. 'Perhaps Andrea was right. I said that everything was my fault, so she snarkily – and I don't blame her – suggested I concentrate on forgiving myself.'

Stig wiped his mouth. 'Thanks for mentioning me to your sister. It's been great living in the barn and making myself useful. But more than that, I feel a small sense of... belonging. I get on well with your mum and I've got a lot in common with Andrea. She's a great person.'

Emma pretended not to notice his blush. 'Belonging means everything, doesn't it? I've got a life now and wonder why I was always so hell bent on finding the bright lights and leaving Healdbury. It's the small, simple, everyday things that matter. It's about doing the right thing and being there for people, isn't it?'

'Perhaps it wasn't really Healdbury you were trying to get away from. Perhaps it was yourself.'

Lately Emma had been thinking the same thing.

He took another bite and gazed around. 'It's so pictur-esque here,' he said in between chewing.

'Beautiful, isn't it?'

'So quintessentially English. The flowers are amazing. So much insect and plant life. It would be a brilliant location for a field trip.'

'There's nothing quite like the sea of forget-me-nots in the spring.'

Basking in the luxurious sun, they both stretched out their legs. What a contrast to the days they'd spend hunched on Manchester's streets.

'That reminds me of an English lesson I had to supervise once,' said Stig. 'The kids were studying a fable about a young woman whose husband had to head off to sea. She pressed some forget-me-nots in a book and told him to take them on his journey so that he never forgot her.'

'That's sweet.'

'Yes, but the trouble was, while he was away, she got led astray by single friends and forgot who she really was. She danced every night, stayed out drinking and had liaisons with several men. When her husband came back home, he'd remained loyal.' He looked at Emma. 'What messed things up was that he'd remembered her but she hadn't remembered herself. Perhaps it's the same for forgiveness.'

'What do you mean?'

'Maybe Andrea unintentionally had a point. You can ask people to forgive you, but it means nothing if you don't forgive yourself. If you can live with what you've done, perhaps it will take the pressure off seeking that peace from another person.' He raised an eyebrow. 'Maybe what matters most is the respect you get back from yourself. The rest is a bonus.'

Then perhaps self-forgiveness was also the answer for Andrea and Bligh, seeing as they thought they deserved some of the blame. Hopefully, with Emma sticking around, healthy and productive, they would begin to think more kindly of themselves.

Perhaps they couldn't forgive right now because the hurt had damaged their own self-image.

Bligh saw himself as her protector. Andrea considered herself a guardian big sister. They both felt they'd failed in those roles, as Emma's life took a downwards spiral. They needed to let go of the responsibilities they thought they carried. Only then would they realise they'd done nothing wrong. Only then was there a chance that the family could go forwards together.

It was a bit like Emma's discovery of those cards. She'd always seen herself as someone whose life would have been better with two parents; letting go of that idea made it easier to forgive her mum.

'Roll up, folks, these pork chops are ready!' Phil's words travelled across from the yard, accompanied by barking from the Duchess and Dash, and mouth-watering smells.

Emma stood up and stared down at Stig. She held out her hand. 'Come on. We're neglecting the guests, and Phil and Joe might have come to blows.' She pulled him to his feet.

Like with Mum's recipe book, it was time to move forwards now – in the same way, but differently.

They stood opposite each other. Stig didn't wear his bobble hat any more. Emma brushed a small fly off his face. He squeezed her hand before letting go. Leaving quiche crumbs behind for industrious ants, they hurried back to the barbecue and joined the hubbub of chat.

Chapter 30

Up in her bedroom, Andrea ignored Phil's voice announcing that the meat was done. She was enjoying a few moments' peace before she was missed. Her right arm reached outwards. Sight was not required to curl her fingers around the blue bottle she knew was there. She topped up her mug, took a large mouthful and felt a whoosh from the warming liquid.

Truth be told, since her operation a year ago, Mum had completely lost her taste for her favourite tipple. Andrea, however, had kept up the ritual, pretending that Gail still enjoyed her nightcap. She'd sip the sherry as she sat at the foot of Gail's bed and watched her fall asleep. One glass had become two, then four. Discreet mouthfuls during the afternoon made the day more manageable. She'd hide the empties under her bed and when Bligh wasn't around take them straight to the recycling plant. In view of Emma's past, she didn't want him jumping to the ridiculous conclusion that anyone else at the farm had a problem.

There was so much to deal with, and she just needed a little lift so that she didn't think about her ex-boyfriend Dean, the finances of the farm, the early loss of her dad, her mum, the places she hadn't been.

But most of the blame lay with her sister. Her nose wrinkled and she thanked the universe that she was nothing like Emma. Sherry was a civilised drink. Andrea drank in a civilised manner. Plus no one knew about her habit, which proved she had it under control. She deserved this one treat.

She stood up and stashed the bottle behind her dressing table mirror. Then she took out her mints, slipped one into her mouth and went back downstairs to wash up her mug before joining everyone else.

Acknowledgements

Dear readers, I so appreciate you following my journey into Women's Fiction. I have loved creating this story and hope you enjoy reading it. You are the people I write for – the words flow from my heart to yours. Thank you so much.

Massive thanks to my talented and caring agent Clare Wallace, at Darley Anderson. Thanks for your incredible help as I've faced the challenge of writing for a new genre. Your belief in me has meant a lot – despite the pages of revisions! Thanks for never being phased – if you have been, you've hidden it well.

Huge gratitude also to Tanera Simons at Darley Anderson. Your efficacy and understanding have made challenges I've faced that much easier.

Thanks to Mary Moody – on a personal level and for answering many research questions. I have a huge amount of respect for what you do and wish you all the very best for the future.

Thanks also to Karen Whitehead from Mosaic Services, Stockport. I'm grateful for the time and know-ledge you've given me and am full of admiration for how you and your colleagues change young peoples' lives.

I have to mention Mark Holder from Acorn Recovery Projects. Mark, you know what a central role you've played in my own personal journey into recovery. I'll be eternally thankful for that. Tough love personified, I wish you every success with your continued career.

Thanks to Tracy Griffiths for your friendship and sharing your story. You are a huge inspiration to me.

Ruth Yates, you've been brilliant – a real rock and such a role model.

Gratitude also to another Karen. You made such a difference when it counted.

To the person I got to know during treatment who is homeless and suffering from drug addiction, thanks for sharing your experience of using and rough sleeping. Your cheerful smile, your banter and kind nature always inspire me.

Thanks to blogger Rachel Gilbey and her super efficiency in organising blog tours. You're a lovely person, so professional and a real cheerleader of books.

I'm also immensely grateful to all the bloggers who support my stories. I have so much respect for the amount of work you put in – and time. It's so heartening to witness your passion for the industry and I love connecting with you on Facebook and Twitter. You are the best!

Jan Wooller and Beverley Ann Hopper, thanks so much for the support you show me and so many other authors – you are both very special people and always brighten my day immensely on Facebook… as does the lovely, funny Sue Blackburn. And thanks to Ian Wilfred for being such a support on Twitter.

Finally, I'm so grateful to my tenacious editor Michael Bhaskar and the team at Canelo Publishing. It's an honour to be published by such an innovative, dynamic company. Your inclusiveness, your enthusiasm and passion for this project and my writing have meant a great deal. I can't wait to work on the next book with you!